"Why is that serendipitous call of one body to another never enough, Lilly?" Alec spoke right behind her in a warm exhalation that curled down inside her. "When I'm near you my blood sings."

Tension surrounded them in the musty, silent house. Dust motes whispered to the floor. Alec touched Lilly's face and her eyes glided shut, her mouth turning eagerly into his palm. She wanted every cell of her body to be imprinted with his indelible mark. She belonged with him; that gnawing sense of constant loneliness was gone. Her mind cried, *why this man?* But there was no answer, only his free hand stroking her thick hair and their mouths meeting with a pleasure that shook them both.

From Twilight to Sunrise

MARTHA STARR

A *Love Affair from*
HARLEQUIN
London · Toronto · New York · Sydney

First published in Great Britain in 1986 by
Harlequin, 15–16 Brook's Mews, London W1A 1DR

© Martha Gordon 1984

ISBN 0 373 16084 4

18-0186

Printed and bound in Great Britain by
Richard Clay (The Chaucer Press) Ltd,
Bungay, Suffolk

Chapter One

The morning mist hung like a straggly white beard over the river valley below Fielding College, shot through here and there with gleaming tangerine light. At intervals, black tree limbs thrust out of the mist like the reaching arms of a drowning man. Help, help! Lilly thought mockingly; that's exactly what I could use right now. With a nervous sweep of her hand, she wiped the steamy patch her breath had created from her office window.

From the hallway behind her she heard the murmur of male voices and her stomach muscles tightened, but she remained staring out the window, fighting the urge to race out of the building, dive into her car and run away from this scary situation as she'd run so often in the past.

Just first-day jitters, she told herself, ignoring the small voice that asked why no friendly face had popped in to wish her good luck on this official start of her career as the newest member of the Fielding English staff. Something more than just first-day jitters was at work inside Lilly. She'd pushed down the feeling during the first few hectic days since she'd arrived in Fielding, but now she faced it.

Lilly had the distinct feeling she wasn't wanted.

That both puzzled and alarmed her, for she'd been around academics long enough to know that the way she was being treated was unusual—especially at a small, private college like Fielding, where new staffers were scarcely an everyday occurrence. Even more puzzling was the fact that Lilly had been assured her presence was badly needly to shore up the weakened composition program.

With a sigh, Lilly turned back to her desk, picked up her notes and the bound copies of her Ph.D. dissertation and went out the door. She walked straight to the end of the hall and with a slightly shaky hand pushed open the door to the lounge.

A group of about ten men huddled near the windows at the end of the large room, and all conversation ceased as Lilly came in the door. Lilly looked around for Professor Curran, the elderly man who'd interviewed her, but not one face was familiar.

"Will Professor Curran be at this staff meeting?" she asked hesitantly, then forced herself to loosen the death grip she had on her papers and lay them on the table that ran down the center of the room. No one answered. With the light behind them they looked like ten faceless accusers to Lilly's agitated imagination.

"Josh Curran had a heart attack and has taken an early retirement," one of them finally said after what seemed ages. A slim man with thinning hair and pale skin detached himself from the phalanx. "I'm David Holmes. Victorian Studies. I don't believe we've met."

"Lilly Burns. Composition and linguistics," Lilly replied crisply, and that was enough to crack the surface ice. Names and specialties flew back and forth, and Lilly tried to keep them straight. They seemed less frightening now as someone suggested they sit down, and Lilly could at least put names to some faces.

"All we need is the twelfth man for the jury to be set," Lilly said jokingly. Immediately all chatter stopped. Several suspicious looks were shot Lilly's way, to her complete puzzlement. And she heard a muttered comment that sounded like "Where's her lawyer?" that seemed to generate some nervous laughter.

"Actually, we're waiting for the present department chairman, Alec Thomas, to arrive." David Holmes once more stepped into the hardening silence. "He's also a playwright, a local man. Perhaps you know him, Miss Burns?"

"Yes, I've heard of him," Lilly said dryly. Fielding believed in getting the maximum out of any faculty member, and she'd been given a total rundown on Alec Thomas by Dr. Curran. Alec's work was fairly well-known, but Lilly disliked it. "Is he working on a new play?"

"Yes." That was the murmured consensus from the group, and apparently the end of their contributions to the conversation. For several long moments the only sound was the buzzing of the fluorescent lights overhead. The table was so polished it gave Lilly back a wavering reflection of herself that was vague in details, but showed the oval of her face and the curly mass of her dark blond hair. With great mental effort she resisted the impulse to fuss with her hair, straighten the tie on her pristine blouse, or worse, bite her nails.

Several of the men lit up. Lilly regarded them enviously, wishing she smoked for the first time in her life. Anything to relieve the tension she felt. And since her first attempt to break the ice had backfired so badly, she didn't feel ready to try again so soon. Try as she might, Lilly couldn't see what was so threatening in her remark, unless they felt she saw them as a jury. Come to think of it, she thought ruefully, that was not too far off the mark.

Time dragged along. Lilly shuffled through her papers, growing angered by the long wait for the seemingly mythical Alec Thomas. She wished fervently he would show up, if only to get the execution over with. Lilly began to realize she was the lone woman on the staff. Perhaps, she thought as she looked at the exceedingly nervous faces around her, they were wary of how well a woman would fit in here?

"Any reason why there aren't more women here? Have you guys got something against us?" Lilly said jokingly when she could stand the continuing silence no longer. Perhaps it wasn't the most tactful remark, but the reaction to it couldn't have been more violent if Lilly had drawn a gun on them and told them to hand over their valuables, she thought in astonishment.

"No, not at all. We love women." From total silence the room erupted with sound. "Actually, we have several women staffers whom you've yet to meet," David Holmes said hastily, with a quelling look at the most noisy of his co-workers.

"That must mean our professional-looking secretary, and a pregnant part-timer who's always on the verge of quitting," sneered one of the younger men, whose name Lilly thought was Todd Godwin.

"I wish Alec would just get here," muttered Al Schwartz, his German accent growing heavier in his obvious distress.

"Look," Lilly broke into the puzzling exchange, trying to sound more confident than she felt. "I think you owe me some kind of explanation. Just what is going on here?" She focused on David Holmes because he seemed to be the authority figure.

"Yes, Dave. Do enlighten us both," a deep male voice commanded from the doorway. "Just what the hell is going on here?" Lilly swiveled to find sharp blue eyes fastened on her as Alec Thomas rolled into the room. "What's this, for example?" he asked with a stab of his finger toward Lilly's tidy blue-suited presence as if he'd never seen a woman before and didn't like them much now that he had. Alec shucked his suit-jacket, thrust back his sleeves, and spilled the contents of a bulging briefcase across the gleaming tabletop. He seemed to draw up the whole room, tightening the strings in his short, capable-looking hands.

So this is Alec Thomas, Lilly thought as she watched him pin David Holmes to his chair, totally ignoring her for the moment. Until this moment what she'd known of him had been only by reputation, since he generated more flamboyant press than any academic had a right to, or so the gossips had it. He'd been involved in everything from protesting the razing of a famous New York theater to becoming a media celebrity as he fought for funding for the arts in every forum he could find. Alec Thomas lived in the limelight, and from all appearances he seemed well suited to it, Lilly thought, wondering how he could be content to make Fielding his permanent base. From what she'd seen of it so far Lilly found it pleasant enough, but surely no cultural mecca of the arts.

"Alec, this is Lilly Burns. She's the newest member of the staff, and as part of the committee that examined her record, I can personally say she's highly qualified for the job." David spoke calmly and seemed to ignore the bulk of Alec's terse demands.

Alec scowled at Lilly from behind wild, bushy eyebrows and said nothing.

"Good afternoon, Mr. Thomas," Lilly said pointedly. "So glad you could make it." Since it was about ten thirty in the morning, Lilly was pretty sure he would get her message.

"Late, am I?" Alec leaned back, lacing his fingers behind his head, then said thoughtfully. "You know, if any of you guys had *told* me what foxy little lady you'd lined up for me, I'd have been here days ago."

Lilly heard the gasp this remark caused around the table, but her attention never left the man at her side. Dislike darkened her hazel eyes to almost black as she struggled to think of a really terrific retort. None occurred, and she was forced to settle for indignation.

"If you think for one minute I'll tolerate—"

"Well, that's just great!" David Holmes broke in with false heartiness. "Now that the introductions have been made, perhaps we ought to move along to other things. We've got a lot on the agenda, and I have it on good authority that we're receiving some of those famous Fielding cafeteria caramel rolls for the break. So let's get started!"

Several people seemed relieved to be moving on, and a few chairs scraped as people drew nearer the table. It looked as if David were going to carry it off.

Alec had other ideas, though. "Hold on just a minute, Dave." He spoke in a soft, seemingly gentle voice that didn't fool Lilly one bit. "Don't you know it's rude to interrupt a lady when she's talking? Honey, try not to take it to heart." He reached across the table to pat Lilly's hand. "Do you think you could try to remember what you were going to say?" he asked, brows drawing together in mock anxiety. "It was something about what you couldn't tolerate," he added helpfully.

Anger the likes of which Lilly had never felt before in her life welled up inside her, and Lilly jerked her hand from beneath his warm one. Calm down, she urged herself. He's just trying a variation on the old harassment game. Lilly knew his purpose was to rile her into speaking impulsively. The trouble was he nearly succeeded.

"I'm a fully qualified professional, as my résumé makes clear," Lilly began in a crisp, controlled voice. "My credentials have been available to you all for several weeks. But since some of you have obviously not taken the time to examine them"—she paused to glare pointedly at Alec—"I'll review them briefly for you. My B.A. comes from Harvard and my Ph.D. from this state's university, where I have taught composition for the past five years in combination with writing my dissertation. That means my knowledge and understanding of students and their writing problems is not just theoretical." Lilly paused to draw breath, moving her eyes over the circle of men around the table.

"I admit I'm puzzled by my reception here so far. Professor Curran assured me my presence was wanted and needed in efforts I was given to understand were underway to revamp the composition program. If I'm under a misapprehension, and my presence is not wanted, as this meeting today seems to indicate, then please, gentlemen, accept my resignation and consider my contract void." Lilly stopped. She felt weak and shaky, but she hoped it didn't show. That last statement had been a gamble, an attempt to force the truth out.

"Your presence is very much needed and wanted, Miss Burns," David Holmes said firmly. "Please have no doubts on that score."

"If you want letters free of caramel to go out of my office today, someone better come and get these rolls," announced a blond woman from the door. Her accent was an attractive singsong, and Lilly thought she must be Swedish. She was a bit surprised that a secretary would interrupt a meeting like this, but since no one else seemed to be, she assumed it was the normal course of events.

"A break might be a good idea now," Al Schwartz suggested, and flashed David Holmes a look Lilly couldn't decipher.

"I'd love to hear more about your credentials," Alec murmured into her ear as they filed out. "Care to come into my private office and lay them out for me?"

Lilly ignored him, keenly aware of the inquisitive eyes of Todd Godwin on this exchange. For the life of her, Lilly couldn't see why Alec felt the need to be so offensive, unless he was always that way. Perhaps that's why there are no other women here, Lilly thought as she headed for the ladies' room that was across from her office.

She raised a white, shaken face and looked at herself in the mirror. She saw that some color was needed in her face, then remembered her purse was in her office. A bit of blush and a comb through her hair wouldn't fix this situation, but they'd make her feel more confident, Lilly knew, and she needed all the confidence she could garner at this point.

Lilly ducked across the hall into her office, and, about to shut the gun-metal gray drawer, she heard voices.

"Man, you did your best to get us in the soup with her! What the hell is the matter with you, Alec?"

"More to the point, what have you and that old fool Curran cooked up between you? I left for New York with the position guaranteed to Gary Felt. He's a good man, and wouldn't give us a moment's trouble."

"Precisely. He's a man." Lilly recognized the other man's voice as David Holmes. She thought about announcing herself, then stifled that thought.

"You hired her because she's a damned female?" Alec asked incredulously. "That's ridiculous!"

"Alec. You don't understand," David said in a low, terse voice. "We had no choice. We had to act and act fast. I agree: Under ordinary circumstances Gary would have gotten my vote, too. But we *are* being sued for sexual discrimination. And at this point our only other female staffer is a secretary."

"What about Glennis?"

"She's only ever been part-time. Now she's having another baby, and doesn't feel she has time for even a few hours a week."

"Well, then," Alec grunted. "I fail to see the problem; that makes it merely de facto, not intentional, that we have an all-male staff right now. So why the rush to hire this...girl?"

"You don't seem to understand, Alec," David said patiently. "Not only is this department being sued, but you are specifically cited in the suit."

"Damn you, Karen Willis!" Alec roared, and slammed his fist into the wall of Lilly's office, causing her partially opened door to swing wider and making Lilly jump for the second time that day. "Why does that woman insist on haunting my life? I knew it. I knew she was trouble. I knew she should never have been allowed to set foot in this department, whatever her talents as a poet—which I doubt. Professor of Malice ought to be her real title!" Alec's angry words exploded into the air, slicing Lilly's skin like glass shards.

My God, what kind of snake pit have I gotten into here? Lilly thought dismally as she sank back against the edge of her desk. The question of whether or not she ought to have listened to that conversation seemed irrelevant in light of what she'd just learned. Evidently, those ten nervous men in that room were doing everything to keep her from learning of the suit. Lilly thought of her innocent remarks about juries and women staffers; the irony of it all made her smile in spite of the gravity of the situation.

The question of what to do with this unwanted, unpleasant knowledge was a thornier matter. The urge to run returned stronger than before. She'd sensed something peculiar going on here, but a sex discrimination suit hadn't crossed her mind. The thought of facing them all again appalled her, and she wished desperately that at least one of those men had had the decency to tell her what was really going on. Lilly felt totally alone.

Having listened to him as well as having been the brunt of his cute little tricks, Lilly could well imagine any normal woman suing Alec. Just thinking about the way he'd treated her made Lilly's anger burn all over again. But I didn't let him get to me, she reminded herself, and that's what counts. And now she had some power on her side, because she knew what was really going on. Of course the easiest thing to do was run. Lilly didn't need the job: she worked because she loved teaching. It gave her a sense of purpose and satisfaction to help a student conquer his dislike and fear of working with words. But Lilly hadn't really relished the idea of leaving Minneapolis for a small, private college. She'd come because getting away from Minneapolis had suddenly become attractive.... The odor of freshly perked coffee wafted into her office, and Lilly sniffed appreciatively. It was a nice, normal smell that she associated with teaching, reassurance that at least some things remained the same.

Lilly looked up when someone tapped at the half-opened door. Hilda Svensen poked her lacquered blond head around the corner and said, "I brought you coffee and a roll before the men demolish them all. I don't blame you for hiding out. I usually take my breaks downstairs in the French office. At least you get some decent conversation there."

"That was kind of you," Lilly answered softly, rising to take the Styrofoam cup from the older woman, the first real smile of the day lightening her attractive features into real beauty. She studied Hilda a bit as she sipped the coffee. The older woman looked a bit like an escapee from a Hawaii travel brochure. She wore a fuchsia, orange and yellow print dress, glazed fruit earrings bobbled from her ears, and her painted toenails protruded from grass sandals at least a full size too small for her large feet. But Lilly wasn't fooled. She had a shrewd idea who kept the department running smoothly on a day-to-day basis—and it wasn't the chairman, Alec Thomas.

She knew why Hilda was here, too, and it wasn't to bring Lilly coffee. She was here to size Lilly up. They exchanged pleasantries for a few moments; then Hilda said, "Look, Miss Burns. Try to have patience with Alec right now. I'm sure he's being as obnoxious as only Alec can be. But he's under a lot of strain. I've seen your résumé and spoken to Joan. She says you're good people—oh, Joan and I are friends from way back," Hilda said with a throaty chuckle when she saw the surprised look on Lilly's face that she would know the head secretary at the university English department. "We go way back," she repeated, and Lilly felt her instinctive respect for this unlikely woman increase.

"Well, I'll leave you to enjoy your roll. The meeting resumes in fifteen minutes," she reminded Lilly in a motherly way as she turned and went out the door. Lilly listened thoughtfully until the gentle swish of her grass sandals faded completely away.

Mmmm, Lilly thought. That wasn't what I expected to hear. She had half expected to be told to clear out of town by sunset from the stern look on Hilda's face when she'd first come in the room. She must have liked what she saw, and Lilly realized her wish to have someone on her side in the department had just been fulfilled. With that, Lilly decided she would go against her instincts and battle it out with Alec Thomas, and for that she needed war paint!

By the end of the long meeting that dragged on past the noon hour, however, Lilly was beginning to regret that decision. Exhaustion was setting in as she began the final section of her planned presentation of changes she'd like to implement in Fielding's composition program. The effort to make criticisms without stepping on the toes of those around her proved much more difficult in practice than it appeared on a piece of paper.

"Here are several samples of student papers. I'd like you to take a look at them. Grade them as you ordinarily would, and then I'd like to discuss your grades with you." Lilly passed out mimeographed pages and tried to ignore the suspicious looks she received. Alec sighed heavily and began to read.

Lilly had tried all morning not to be overly aware of him, but now she admitted that she was failing. Every breath he took, each flick of his sharp, blue eyes was felt and recorded inside her. Lilly was incredibly sensitive to every move he made, and she tried to tell herself that it was just because he'd irritated her so much earlier. But it was more than that. He was a compelling man. She found herself trying to figure him out, make excuses for his bad behavior, and that made her wonder.

"Okay, what about Sample A?" Lilly asked when it appeared most of them had finished. Lilly knew "A" to be the best piece of writing of the lot, but suspected they wouldn't think so. She'd done similar tests with high school teachers and business executives in the course of preparing her thesis, so she knew what to expect.

"Although the student makes a few good points," Al Schwartz began condescendingly, "his style is too elementary, too childish to be acceptable at the tertiary level. Vocabulary is poor, and his logic seems weak. I would give this paper a C."

That seemed to be the consensus of the rather anemic group response as Lilly heard murmured phrases such as "lacks sufficient depth of sentence structure" and "ideas just don't seem developed."

"All right," Lilly said gently. "Can any of you give me specific places where the logic is poor or the sentences are poorly put together?" She smiled encouragingly when what she felt like was a satisfying scream as they began to answer. Time and again she directed their attention back to the texts and away from their own unexamined prejudices. Finally they began to see that the piece, far from lacking logic or sentence strength, was actually a solid piece of work that simply lacked the verbose prose they'd grown to think of as "college level" or intellectual.

"Actually, ornate writing just seems strong because it's fuzzy and difficult to understand," Lilly went on.

"Are you trying to say we should reduce all written language to words of two syllables or less?" Alec asked skeptically, holding Sample A up gingerly between thumb and forefinger.

"No, I'm not. Although that's a common *student* complaint," Lilly told him, implying he sounded just like the average student without actually saying so. Lilly wasn't sure why she felt she had to make these little digs, but they kept slipping out.

"All I am saying—" Lilly turned to the room in general—"is that we as teachers are guilty of accepting polysyllabic words and ornate, passive-verb sentences in lieu of strong logical thinking and well-supported argument."

Lilly had made this argument many times, and she still felt it just as strongly as she had the first time. Today was different only in the audience to whom she addressed it.

"I guess I see several of the points you've made, Miss Burns—"

"Please, call me Lilly."

"Lilly, then," David agreed. "But my question is what holds this all together? How do you put this into effect in the actual classroom?"

"The underlying theme is that writing is a process. In practice, this means the class differs quite a bit from conventional composition courses that emphasize the final product and care nothing for the thinking process *behind* a student's errors. Therefore I do not teach grammar, and I encourage students to find an angle of assignments that they are really interested in, not try to read my mind and write what they think I want to hear. Nothing creates more boring, stilted papers than writing to the teacher."

The uproar that ensued rivaled that which followed her remark about the lack of women in the department. Alec shot her an exasperated look as if he suspected she was doing this merely for effect. And it was effective.

"How in the world can you expect improvement without drilling on grammar? One must have standards!" they cried in dismay.

"All you do by forcing students to submit to you as the ultimate authority figure is create boring, stilted papers," Lilly insisted.

"Then you advocate total anarchy in the classroom?" Alec slipped in slyly, thinking he'd trapped her now.

"No. Just the opposite. Because the discipline comes from within each student. I teach them how to edit their own prose and examine their writing critically. Thus when the student leaves my class he can find the weak spots in his own writing, and doesn't need to submit it to some ultimate authority for 'correctness.'"

"Sounds noble," Alec said dryly, "but how do you bring it down into the world of reality?"

"Yes, and what grammar and textbooks do you use to do it?" someone else asked eagerly.

"I don't use any textbooks, although I sometimes recommend some to those among my students who feel more secure with some handbook to fall back on." Lilly admitted, and heard another gasp of disbelief follow this admission. "I rely on their own drafts of their papers, which they discuss in small groups, honing their skills and getting immediate feedback at the same time. They critique each other's work based on a set of questions we establish as a class. So please, don't confuse this with some standardless, do-as-you-please method. This rigorous set of questions that they pose to themselves as they write becomes part of their mental landscape."

Lilly paused, and looked around, feeling for the first time today she had everyone's undivided interest. She pushed back a lock of hair that had fallen toward her face and went on. "I don't lecture, but I do continually take sentences and paragraphs from their papers and draw lessons from them for the class as a whole."

"But the grammar?" asked one wistful voice.

Lilly shook her head ruefully. "I've had too many students who could pass every complicated test on English grammar but were unable to write a clean sentence to put much stock in grammar."

She stopped to take a sip of her cold coffee to wet her parched throat and mouth. Time to sum it up, she thought. "Most of what I've said is laid out point by point in my dissertation, where I hope I've practiced what I preach. I'm hoping today will at least pique your interest in my methods. I can assure you more lively classes and much greater improvement in your students' writing over the course of the semester."

Lilly left the building more tired than she could remember being in her life. David and a few of the others were headed for the Alumni Center for a late lunch, and invited her along. Lilly knew she ought to go, but she just didn't have the strength.

Alec had disappeared behind the frosted-glass door marked Department Chairman, although Lilly tried to pretend she didn't notice or care what happened to him. He'd been fairly quiet after the break, making a few notes here and there that Lilly would have dearly loved to have read. He'd also been one of the few to pick up a copy of her dissertation, and Lilly had no success telling herself she didn't care what he thought of it, either.

From the sounds of what she'd overheard Lilly thought the possibility of being fired was nonexistent, and she knew her main worry ought to be—as her father had told her time and time again, doing her best—not everyone else's opinions. Still, she had hung around the building for a while after everyone else had left, like some bashful freshman waiting to get up the nerve to approach a professor. She'd gotten a drink of water; she'd checked her mailbox. Why do I care what that awful man thinks? Lilly demanded of herself irritably, and forced herself to walk away, down the stairs and out of the building.

She still didn't have an answer for that one. But honesty forced Lilly to acknowledge that she felt compelled to prove herself to Alec. That wasn't logical, or necessary, but it was true.

A light breeze had long since cleared away those morning mists that hung over the valley, and the sun hung heavy and wan in the late afternoon sky as Lilly turned her snappy red Corvette into the driveway of her rooming house. Lilly had wanted quickly to buy or rent a house in Fielding, but her father had strongly advised her to wait before getting too deeply committed. "You just think I won't be able to handle it," Lilly had accused. But now with the situation in the department, Lilly had to admit waiting had been a smart idea.

No one was at home, and Lilly swiftly changed into snug jeans, a checked shirt, and her favorite bright red jacket. She grabbed a crispy green apple from the bowl Mrs. Jordan kept in the kitchen and went out the door again.

The creek beckoned to her weary spirits, so Lilly crossed the street and walked the two blocks to the wooded shore. She ducked down the embankment, crunching the apple as she walked. The water in the creek was low, amber-colored and, when she bent to trail her fingers through it, cold. Shadows pooled beneath hollowed cottonwoods whose limbs had gnarled with years of trying to protect themselves from the harsh Minnesota winters.

From the fields beyond the creek Lilly heard the bugling of a male pheasant proclaiming his territory to the world. Lilly felt the cares and tension of the day fading a bit as she walked. Then there was a violent crackling of undergrowth and two large golden retrievers bounded down the embankment, headed for Lilly. They rushed at her in a prancing, well-mannered show of enthusiasm that she found entrancing.

"Aren't you gorgeous!" she exclaimed, and knelt to pet them. "But don't you belong to someone?"

"To me, I'm afraid," Lilly heard an attractive male voice admit wryly. "They get a bit out of hand. Apparently it never occurs to them that not everyone will love them."

"Oh, but I do," Lilly said unnecessarily, unable to resist giving them each one more hug before scrambling to her feet, brushing the dirt and bark from her knees. "I envy you. All my animals are in Minneapolis until I find permanent housing here."

"Ahh. I didn't think I'd seen you around Fielding before," he commented, managing to imply with the twinkle in his dark blue eyes that he'd have remembered her if he had. Lilly smiled, unable to find fault with such a genuinely heartfelt compliment, especially after the beating her ego had taken earlier in the day.

"Are you a farmer?" Lilly guessed, studying him for a moment. Nearing forty, he looked successful despite his casually worn cord pants and blue work shirt, his face full of a calm authority Lilly liked.

"Not exactly," he answered slowly, as though she'd amused him with a view of himself he'd not thought of before. "Although I guess you could say that I have interests in the farms around here." He picked up two sturdy sticks and tossed them far down the creek bed for the eager dogs. Without a word, they turned and began to follow the racing dogs, who covered twice the distance they did, dancing around them like burnished patches of sunlight as they walked.

"What do you do to earn your crust of bread?" he asked, casually wrapping a guiding arm around Lilly's

small shoulders as she nearly walked into a rocky out-
cropping.

"Not mountain climbing, obviously!" Lilly said
wryly. Their laughter had a shared quality that was rare
for such new acquaintances. Now they had moved
between steeply rising bluffs of limestone. A lone crimson maple clung stubbornly, seemingly finding an impossible toehold in solid rock from which to spread its
limbs. Lilly stopped, filled with a piercing sense of life's
wonder as she stared at this example of pure tenacity.
The magnitude of her own problems seemed dimin-
ished in this setting.

"I often come walking here to think," he said. "The
dogs make a good excuse, of course, but I'd come anyway. Problems have a way of growing smaller, less
overwhelming somehow."

"Oh, I know just what you mean." Lilly was amazed
that his thoughts so closely echoed her own. "In fact, I
came here to decide what to do about my job at the
college. I thought I'd be welcomed with open arms. Instead I found the department embroiled in a discrimination suit and the chairman snarling that he'd had
someone else picked out for the job!"

"I know quite a few people up at the college. What
department are you in?"

"English. My chairman, Alec Thomas, is being completely unreasonable about this, too." When he said he
knew people in the college, Lilly ought to have felt a
prickle of warning, but she was just warming to her
subject. "No, he's worse than unreasonable. He's a
pompous ass!

"I'm sorry!" Lilly exclaimed apologetically when she
saw the startled expression on her companion's face.
"Here I am rattling on and on, and I haven't even in-
troduced myself. My name is Lilly Burns," Lilly added
warmly and extended her hand.

"I'm pleased to meet you, Miss Burns. My name is Jonathan Thomas. I'm the president of Fielding National Bank, and I'm afraid that pompous ass boss of yours must be my brother, Alec."

Chapter Two

Lilly shut her eyes and wished she'd done the same with her mouth. "I apologize for my remarks. They were out of line," Lilly said, and she meant it. "I suppose this means I won't get the loan?"

Jonathan threw back his head and roared with laughter. "You forget one thing: I grew up with Alec. I think your remarks are mild in comparison with the things we used to call each other."

"That's different," Lilly murmured, knowing he was being kind, and glad her joke hadn't misfired—for the third time in one day would be just too much! "I truly wouldn't have spoken as I did if I'd known you were his brother, but I stick by my sentiments. He's being unfair, and unprofessional." Lilly fixed Jonathan with a challenging glance that he returned squarely.

The dogs had disappeared up an angled path and the two of them were alone except for the wind and the water in the dying light of the autumn afternoon.

"Care to come up to the house for a drink?" Jonathan offered, and Lilly knew that meant more than just a cup of coffee. Strange as it seemed, she felt they'd established a friendship, and Lilly was glad that it could be based on honesty. She'd had enough of dishonest relationships to last her a lifetime. Jonathan held out a helping hand to start her up the path.

Lilly was breathless as they reached the top, but

Jonathan breathed easily as he lead the way to a large, attractive stone and glass house. They entered through the patio door, where the two dogs waited patiently to be let in. Jonathan soon had the coffeepot on, and he seemed to know his way around the kitchen very well, Lilly noted.

"I can only urge you to give Alec more than one chance. He's under incredible pressure just now trying to round up funding for his latest play. All that fundraising doesn't mix too well with the creative process of playwriting, and I can tell you from personal experience that when things become difficult for Alec he tends to take them out on those around him."

Lilly held her tongue as Jonathan brought her a mug of steaming coffee. He didn't sit down, though, but fished around inside the refrigerator and unearthed a half-eaten coffeecake that he slid into a microwave, punching in the numbers he wanted with the ease of long practice. He brought butter, plates, and broad-bladed knives to the table when he'd retrieved the heated coffeecake.

In a state of bemused envy, Lilly watched him pile on several hundred calories of butter and pop the whole thing into his mouth. While good-sized, certainly much bigger than Alec, Jonathan was by no stretch of the imagination fat. Oh, what it would be like to eat like that! Lilly thought, and picked up her mug of black coffee. Jonathan quirked his brows. "I take it from your silence that you don't agree with me?"

"I just think we all have to deal with stress. If you let people get away with taking their stress out on you, then they'll keep doing it. Alec was determined, ruthlessly determined, to get me to quit by any means that came to hand."

"That just doesn't sound like Alec," Jonathan said with a shake of his head. A bar of concern deepened between his eyebrows as he thought about Lilly's remarks. "He's hot-tempered but not vicious, and I'd think you would be someone he'd like. I certainly do, and I'm rarely wrong," Jonathan added with a decided twinkle.

Why couldn't Alec be more like this? Lilly asked herself. Why wasn't Alec the banker and Jonathan the playwright? She knew the answer immediately. Lilly guessed that it was true that she hadn't seen Alec at his best today; the news of Karen's suit must have been a terrific shock, but even so, Alec was much more volatile, more intense in every way than his almost placid brother. Thank you, Dr. Burns, for your instant character analysis, she teased herself as she gazed around her, taking in her surroundings.

"This is a lovely house." Built low to the ground, the house nonetheless gave the impression of spaciousness and height. Bushy philodendrons sat in squat wicker baskets along the wall of windows that faced the creek, and an area rug of ochre, bronze and gray carried the eye through to the living room. In one corner sat a black baby grand piano, and on it was a dramatic studio photo of a flame-haired woman in a flowing dress. "Is that your wi—" Lilly never got to finish that sentence because of the growing commotion outside. But as she turned back to Jonathan, Lilly glimpsed a look of intense pain that made her rethink her analysis of Jonathan as the placid one. And instinctively Lilly knew it had something to do with the mysterious-looking woman in that picture.

The dogs, barking wildly, rushed to the patio doors to greet someone. Somehow Lilly was expecting the flame-haired woman to appear, and was totally shocked to see Alec instead.

"What the hell are you doing in my house?" he barked out at her, evidently as glad to see her as she was to see him. He tossed his briefcase onto the low, gray suede couch and glared at her. Immediately the room grew smaller and Lilly had trouble just breathing easily in and out, although she'd been doing it all her life.

Confused by the blatant hostility in the air, both dogs growled, then whined and looked to Jonathan for guidance in this very confusing situation.

"Your house?" Lilly choked on the possessive, feeling ill. This house, where she'd felt so at ease, belonged to Alec? She just couldn't take it in and, like the dogs, looked to Jonathan to sort this one out for her.

"Actually we both own half." Jonathan dropped more confusion into the brew with that comment.

"You mean you live together here?" Lilly found that hard to imagine somehow.

"My God!" Alec exclaimed with complete exasperation. "Would you like to see how we divide up the bills, too? Jonathan, what is she doing here?"

"Lilly and I met by the creek this afternoon, Alec. Nothing sinister in that," Jonathan answered him quietly. "Coffee's fresh, would you like some?" This was said in an effort to diffuse some of the crackling tension in the air as Jonathan looked from the stiff, angry figure of his brother to Lilly's bewildered face.

She just couldn't take it in. Lilly's eyes moved around the room and fell once more on that picture on the piano. Who was that woman? It was the sort of picture one gives to a lover, which discounted a sister or relative in her book. That left only one likely category. Lilly didn't like that category, but disliked the fact that it bothered her even more.

"Look. I have to put up with you at work. Do I have to do the same in my own home?" Alec demanded offensively.

"Alec!" Jonathan said. "This is my home as well as yours and Lilly is my invited guest."

"It's all right. I have to be getting back. I have some phone calls to make, and lesson plans to finalize too,"

Lilly said, and stood up hastily. She didn't want Alec to be able to add creating a rift between the two brothers to her sins, even if he was being incredibly obnoxious.

"Great. I'll see you off the property," Alec said with no attempt to hide his satisfaction at having won this round.

"No thanks. It's not far."

"Nothing is in Fielding, as I think you'll find once you've been here awhile," Jonathan said with that twinkle that Lilly liked.

"If she lasts that long," Alec muttered, not quite under his breath.

Then the phone rang, and Jonathan leaned over the counter to hook the receiver with one long arm. Half-listening as she slipped into her red jacket again, Lilly was astonished to see an entirely different aspect of Jonathan. He became instantly businesslike, almost austere, and she could see that her little analysis had been too hasty all around. The family resemblance was there between the two brothers; the edges were just a bit more polished, more honed down in Jonathan, that was all.

"Let's go," Alec said impatiently, and grabbed for her elbow. Rather than make an issue out of it, Lilly allowed herself to be almost dragged to the door.

"Willis has managed to come through with partial payment," Jonathan said with evident relief as he replaced the receiver. "I sure didn't want to start foreclosure actions."

"You shouldn't give the man so much rope. He'll just take longer to hang himself," Alec said darkly, and jerked Lilly through the door.

"Are you always this pleasant about everyone, or is this just a performance for my benefit to scare me away from the job?" Lilly asked sweetly as they took off at a rattling pace down the nearly dark driveway. Jonathan's good-bye floated after them in a vain effort to catch up.

Stupidly, Lilly at first tried to keep up with Alec's blistering pace, then she slowed. She had no intention of embarrassing herself and delighting this blue-eyed devil by falling on her face.

"Just stay away from my brother, do you hear?" Alec ordered over his shoulder. "You'll eat him alive."

"Drop dead," Lilly shot back, head lifting defiantly, face a white blob in the near dark. "You have absolutely no say in my private life, and a *lot* less in the execution of my job than you think you have, buster!"

"Just what does that mean?" Alec stopped.

Lilly stopped too. They faced each other. Energy snapped between them like the crack of sails on a gusty day, a bitingly painful kind of energy that Lilly had never experienced before. She felt aware of everything around her: the dry whispering of the wind in the pines that spread their cool scent in the air; his outline against the faint light from the road; and so close were they, she knew each exhalation of his breath and the hard, set expression on his beaky face.

"I don't find much ambiguity in that remark," she added sarcastically. "But since you seem to have a problem with the language at which you're supposed to be such an expert, I'll put it in one-or two-syllable words that you'll understand: Mind your own damned business!" Lilly shouted.

"You think you've got life pegged, don't you?" Alec shouted back furiously. "Little miss rich girl out doing her civic duty to educate the less-fortunate masses."

Lilly swallowed hard. There was just enough truth in that to sting like mad, but she was damned well not going to let him see that. "What would you know about it? You're too busy writing sneering, misanthropic plays that pass for serious art these days just because you can't bear to let your characters be happy!" Lilly had to stop because she'd run out of breath. She took a deep one, hands clenched at her sides as her ribs heaved up and down. "Your play reeks of hatred of women, so I fail to see that your judgments have much validity."

Lilly knew she'd hit home. They both had, and were both breathing hard, as though the words they'd hammered at each other were physical blows.

"Run on home now, little girl, because you're starting to play with the big kids now. You just might end up having to ask Big Daddy to buy you another position at some other college that's in need of endowments."

Lilly longed so intensely to hit him that she could almost see her fist flashing into his stomach with all the power of adrenaline-pumping muscle behind it, and could almost hear the sweet, satisfying grunt as the air went out of him. Instead she stalked regally past. His breathing did grow more ragged as he struggled to control his temper and Lilly quickened her pace. She refused to run, but hurrying seemed like a good idea.

She ought to have paid more attention to her footing and less to what Alec was doing behind her. A stone caught the toe of her shoe, her arms flailed, and Alec shot forward to grab one of them. Lilly thrashed wildly as his fingers twisted in her thick hair. "Apologize for that remark about my work, or I swear you'll regret it," he said in her ear.

He barely got the words out before Lilly kicked him. Instead of letting go, he forced her closer, and their struggling threw them both off balance. Alec pushed her against the trunk of a pine tree, his mouth finding hers as Lilly moaned in combined response and frustration, digging her nails into the thin material of his shirt. Suddenly the seemingly solid form of the tree trunk gave way, sending them tumbling over and over into the shallow ravine that fell away from the driveway. Alec ended up on top of Lilly, and his mouth careened over her face in an unrelenting search for her mouth that left her weak and panting. One bare white shoulder protruded from her red jacket, and Alec trailed warm fingers along the hollowed flesh, which sent an unwanted express train of desire through her, and she pushed her fingers into the dank soil to stop them curling into him.

"Satisfied?" she asked in a voice that was meant to be scoffing but that came out a whispered plea, an unconditional surrender. This wasn't how it was meant to turn out. The enemy had weakened her with a surprisingly potent flank attack that had put her forces into a total rout.

"No. No, I'm not. Are you?" he asked, and for a tense moment the only sound was their still rasping breathing.

"Get off me," Lilly ordered quietly, and he obeyed, not helping but standing back to watch as she straightened her jacket and brushed down her clothes with shaky hands.

He looked strangely out of place in the dim forest, a man dressed in pinstripe pants, dress shirt and Italian shoes—more ready for a board meeting than a battle in the forest. Lilly took a few steps back and away from him. She found she could think more clearly when he wasn't physically so near.

She longed to say something dramatic like she never wanted to see him again, but as she knew she'd see him at the college in the morning, she was denied that very satisfying gesture, and instead flicked pine needles vigorously in his direction as she stripped them out of her tangled hair. She winced at one too hard a tug on her hair, and glared at Alec.

"You look fine. No permanent damage, so let's go." He gestured impatiently with his arm for her to move out. The breeze lifted the collar of his shirt and ruffled his black hair. He's probably feeling the cold, Lilly realized, and thought it was only what he deserved.

The walk back to her rooming house was a silent

one. They went past homes filled with the golden warmth of homecomings that made the chill all the more marked between them. Leaves whirled in aimless, forlorn patterns around their feet, and somewhere a dog barked twice, his voice deep and rough and full of warning to someone invading his turf.

"Mission accomplished," Lilly said bleakly when they stood on the porch of her rooming house. The house was completely dark, which meant her landlady was in Mankato visiting her married daughter. Lilly would be alone for the night.

Without another word Alec turned on his heels and left.

Lilly went into the house, turning on lights as she went.

Mrs. Jordan had warned her that she often spent time at her daughter's home in Mankato, but Lilly was glad there was no one to see her disheveled appearance and wild eyes that shocked even her as she passed the hall mirror on her way upstairs. A hot bath was what she needed, she told herself as she raised an arm experimentally and felt the muscles tweak in protest.

Halfway up, she reluctantly turned around and went back down to lock the doors. Fielding might be a very safe place, but Lilly knew she wouldn't be able to sleep if she left the doors unlocked all night. The phone rang as she passed it, and, to her surprise, it was Jonathan.

"Something wrong? Is Alec all right?" Lilly asked quickly and then could have kicked herself. "He just left here in kind of a hurry," she added lamely when Jonathan asked her why she thought something might be wrong.

"Actually, I'm calling on Alec's behalf to see if you're okay. He said it looked like no one was home and he wanted to make sure you got in with no trouble." Jonathan spoke the lines like someone reading off a cue card. Lilly smiled.

"Why couldn't he call me himself?" she asked, knowing he was too angry with her to do so, but also secretly pleased that he was worried enough, and gentleman enough, to get someone to do so.

"You've got me," Jonathan said exasperatedly, evidently abandoning the script Alec had written for him in favor of brotherly candor. "All I can say is that there are some wild days ahead for the Fielding English department if you two can't make peace."

"Oh, whatever do you mean?"

"Well, all I know is that forty minutes ago the two of you left here for a walk that shouldn't take more than five minutes, and then Alec comes back in with his shirt ripped and dirt—" The phone went dead, but just before it did, Lilly was sure she heard Alec's voice in the background.

Lilly felt her spirits rising for no reason she could really pinpoint as she once more headed for the stairs and a hot bath. From the warm and steamy comfort of a hot tub, that fight in the cool, dank woods seemed unreal, something that happened to someone else, not her. Yet the ache in muscles unused to violent motion was proof enough. What a day this has been, Lilly thought as she reluctantly got out of the tub and dressed in a cherry-red robe and fuzzy slippers.

Lilly wondered how Alec knew so much about her family. Those remarks had hurt, but they weren't the kind of casual insult that just pops into the mind. No, he had to have done some checking on her today, and that meant he hadn't just gone behind the frosted door marked Chairman and forgotten about her. Lilly considered it only justice that if he was haunting her thoughts she been haunting his, too. The idea of her father buying her this position was ludicrously funny. If he only knew the truth, Lilly thought. He'd find it was just the opposite. She'd interviewed for this job almost in secret, afraid that if her father knew he'd pay them not to hire her! He wanted Lilly in Burns Electronics, but faced with a fait accompli, he'd been forced to give in. She actually preferred Alec's version of things. Because if he knew how shaky Lilly felt about this bid for independence, he'd have a much more powerful weapon than thinking she was a little miss rich girl who got everything her heart desired.

Lilly knew the time had come for the call she'd been putting off. Just call them and get it over with, she ordered herself. Lilly knew her parents well enough to know that if she waited for them to call her, they'd assume she had something to hide. Better to take the initiative than to be called out of a class to take an "emergency" call from her mother!

"Things *are* going well, Mother," Lilly was insisting just moments later.

"Well, we were about to call; I thought something might have gone wrong since you didn't call when you said you would," Millicent Burns said.

"No. I gave my presentation to the faculty today, and have offered to assist anyone interested in incorporating portions of my system into their course work." Lilly sighed, twisting the black phone cord into contorted figure eights as she listened to her mother's reply. She could imagine her mother sitting in bed, black half-glasses on her thin nose, knees drawn up to support her papers. Millicent Burns didn't believe in wasting time, and knew herself to be totally capable of managing her daughter and getting paperwork done for the business at the same time, Lilly knew.

"You know your father and I have only your best interests at heart, darling," Millicent went on. "I'm glad things are going fine so far, but please remember that if this should fall through, we would want you back here in a minute."

"Of course, Mother. If I fail at this, I'm sure you'll be right there to tell me you told me so."

"What a nasty, uncalled-for remark," Millicent said evenly.

"I'm sorry. It's been a very, very long day. And I don't have much more to report."

"Well, you needn't sound as though I were the police," her mother said, her voice sharpening with authority nonetheless. "I just think it was a mistake moving down there so soon after breaking off your engagement. I'm not sure you're fully recovered from it yet."

You mean I'm inconveniently beyond the influence of you and Martin down here, Lilly added mentally, but she said, "I just think a change of scene was a good idea."

"It makes reconciliation difficult, though. How can you and Martin work out your differences with you in the poky little town and he in Minneapolis?" Genuine appeal emanated from her mother's voice, and Lilly steeled herself against it.

"We can't. That's the whole point, Mother. There will be no reconciliation, no tidy corporate merger. I don't know how much plainer I have to make it that I want nothing more to do with that man."

"All right, don't upset yourself," Millicent said hastily, and Lilly heard the crackle of paper as her mother sat up and put her work aside. I ought to be flattered that I'm getting her full attention, Lilly thought caustically.

"I have to get some sleep, Mother. Say hi to Ben and Daddy for me, will you?"

"Of course. They miss you, too. Try to come home for the weekend soon. Your animals miss you also."

Lilly grimaced as she hung up the phone and trudged back upstairs to her bedroom. As always, her Mother managed not only to have the last word, but to plant a zinger in it. She knew Lilly disliked leaving the animals there, but this job offer at Fielding had come up, a fortuitous opportunity she didn't want to pass up. The one snag had been the lack of time to find proper accommodations for her Irish setter and cat, Mongo. Her mother had also managed to imply that she personally slaved over a hot can opener and letting a dog in and out had tied her to the house. In fact, Lilly's young brother, Ben, was thrilled at the chance to care for them.

For a long time Lilly stood in the cool embrasure of the bay window that looked out over the straggling bluffs leading up toward Fielding College. The college was a beacon, the only bright lights in an otherwise dark sky. *What if mother is right, and I fail at this, too?* Lilly wondered, knowing there was more than a slight chance of it. The situation in the department was nothing like what she'd been led to believe. Tired and alone, it seemed to Lilly that all around her were willing her to fail.

She sighed, resting her forehead on the cold pane, listening to the wind brush the limb of an old elm tree in squeaky patterns across the glass. Just three months ago the future had seemed so assured: her Ph.D. completed, she was ready to move from the part-time consulting she'd done for Burns Electronics to full-time work, traveling the country, giving writing seminars to the secretaries and executives at the various branches of her father's company. She would marry Martin, of whom her father and mother heartily approved, and live happily ever after.

It's always disheartening what a fool a seemingly intelligent person can be, Lilly thought without much amusement, and Lilly considered herself one of the biggest. Once she'd seen through Martin, actually heard him bragging that marrying her would be his best career move to date, Lilly began to see all the little things that had constantly given him away. A small measure of her pride was restored as she allowed Martin to betray himself. What was the phrase Alec had used about this Willis person? Lilly dug back into memory and found it. She'd given Martin enough rope and he'd finally hung himself with it.

Something nagged at Lilly. She dragged her thoughts away from pointless recriminations back to the present. That name Willis sounded familiar, and for a moment Lilly couldn't remember why. She knew no one in Fielding...the discrimination suit! Karen Willis was the name of the woman who was suing Alec; there was something very odd going on here, Lilly thought with a frown. She hurried out the bedroom and down the stairs, holding her robe up carefully on the steep stairs. All her weariness was forgotten momentarily as she shifted through the pile of magazines Mrs. Jordan kept near the phone. The familiar yellow surface of the phone book was at the very bottom and looked as though its stiff pages got little use. Lilly picked it up and thumbed through it until she reached the *W*'s, which in a quarter-inch thick phone book didn't take long, Lilly thought in amusement.

Ahh, there it was: Henry Willis, R.R. 3. Quite an address, Lilly thought with a quick grin. It was the only Willis in the book, so either Karen was from a different town, or she was related to this Henry Willis by marriage or family. Either way, it seemed odd to Lilly that Jonathan was so obviously relieved that "Willis has come through with partial payment."

The plain, old-fashioned clock on her bedside table read quarter to two when Lilly finally pulled back the quilt and got in. Sleep swept over her, and only when strong sunlight touched her eyelids with warmth did she stir.

She rolled over lazily to look at the clock, then shot upright as if electrified. The clock told her she was late, and on the first official day of classes! Dressing took only minutes, since Lilly had yet to bring most of her wardrobe to Fielding, and she took a precious ten minutes to eat breakfast, since she'd had no dinner the night before.

One of the nicest things, Lilly thought as she roared into the faculty parking lot, about living in a small town was that nothing was too far from anything else.

"Good morning, Miss Burns," Hilda greeted her warmly as Lilly rushed in to check her mailbox. Lilly pulled its contents out and said, "Please, call me Lilly. Did you get a chance to run off those syllabi for me?"

"Of course," Hilda said with an audible sniff, visibly offended that Lilly should dare to imply she'd forget something like that. "I saw that red car of yours out of Mr. Thomas's window, and put a cup of coffee on your desk too."

"Thank you, you're an angel," Lilly said with a lovely smile over her shoulder, and thought that small-town secretaries were another thing she liked. Her box contained reminders of deadlines for grade changes, book orders for next semester, and a note from David Holmes that said he would appreciate her sitting in on one of his classes, and included a brief schedule of his day. That gave Lilly a lift. She knew David Holmes wasn't the toughest nut to crack in the department, but still, this was a beginning.

She sat down at her desk to sip the hot coffee and compare their schedules in an optimistic frame of mind. Looking over her own schedule, Lilly knew her colleague thought they'd given her the dregs: two courses in introductory composition and the introduction to linguistic studies. But the truth was that Lilly didn't mind a bit, except for the politics of the thing. Unlike so many academics, she liked teaching composition and wasn't eager to pay her dues and move to more upper-level courses. She was also eager to show how well her system of teaching composition worked, and the more sections of composition she had the better she could do that. Lilly had no doubts about her teaching method, but many about the professors she'd like to get to employ them.

The bells sounded for the opening classes, and Lilly's stomach tightened, this time with good nervousness, the kind that made Lilly a superior teacher. Lilly got "up" for every class, and her ability to focus her attention solely on the subject at hand, no matter how many times she'd been through it before, was one of her greatest strengths.

Yet like many people, she had a tendency to take for granted the things she did well, and focus all her attention on things she thought she did poorly—and a glimpse she caught of Alec's sturdy back disappearing into his office sent her spirits plummeting.

How in the world did I allow myself to get into a brawl with the man? Lilly demanded of herself as she walked to her class on the first floor. Then she pushed open the door, all noise ceased and the teaching day had begun.

Lilly got to see David while she was picking up her second cup of coffee. They stood chatting in the same room where they'd had the staff meeting the day before, a room which was also full of shelves containing reference materials used by the entire staff.

"I got your note. This week's a bit hectic, but would next week sometime suit you? That way you'll get a chance to get to know their problems before I descend on them."

"Yes, that's fine," he said easily, and pushed his gold wire-rimmed glasses up absently. "I reread your dissertation last night. It's excellent. I think Fielding College is lucky to have you on the staff."

"I'm flattered," Lilly said, but privately thought David probably had a fair stake in seeing that she lived up to her résumé. Otherwise she guessed he'd never hear the end of it from Alec. But maybe I'm just getting cynical in my old age, Lilly told herself. David was a genuinely nice man; he lacked the extraordinary vitality of Alec, but he was a nice man.

"A week from Friday my wife and I are having some people in for a party. We'd really like to have you come, if you're free."

"I think I'm free. Can I bring anything?" Lilly was already doing a swift mental survey of her limited wardrobe and wondering if she'd have to go home to get some more clothes. She really hadn't thought about party wear when she'd packed. Lilly's thoughts had been a bit scattered, and she'd mostly pulled working clothes from her closet in Minneapolis, along with the usual casual attire that she always wore.

"No, just bring yourself, and a date, if you wish. Anyone can give you directions, but we live on 23 Walnut Lane, which is just beyond the Dairy Queen. Come around eight."

"I'll look forward to it, David," Lilly said, not entirely truthfully. Lilly didn't enjoy business parties, or parties in general, for that matter. The black dress would have to do, she thought in resignation, and told herself it might not be that bad. She went down the hall and into the room where her second composition class of the day met, and pulled the door shut behind her.

"Good morning. My name is Lilly Burns, and this is Composition 101, section five. Please check your registration cards before you hand them in to me to make sure you're in the right place." Twenty-five heads bent in obedience, and Lilly thought in mild amusement of the power she wielded. She collected the cards and handed out an information sheet meant to gather facts about how much writing they'd done in the past and what they thought their problem areas were. While they did that she read through the cards to give them a few minutes to write.

"Remember to answer in complete sentences, as I'll be looking at the form of your answer, not just the content," she warned good-naturedly as she saw several of the male students jotting yes or no answers to questions she'd specified must be answered with complete sentences. Patience, Lilly had found, was a prime necessity for good teaching, and Lilly thought Alec must have a secret supply of it that he hadn't shown her yet, if he was any kind of a teacher.

She read through the names and attempted to attach a face to each name. She was good at it, and usually had a whole class down by the end of the second or third class.

"John Sonntag, Susan Thomas," Lilly paused at that name. "Any relation to some other Thomas in this department?" she asked teasingly. Thomas was a fairly common Welsh name in the area, and she was merely trying to establish contact with the rather stony-faced young woman in the front row.

"He's my brother," she acknowledged in a smoky voice that held a tinge of hostility.

"Well, good for you," Lilly said with not entirely genuine enthusiasm. Inwardly she accused Alec of spying on her, and knew she'd have a word or two to say to him.

She straightened from the podium where she'd been leaning and picked up her syllabus. Walking to the front of the class she said briskly, "Let's get started, shall we?"

Chapter Three

By the time her class ended Lilly had calmed down quite a bit. She went to her office, shut the door, and dumped the rest of her handouts on the desk. She felt the usual sense of tired exhilaration. After the first class of a semester she usually had more questions, but the students here at Fielding seemed just a touch more mature and organized. Besides, it was a lot easier to find your books in a college bookstore that catered to five thousand students than a university bookstore that catered to sixty-five thousand, Lilly reminded herself. Already, the differences between the two student populations were becoming evident.

Still, Susan's presence was going to make Lilly more careful. And she was seriously beginning to wonder just how many Thomases there were! With a clunk, her dark blue pumps hit the floor under her desk. When she looked at it objectively, spies didn't seem much in Alec's style, either, Lilly had to admit.

"Miss—er, Lilly, I mean. Alec would like to see you in his office."

"I'll be right there, Hilda," Lilly told the older woman, and her toes stroked the cool linoleum in search of her shoes. Hey, wait a minute. Lilly stopped and asked herself why she was in such a hurry to jump through his hoops. Let him wait a minute, she urged herself. She sat tapping a pencil on her blotter to the rousing beat of the Fielding College band, which was rehearsing on the athletic field not far from the English and Foreign Language building.

She lasted close to five minutes. Since she'd been the victim of power games in her own family, Lilly disliked them. They made her feel uneasy and ashamed. So with a decisive backward thrust of her chair, Lilly stood and left her office.

Typewriter keys clacked in a painfully intermittent fashion as she neared the chairman's office. Lilly felt her insides tighten in anticipation of seeing Alec again after their struggle the night before.

"That was quick," Alec said approvingly after her light tap was answered by a gruff 'Come in.' "You didn't have to drop everything and run down here."

"I didn't. I was at a point to take a break, anyway," Lilly answered coolly. So much for making a dent in his ego, she thought, and added, "What did you want to talk to me about?"

"First of all," he began, and made a gesture for Lilly to take the battered chair in front of his desk, "I wanted to apologize for my horrendous behavior last night and yesterday afternoon. My remarks and actions were totally uncalled for. My only excuse, such as it is, comes from the pressure I've been working under lately." He smiled at Lilly, and unwillingly she felt her dislike soften.

"I didn't exactly act like my normal self, either," Lilly admitted.

"Ahh, now I think you're being generous! I know my faults. A quick temper and a tendency to allow frustrations to spill over onto those who don't deserve it are certainly high on the list."

Lilly laughed at his rueful expression and said, "You're not alone in that."

"Now I'm hoping you'll extend that generosity a bit further and call my behavior yesterday a bit of temporary insanity brought about by overwork. Could we start over, Lilly?"

A shudder and a sigh released some of the tension she'd been holding inside, and Lilly nodded. She was frankly bewildered by this turn of events, but try as she might, Lilly could see nothing but sincerity in Alec's intense blue gaze.

"Good." Alec's tone grew brisker, a shade louder as he moved quickly on. "I've read your dissertation, and I give you full credit for practicing what you preach. Your prose is crisp, elegant and clear."

"Why, thank you." Where was the chauvinistic, sarcastic man of yesterday?

"That's where I thought you might be able to help me out," he added smoothly, shuffling through several piles of papers with a trace of his earlier self showing in the impatience that flitted over his face as he searched for what he wanted.

Aha, he wants a favor, and that's the reason for the big apology. "What can I do for you?" she asked, a touch of dry humor in her voice. The humor was directed at herself, mostly, for not guessing from the start the reason for his lavish apology, because it had seemed strongly out of character.

"Maybe a great deal," Alec said. He shoved back his chair and paced to the narrow window overlooking the parking lot. "I like to assign work to the best-qualified person. Your dissertation and your evident enthusiasm for clear writing makes me think you're perfect for this job."

"What job?" Lilly asked. She had her doubts, after what she'd overheard yesterday, about how impartial Alec's choices were. And her suspicions were thoroughly aroused, despite his gracious apology.

"Things are changing here at Fielding. I want the English department to be part of that change. Right now we're in the process of revising the statement of this institution's philosophy. But...." Alec paused, fingers riffling through his black thick hair in a disgusted gesture.

"But you're having difficulty with it?" Lilly said quietly, remembering the intermittent pecking at typewriter keys that she'd heard as she neared his office.

"You wouldn't believe what these administration boys are capable of generating!" Both palms slapped down on the desk and Alec leaned over it, blue eyes electric. "So what do you say? Are you willing to take on the language of the bureaucracy?" His tone was challenging as he held Lilly's gaze and refused to let go.

"Give me the proposal, and I'll take a look at it." Lilly stretched her hand for the tattered piece of paper just as Alec pushed it her way. Their hands brushed and awareness snapped taut between them.

Lilly pulled the paper away and bent her head, but the words refused to focus. She felt Alec's restless energy zinging around her impatiently as he waited for her comments, and that didn't help her concentration. She didn't want to acknowledge the urge she'd had to stroke his hand; she wanted her mind to be strong and confident, not this pulsing mass of feelings.

It's just one of those physical things, she assured herself, the result of an unusual combination of factors. Lilly was sure that if they hadn't started out so angry with each other she wouldn't be so ridiculously aware of Alec's every breath. Lilly closed her eyes momentarily at the remembered scent of cool, dank earth beneath her naked shoulder. Last night's tussle in the woods seemed suddenly very near in the sunny light of morning.

"Well?" Alec demanded brusquely. "What's wrong with it?"

Scrambling, Lilly scanned the piece and saw many places to start. "In general, a lack of directness. Many of these long, ornate sentences lack true verbs."

"Mmmm." Alec sounded unconvinced.

"However, the lack of true verbs is hidden from the casual reader because the sentences are so long. By using fancy clauses the writer manages to obscure his meaning."

"I noticed a lot of passive voice," Alec agreed, and Lilly nodded.

"Absolutely. This writer has no guts. He'd be getting straight *F*'s in my class." Lilly's tone was stinging. Inwardly she thought the administration staff could benefit from the type of seminars she'd given at her father's electronics branches around the country.

Alec gave her a startled look and said, "What do you mean?"

Lilly knew she had his attention now, and she stood and walked around to the other side of the desk. Slapping the piece of mangled prose in front of him, she demanded: "I challenge you to tell me in plain English what this sentence means." And she pointed to one at random.

To her amusement, Alec squirmed like any first-year student as she read it. "Employment of prioritizing necessitating student input positively impacts on future career choices and facilitates maximization of student potential."

This close Lilly could smell his skin, could see the pinprickly beginnings of stubble along his jawline. He smelled . . . sensual like the moist earth. Her heart raced as she realized he was looking back at her; they were only inches apart. Lilly could see the thin yellow striations in his blue eyes. "Do you notice anything about this sentence, Alec?" she asked, her voice a trifle ragged with the effort to control her physical reaction to him.

He ran his short, square-tipped fingers along the lines again until they brushed her own, following the arch of index finger and thumb upon which Lilly supported herself. Lilly moved her hand away jerkily.

"Too wordy?" Alec offered, and tilted his head back the fraction necessary to touch her breast and sensation fired inside her.

"Uh-huh, but can you tell me the verb in this sentence?" Lilly asked, moving back to fold her arms protectively across her breasts. She was determined not to dignify his behavior with a comment, yet equally determined to see that he went no further.

"Impact?"

"No. Impact isn't a verb."

Alec scanned the sentence again. "You mean—my God, you're right! The sentence has no verb. No wonder all the minor tinkering I was doing didn't help!" He turned in his chair, their knees brushed, and a sensation like liquid fire seared through Lilly.

"You still haven't told me what this sentence means," she reminded him huskily. She moved to the other side of his desk and sat down unsteadily, her flesh still hot from the contact with his. She raised her eyes to his, and her breathing quickened. It took all her will to remain seated, because her body wanted to melt into his. But her mind prodded coldly with reason after reason why she couldn't.

"I'd say that the sentence is an attempt to say how important it is to have goals," Alec said, blue eyes compelling. "Will you have dinner with me, Lilly? Just to prove there're no hard feelings?"

"No."

The bells sounded for the end of the class period and the shuffle of feet began. "I have a class now. Do you want me to edit this policy statement or not?" Lilly stood, her hazel eyes flaring bright yellow with emotion. Her voice was dry and cool.

"Yes, I do. And I wasn't trying to put you on the spot with my dinner invitation—"

"Oh, really?" Lilly's voice interrupted, sharp with disbelief.

"Really," Alec said quietly, and his expression was puzzled as Lilly crammed the tattered paper into a folder he handed her. "But if that frightens you somehow, think about joining the group of us that meets on Tuesday nights at Duffy's Bar."

"It doesn't frighten me; I'm just not interested, and now I have a class to teach."

But as she taught, Lilly thought only of Alec. As she discussed phonemes and nasal passages, Lilly thought about Alec's dinner invitation. She realized as far as he was concerned, after apologizing for his behavior of yesterday, he probably couldn't see any reason why she would refuse to go out with him. But *afraid*? Lilly contemplated that idea and dismissed it. Just wait until next Tuesday.... She'd refused his invitation to eat alone with him, but Lilly saw no reason to avoid group gatherings. She alternated between indignation that he'd thought a dose of boyish charm could make amends for his behavior, and a sense of disgust with herself for having responded to it.

Overlying this was the uneasy realization that nothing he'd done either today or yesterday made his guilt in a sex discrimination suit anything but plausible.

Lilly's exhausting first day ended by three, and she drove the short distance to Mrs. Jordan's with a sense of relief. Just a quick shower and a change of clothes helped. She walked into the kitchen determined to shed Alec Thomas, too. After a salad filled with good things from the garden, Lilly settled back to read through the student's in-class essays. In general, the writing seemed a cut above that of her university students. Still, there was room for improvement.

Also not surprising was Susan Thomas's response. Lilly read it with frank interest. The assignment had been to describe the ways in which she thought her life would differ from her parents' lives. Students could answer from a personal or a global stance. Susan's answer was very personal: "I come from a family of five in which I am the youngest and only girl," she wrote. Shades of a long Russian novel, Lilly thought. "I don't want my life to vary greatly from that of my parents and two older brothers. They are both single and pursuing successful careers. I wish to do the same, except that I have chosen the field of neurosurgery." Nothing like knowing where you're heading at age eighteen, Lilly thought wryly. The essay went on from there, and technically Lilly couldn't fault it much, although its youthful arrogance made her smile a bit. She finished it and put it aside.

She thought for a moment of herself at eighteen; she felt much more than ten years older than Susan Thomas. But then, Lilly acknowledged ruefully, at eighteen she had very much wanted her life to differ from her parents' lives. Studying English literature had been as much of a rebellion for Lilly at eighteen as she could manage. Harvard had been a delicious freedom. She didn't want a degree in business, thank you very much, Daddy, and that was the beginning of a nearly four-year campaign. Next came the struggle over graduate work. "You've had your fun, now get serious and earn an M.B.A." had been her father's attitude. Instead, Lilly had come home and gotten a Ph.D. in composition. Yet in the end, she'd almost ended up where both her parents wanted her: in the family firm. Thank you, Martin Stone, Lilly thought, for rescuing me from that!

Even as she continued to read her students' essays, lightly marking the main problems in each one, Lilly's thoughts kept returning to the Thomas family. If neither of Susan's brothers were married—and Lilly felt a stab of jealousy at the thought of Alec being married that she didn't want to examine too closely—then who was the mystery woman on the piano? She sensed that the woman was important in the Thomas brothers' lives, and had the strange sense she would affect Lilly's own life as well.

The first week of classes passed swiftly. She'd seen surprisingly little of Alec, and found out from David Holmes that he'd been doing readings of his new play in New York for possible backers. "Doesn't the administration object to his running off like that?" Lilly had asked casually. David had assured her that Alec was beginning to have enough of a name for himself that they made allowances for him. "And he doesn't shirk his workload here in the department, either." David had shaken his head, careful not to dislodge the thinning strand arranged over the top of his head. "He's got enough energy for three men."

Tuesday night found Lilly strangely restless. She'd been working hard for the past week and needed a change, she thought, and remembered Alec's casual suggestion that she try the group get-together they had at Duffy's Bar. At the time Lilly couldn't have been less interested but it suddenly sounded . . . well, fun.

She found Duffy's without difficulty: it was one in a line of neon-decorated places that were loud, scruffy, and unappealing. But Lilly forced herself to overcome the squeamishness she felt at entering such a place on her own, and was hit by a blast of country music that nearly knocked her off her feet.

At first glance, smoke and dim lighting kept her from seeing anyone she recognized, but then at the back of the narrow barroom she caught sight of Hilda's brassy head next to Alec's dark one. They were at a long table of about six or eight people. Lilly had to circle a few overturned chairs to reach them. They had obviously been there awhile, since the table was littered with empty beer bottles and bits of popcorn and peanut shells crunched under Lilly's feet.

"Hi!" Lilly spoke brightly to cover her sudden shyness. "May I join you?"

"Go right ahead," several people chorused at once. Lilly slid into the booth side of the long table, next to Hilda and David. She and the secretary exchanged greetings. Lilly was becoming fond of this middle-aged woman, and had to admit she was a bit surprised to see her here. Lilly would have imagined her to be the home-and-hubby type. Obviously that wasn't the whole picture, Lilly thought, as she watched Hilda polish off what was definitely not her first beer. Tonight she wore a yellow polyester pants suit with several large-beaded necklaces of amber, orange, and blue.

Now that her own initial nervousness had fled, Lilly had the distinct feeling she'd interrupted something.

"What'll you have to drink?" David stood up abruptly and asked. "The first one is on me, and after that you're on your own."

"Chablis, if they have it." Not even for camaraderie would she drink beer. Lilly looked around at the bent heads and sudden silence. She felt certain she'd been at least partially the topic of the now-defunct conversation. Too many of the participants were looking anywhere but at her.

With the exception of Alec Thomas. He calmly pulled a wicker basket of peanuts closer to him, and crushed one open between his fingers.

"Oh, thank you," Lilly said as a dripping wineglass appeared over her left shoulder.

"Got bumped on the way back. Sorry," David explained as Lilly took the dry napkin Hilda silently handed her.

"Don't worry about it," Lilly reassured him as she saw his anxious expression. Lilly took a deep breath, then plunged into the cold conversational abyss. "I'm looking for a house to rent, possibly with the option to buy. Does anyone know of something available in the area?'' She looked around the group, then added, "I'd like a medium-size place that allows animals."

Just then someone put another coin into the jukebox and a singer claiming it was still rock 'n' roll to him blasted into the room like well-placed dynamite, and Lilly had to shout to the man who'd just touched his lighted cigarette to the back of her favorite red jacket that, no, that was perfectly all right. So she missed Alec's first murmured comment.

"I'm sorry, what was that you said?" Lilly leaned forward to hear.

"I said there's always the old Higginboom place out on Route 8," Alec repeated patiently, blue eyes bland as a baby's bottom.

"Oh, would they allow animals?" Lilly asked eagerly, and was surprised to hear snickers from some of those around the table. Hilda was giving Alec a long-suffering look, and Lilly noticed the subtle twitching of his upper lip.

"Isn't that place too close to the fields where they hold those all-night fraternity parties?" David asked gingerly. His skinny fingers plucked at his napkin, rolling bits of it down into tidy balls that he then threw into the overflowing ashtray.

"The old Higginboom place! Now there's a spot of history, miss!" A beery voice boomed into their conversation from the next table.

"Oh?"

"Yes, ma'am! Old man Higginboom hung hisself and they didn't find him for four whole days. Blowing in the wind he was, and his milk cows bawling their heads off!"

The table rocked with laughter. Lilly met Alec's gaze steadily. "Please let me know when you're in the market for property in the Minneapolis area, Alec. I'm sure I can steer you in the right direction." There was more laughter and some approving glances for the swift comeback Lilly had to Alec's teasing, then the normal conversations resumed. Lilly was only marginally aware of the others. Alec drew the bulk of her attention as he always seemed to do. It was as though the rest of the room was fuzzed, and only Alec was in sharp, biting focus. Lilly wasn't sure she liked that, but that was the way it was—she felt his every breath, could smell the cool, subtle scent of him above all the competition in the smoky room. "Nice comeback," he said softly, and Lilly stared, trying to figure him out. "Why?" she asked aloud.

Just then another round of beers appeared and was passed around the table with noisy, good-natured arguing about whose turn it was to pay. The good-naturedness sharpened, though, when it focused on Todd Godwin. With an effort, Lilly pulled her attention from Alec to watch this byplay. As she sipped her chablis, she wondered if Todd often let everyone else pay.

"Better start drinking up," Todd advised. "Only three hours until closing time."

Lilly gave him a wry look and raised her wineglass as evidence that she was doing just fine the way she was. Next to David, Todd was the youngest member of the staff. Unmarried, he had that kind of tousled, boyish look that appealed highly to some women. Lilly wasn't one of them. Todd had already tried to fill Lilly in on everyone in the department, even though Lilly had done everything she could to politely discourage it.

"If you're seriously interested in some property, I might be able to help you out," David said a bit diffidently. "Or rather my wife might. She's a real estate agent here in town, and a good one, if I do say so myself."

"Does she operate out of one of those national companies?" Lilly asked, more to make conversation than out of any real thought that she would use the woman's services. Without doubt, Lilly knew her father would have someone out here in a minute to deal with any housing arrangements Lilly made. And even though she chafed at the control that gave him over her life, Lilly also felt it was comforting to know she'd have the best and quickest services available.

A muttered, forceful comment from Alec made David and his polite commentary fade into the background, although Lilly tried to give every appearance that she was attending to him. But her real attention turned to the heated exchange going on between Alec and Todd. She listened so hard to hear above the noise and other chatter that her ears hurt.

"All I know is that she had a temper to match that hair," Todd said defensively. He shifted under Alec's unwavering gaze. "I'm sure no one here misses those daily temper tantrums she treated us to in your office. Right, Hilda?" He evidently assumed that she would back him up, and indeed, Lilly had noticed Hilda had a tendency to baby Todd and make excuses for him. Not this time, though.

"I don't know what you're talking about, Todd. I think you've had a few too many beers, dear." She sounded calm, but Lilly noticed her fingering the amber beads hanging around her neck in an agitated way as she spoke.

"I think ol' Alec boy knows what I'm talking about, don't ya?" Todd said sneeringly. "I think this thing has ol' Alec boy running scared."

Alec half-stood and slapped both hands flat on the table in front of Todd. No one at their table made any pretense of paying attention to anything but this escalating confrontation anymore, not even David. Alec emanated intense, focused energy that trapped everyone's attention although he spoke softly.

"You've been riding and riding about this, kid. And now its going to end. One way or another."

"Oh, a real small-town tough guy. I guess we can all see how you kept Karen in line, too," Todd came back, but he looked green around the edges, as though he wished he'd never started the whole thing.

Alec reached across and grabbed the front of his shirt and the combined weight of the two men sent the table over. Lilly was the only one not quick enough to snatch up her drink and the remainder of her wine splashed down her jeans. "All right, all right," Todd said in a choked voice. "Just forget the whole thing."

Alec released him in contempt and righted the table. Seeing that the excitement was at an end, the few other remaining patrons returned to their drinks. Todd straightened his clothes, his face bright splotchy red. "Excuse me," he muttered in the direction of Hilda and Lilly, and flinging his jacket over one shoulder, he left by the back door.

"You know," Hilda said meditatively. "I think I know of a place you might like. Does a cottage appeal to you, Lilly?"

"What?" Lilly couldn't adjust to the way the violence had erupted between the two men.

"My uncle has a property by the creek. I think he's interested in selling or renting."

"That's a switch, then," Alec said with a disbelieving grunt.

"He's getting on in years, Alec. I'm sorry he gave you such a hard time, but five years ago, when you wanted to buy it, he just wasn't interested in selling."

"I'd like to see it. The creek is a very attractive area."

"I'll just pop in to the farm and have a visit," Hilda said happily. "Then the keys will be available for you to pick up and you can look the place over at your leisure."

"That sounds very generous of you. I'll go out and see it right away." Lilly hoped she wasn't getting into something she'd regret. But living by the creek sounded wonderful, and she wasn't committing herself to anything.

Lilly pulled her red jacket closer around her shoulders as a blast of cold air shot through the emptying bar. She looked around at the unattractive layers of stale smoke, the littered tables, and felt an inexplicable rush of loneliness that had nothing to do with the time or the place.

Lilly pushed at the ache that seemed determined to wrap around her heart. Since her break-up with Martin, she had these flashes of feeling and had vigorously repressed them. It annoyed her that she could still be affected by someone who'd just been using her. The experience had left her saddened and suspicious of her feelings in a way she'd never been before, and Lilly sometimes thought what swept over her was an alienation from the innocence she'd known before Martin damaged her belief in herself.

"Good night, everyone." Lilly stood up, suddenly needing to be on her own and away from them. "See you tomorrow!" she added with forced cheerfulness as she buttoned her coat and turned to pick a path through the debris.

Outside the air was crisp and she breathed in deeply. She was grateful for its smoke-free quality. The gleaming curves of the Corvette beckoned to her, but as she approached it she sensed something was wrong. Lilly slid into the low seat, turned the key and examined the gauges in front of her with experienced eyes. With a sinking heart she saw the fuel gauge read empty.

"Problems?" Alec's deep voice grated along her nerves. "Not out of gas, are we?"

"We've had our tank siphoned," Lilly snapped.

"Oh, that's a new one!" Alec said admiringly.

Without a word, Lilly swung her legs back out of the car and pushed past him. She went to the back of the car and when she touched the gas cap it came off in her hand.

She felt Alec watching her, hands scrunched into the

pockets of his jeans, and rocking slightly on his feet. Lilly searched up and down the street for a lighted service station, but she knew it was pointless. Only one station in Fielding had the high octane premium the Corvette needed to run well, and that place was a few miles out of town along the freeway. Lilly knew she wasn't walking several miles along a highway in the pitch dark.

"Where's your car?" Lilly demanded.

"It's that gray Omega." He gestured toward it with a jerk of his head. "But I'm almost on empty myself."

"Doesn't matter." Lilly gave her rear tire a disgusted kick. "That thing uses unleaded, anyway. I wouldn't put that stuff into the Vette."

"Well, excuse me," Alec drawled. "I wasn't aware that social classes existed in gasoline, too."

Lilly shot him an exasperated look as she locked the Corvette, slung her purse over her shoulder, and slammed the door shut. The bright parking lot lights shadowed his eyes, but the sting in his words was enough.

"Why do I let him get to me?" Lilly muttered. She couldn't wait to get away from him, but the dark street leading away from the bar was far from inviting.

"Hey! Where are you going?" Alec shouted after her as Lilly took off, walking briskly.

"Home. Where else?" she said over her shoulder. "Standing in a bar's parking lot at one o'clock in the morning arguing with you isn't my idea of a good time."

"I'll give you a ride home," Alec said.

Lilly stopped walking. Then she turned and went to stand silently by his car. He came slowly after her. Lilly wanted only to be in a warm bed with the covers over her, and the long day at an end. "Your door isn't shut," Alec reminded her after she'd gotten in. He leaned over her and pulled it shut to still the insistent buzzer before Lilly could respond.

She shivered at the hard press of his forearm on the point of her hip, a heavy bar of heat she felt through her jeans. "Cold?" She shook her head, but Alec switched the blower on anyway. Depression sank like a weighted net around her, bowing her neck and pinning her arms to her sides.

Lilly watched the slow disappearance of tar beneath the headlights of the car, feeling almost as though she were holding her breath until they reached the Jordan house.

"Thanks for the ride." Lilly shoved open the car door and jumped out almost before the Omega had stopped.

"You forgot your purse." Alec got out and calmly followed her with it. The two of them stood in the cold air on the deserted porch and looked at each other. Lilly's breath caught as Alec put out a slow, gentle hand and touched her face. His thumb brushed the arch of her eyebrow before sliding to cup the back of her head. He applied no pressure, yet Lilly found herself moving closer to him, found her arms lifting to hold him, her fingers spreading over the warmth of his ribs.

She felt his breath catch in his throat and beneath her fingers. She lifted, feeling her lips parting on a sigh of desire. She was all softness, eager for the imprint of his hardness. Their mouths touched. Lilly moaned softly, wanting more, and tried to pull him closer.

"Invite me in for coffee, or something?" Alec asked from deep in his throat.

Straightening, Lilly stared at him in the harsh streetlight. Cool air filled the space between them, tempering her desire and Lilly said, "No. It's been a long day. I'm tired. I'll say good night." Her voice was jerky but firm, and she held out her hand for her purse, which still dangled from Alec's left hand.

He reluctantly gave it to her, and she clutched it to her

for a moment, waiting for him to go. When he didn't move, Lilly began digging for her keys. She opened the purse wider and dug some more, but the sickening image of her keys dangling from the ignition of the Corvette grew sharper by the moment.

Frantically she began tossing things out in an effort to clear a way through the mess. No good. She was locked out of her house and her car, and her landlady was in Mankato!

"No keys, huh?" Alec prodded with an irritating twist to his lips. "Let's see," he went on, ticking things off on his fingers in a way that made Lilly long to strangle him. "No keys, no gas, nobody home, and no idea what to do about it. You might have to spend the night with me...yet." That final word trailed away into the night air, almost but not quite inaudible.

"No way!" Lilly said, and she'd never meant anything more in her life than those two short words. "No way on this earth!"

Chapter Four

Lilly just left him standing there. She dropped her purse on the porch swing and walked swiftly to the back of the house. No good; that door was tightly shut and locked too. Then she circled the house looking for open windows; she was in luck, because on the stairway to the second floor Mrs. Jordan had left the window open a few inches. Now she needed a way to get up there.

Out to the garden went Lilly, and she came back pushing the creaking wheelbarrow Mrs. Jordan used to spread dirt and manure over her enormous garden. Because it was heavy with dirt, pushing it was no easy task, and Lilly was breathless by the time she got its noisy bulk wedged up against the side of the house.

By standing on the mound of dirt she could almost touch the windowsill. But not quite. She made a few half-hearted leaps, but the wheelbarrow wobbled ominously, and banged into the house. All I need now is for some neighbor to see me and call the police, Lilly thought as she stepped down.

"Need some help?"

Alec was leaning back against a tree watching her efforts. Lilly was too angry to even answer, and went off toward the garage in search of a box or something sturdy to stand on. That insufferable man! Lilly thought; he's enjoying this. The garage was locked, which was so unexpected that Lilly didn't believe it for a minute. She went on trying to heave up the door even though it wasn't budging. Where was all this small town open-door policy when she needed it? Lilly wanted to know.

Her steps were slow and dragging as she returned. There was no way around it. If she wanted to get in she'd have to have his help. That stuck in her throat.

"Could you give me a push up to the window?"

"It'll cost you," Alec warned, and Lilly thought: It already has. "Oh, no, I'm not standing up in that thing. I'll lift you up on my shoulders." Alec gave the wheelbarrow a scornful look.

With one hand supporting her on the wall, and her teeth gritted so hard her jaw ached, Lilly stepped onto his shoulders. He straightened slowly. Lilly hit the window ledge a bit hard, and knew she'd have a few bruises to prove it, but basically things went according to plan. The temptation was great to slam the window shut and crawl into bed, but she had to retrieve her purse. All her identification was in it, and she didn't put it past Alec to hold it until she let him in.

How, Lilly demanded of herself viciously as she opened the door to his grinning face, could I ever have thought he was charming?

"I'd say I've earned my coffee," he said, still grinning as he handed her her purse, then tossed Lilly a tube of lipstick that had gotten caught behind the door.

"Okay." Lilly reluctantly led the way to the back of the house. The plain black clock on the kitchen wall read one thirty, but sleep seemed to be receding into the land of illusion for Lilly. Her eyes felt gritty, and her head ached.

Alec, on the other hand, seemed to get fresher as the night went on. His eyes were bright blue with curiosity as they surveyed the kitchen. It was worth a second look, but right then all Lilly wanted to be seeing was a smooth white sheet. He walked around picking things up and putting them down in a way that irritated Lilly.

But she ignored it for a while, and made the coffee. Ten minutes later he was still at it. "Are you memorizing the place or just naturally nosy?" Lilly demanded as she sipped her coffee. His lay cooling on the table, untouched.

"Both, actually. Make me a sandwich, will you? Anything would do. A ham sandwich, perhaps?"

Lilly gave him a long, steady look. He looked back, then brushed at the shoulders of his cream sweater. "There seems to be an awful lot of dirt on this thing."

"I'll have it cleaned for you," Lilly said evenly, and didn't move.

"Okay, okay! Could you *please* get me something to eat, since you're just sitting there?" His smile was boyish and meant to charm. But with the clarity brought on by total exhaustion, Lilly realized he didn't even see her at all. She was merely a female there to feed him, and he turned on the charm because it worked every time. He was so sure of himself that he'd already returned to examining the pot-bellied stove that sat along the far wall of the kitchen. Don't bother to dole out more charm than the exact amount needed for the task, seemed to Lilly to be Alec's maxim. Lilly couldn't believe she hadn't noticed that until now.

Yet she found herself at the refrigerator without quite knowing how she got there. "Is roast beef acceptable?" she asked dryly over her shoulder, lettuce, bread, and pickles piled against her crooked forearm.

"Oh sure. Just put plenty of mustard on mine," he said cheerfully, and banged the lid of the stove down with a clang that reverberated in Lilly's aching head. Yet when all the ingredients were assembled, Lilly found the idea of a sandwich appealing too. Supper seemed eons ago, and Lilly'd had only fruit and salad.

"This," Alec said with an enthusiastic gesture, "is a stunning kitchen!" He took an enormous bite of his sandwich and patched two halves of his paper napkin together. Each half had scribbled notes that looked like some kind of shorthand.

"I was completely bowled over by this place myself. Mrs. Jordan says she's going to redecorate—"

"Then I'm glad I got here before she did anything so foolish," Alec said fervently. "Say, do you have some paper I can use? These napkins are hard to work with."

What in the world was I worried about? Lilly asked herself as she went into the hall and got the pad of paper Mrs. Jordan kept by the phone. The only layout Alec Thomas is interested in is that of the damned kitchen, and then she was immediately angered by her own contradictory thoughts. She didn't really want Alec to make a pass at her, did she?

Lilly slapped the paper in front of him and he pulled it close without looking up or offering a word of thanks. A credible drawing of the enormous room took shape beneath his swiftly moving fingers. The sandwich he'd ordered lay half eaten beside him, and the black clock ticked on and on.

"What are you going to do with all this?" Lilly wanted to know when he leaped up and began pacing off the room, writing down dimensions, and muttering about pacing and blocking. "Are you going to put this place in a play?" She said it to be provocative.

"Shh. Could you be still for a while, please?" he murmured with an impatient wave of his hand. He began filling in the pieces of furniture, and Lilly had to admire his skill.

The whole room, Lilly had decided, was constructed on the cornucopia theory that if one of something was good, then several were even better. The three stoves that sat along the far wall were like a history of man and fire. In the corner furthest from where Lilly and Alec sat was an open, blackened brick fireplace where Mrs. Jordan hung bundles of wild goldenrod, purple thistle, and herbs to dry. Next to the fireplace was a pot-bellied Franklin stove that burned coal, and next to that was a modern gas range. Mrs. Jordan used all three.

At right angles to the stoves canning shelves set in yellowing accordion-like racks stuck into the room like the splayed fingers of a giant hand. Row upon row of jars bulged with bright green pickles, tender red tomatoes, and yellow peach halves studded with cloves and straight sticks of cinnamon—all fastidiously labeled in Mrs. Jordan's precise script.

"What's over there?" Alec pointed with one finger toward the left without looking up.

"It's a root cellar," Lilly said, on her fourth cup of coffee now, and no longer tired, but increasingly angry.

Alec was gone in there a long time, and emerged carrying a dirty potato and a waxy turnip with a purpling ring around its plump middle. He examined the papery coverings of the strings of garlic and onions Mrs. Jordan kept hanging in the doorway to the root cellar, muttered alternately delighted and staccato comments to himself. To say Lilly felt superfluous was certainly an understatement as she watched the corners of his sandwich dry and begin to curl.

On the other hand, this was the first opportunity Lilly had had since she met Alec to really study him with complete safety. A few strands of gray threaded the top of his black hair, which didn't seem to be cut in any particular style. Lilly guessed that he did his own cutting. Studying his bold nose, bristling blue eyes and darkening jawline, Lilly was hard put to explain how he managed to generate so much charm. Right now he looked... well, certainly he was dark, but tall and handsome were definitely out. Short, Lilly thought succinctly, described him well.

But Lilly wouldn't have been human if she hadn't

felt a twinge of pique that all the intensity in him was now focused on bits of torn napkins and turnips instead of on her.

He looked up suddenly and caught her. Lilly felt naked, as though he'd read her thoughts. It was almost as though the heat of them had penetrated the cave of concentration he'd been in and pulled him to the light. Lilly felt suddenly that she knew every pore and eyelash on Alec's face, would know them for the rest of her life. She shut her eyes in a rush of panic and self-preservation that came too late.

"I didn't know it was this late," Alec said, running a forearm over his face in a tired gesture. Lilly jerked painfully, then realized he meant the literal time as she followed his gaze to the wall.

He gathered up the piles and bits of paper together and stuffed them into the pockets of his leather jacket that hung over the back of the chair. He left behind scrunched pieces in balls over the floor and table that Lilly knew she'd have to clean up before Mrs. Jordan came home tomorrow.

"Guess I have to be getting along." Alec stood up and stretched, and Lilly wished she was not responding to the flexing of his muscles.

"One minute," Lilly halted him in mid-stretch. She brought the plastic garbage pail to him and plonked it down.

"What's that for?" Alec asked with the genuine innocence of a man who never cleans up after himself.

"A garbage pail," Lilly said distinctly. "For the garbage you've left behind."

"This stuff?" Alec's usually deep voice rose in surprise. "But this isn't much."

"Then you won't mind taking care of it before you go," Lilly retorted promptly, and watched in satisfaction as he held the beige pail to the rim of the table and swept the debris inside.

"Here you go." His tone made it clear that he thought she was childish in the extreme. "And thank you for the sandwich. Sorry that I didn't get a chance to eat all of it. It was really good."

"Oh, knock it off, Alec!" Lilly really didn't feel up to another dose of his practiced charm. "I'm not in the mood."

A calculating expression washed over his face, and he came nearer to her. "I'm sorry, honey. I've been a selfish, thoughtless fool. Here I've had you all to myself for hours and I didn't take advantage of it." He wrapped an arm around her and tried to lift her chin with one hand. Lilly resisted, cursing her body for responding to him, even though she knew each word and gesture were a knee-jerk reaction with him.

"Get out of here, right now," she spoke quietly, but firmly. Alec released her, nonplussed.

"You're just angry because I didn't make another pass at you," Alec said disgustedly. "You women are all the same. You say you want equality, to be treated based on your capabilities, not on your sex. Yet when a man acts on that you pout and get offended."

There was enough truth in that to silence Lilly for a moment. She rubbed a hand over her tired eyes and tried to think. A line existed between Alec's accusation and what she'd meant, but right now Lilly was too weary to pursue it.

"Once again I have to apologize for shooting my mouth off," Alec said quietly. Lilly looked at him in surprise at this change in mood. "I didn't really mean all that stuff. I guess I just lost my temper—I'm beginning to think I don't know what the hell I'm doing around you most of the time."

Lilly's brows rose a fraction in disbelief. "Then you don't think wanting my wishes to be considered makes me a pouting—"

"No! Look, I said I was sorry, and God knows I've

apologized more times to you in a week than I have to any other human being in my life!"

"Now that I do believe," Lilly murmured, but with a smile that took any sting out of her words. "But they do say that practice makes perfect." Hands behind her back, Lilly leaned back against the brick wall, mischief dancing in her hazel eyes.

"Something tells me I might be headed for perfection sooner than even I thought if you keep looking at me that way, Lilly Burns."

"And what way is that?" Lilly whispered, knowing what a dangerous question it was, knowing how it contradicted all her inner urging toward caution and not caring. "Is it anything like the way you're looking at me?"

For a moment she just watched the expressions scudding across his face. For the first time in her life Lilly found herself wanting passionately to know another person. She wanted more than just to see a reflection of her own desire in his eyes. Lilly wanted to know him, not his reactions to her, and that kind of desire made her feel very vulnerable. Her lids dropped to cover her eyes.

"You're tired. I think it's time for me to go," Alec said in a gentle voice Lilly had never heard before, and she swallowed to keep back the sudden tears that choked her throat.

"Good night."

"Lilly—"

"Good night, Alec. You're right; it's very late." Lilly stood straight and motioned in front of her toward the door. Alec hesitated, then did as she silently requested, grabbing his jacket off the back of the chair as he went past.

Lilly locked the door behind him, turned out the lights, and went up to bed. She undressed and put on her nightgown, folding and putting everything in its proper place as though ritual could keep her thoughts at bay. The face that stared back from over the sink as she brushed her teeth looked sallow. The seesawing between caution and passion had drained her. Lilly had just gotten herself clear of those awful nights after her break-up with Martin, and she asked herself if she really wanted to start them all again. Something about Alec, about the way she was reacting to him, told Lilly this time could be far worse. Alec had twice the charm, twice the energy and was a far more complex man than Martin Stone. Tonight was a perfect example of that, Lilly acknowledged as she got into bed. Things happened around Alec; he brought a stingingly alive quality to everything.

Now that she could snuggle down in the cool, white sheets she'd longed for hours ago, Lilly had trouble relaxing and letting go of the day. She couldn't put Alec out of her mind. Was there some way she could've handled this evening better? she asked herself, and found no definitive answers. She was struck by the different attitudes Alec had displayed toward her in only a short time. At their first meeting he'd been nasty, sarcastic, and unyielding; yet the next day in his office he'd apologized sincerely and had been funny and sensually appealing. Lilly felt that he'd treated her as an equal that day and that feeling gave her hope. It seemed almost a kind of Dr. Jekyll and Mr. Hyde transformation. She never knew what side of him she'd see next.

Tonight, for example, he'd begun by treating her like a servant, there to jump to his every wish and otherwise remain silent. Lilly would have liked to relive that scene and ask him if he'd have treated a male colleague the same way. Lilly doubted that he would have felt so free to demand food and drink, or to ignore a male colleague when he said he was tired.

Lilly found herself curious about his mother and the

rest of the Thomas family. She had the impression that their father was dead; Jonathan had said something about his mother living on a farm outside of Fielding, but Lilly thought she could be wrong about that.

Lilly also, as she began finally to drift toward sleep, found herself very curious about Karen Willis. What kind of woman was this that, as Alec himself had said, "haunted his life"? Lilly could no longer dismiss her suit as a personal grudge against Alec, and she knew that if Alec and she were ever to have the kind of relationship she wanted, he would have to change. Right now, as tonight's disaster proved, they were far from even agreeing that there was a problem, let alone what the solution should be.

Lilly slept until eight o'clock the next morning and awoke refreshed and clear-headed. She dressed in a corduroy skirt and jacket, and after a breakfast of fried potatoes and scrambled eggs, she sat down to do some work on the questionnaire she was using to gather information for the Composition Conference in a few weeks. As she settled at the kitchen table, a bit of scrunched paper caught her eye. She reached across the table, her narrow fingers slowly unfolding the crumpled sheet, smoothing it with a rhythmic gesture as the night before flooded back into her mind.

Already she had memories of Alec sitting at this table, and Lilly's hazel eyes grew cloudy as she acknowledged how deeply Alec had already gotten under her skin.

Lilly forced her attention back to questions of what student writers thought of their audience, but images of Alec crowded in and refused to be banished. She could see him sitting across from her now, the way his black hair grew up sharply from a strong widow's peak, the taut flow of skin beneath his eyes, and the healthy pink of his nails as his fingers pressed the pen to the paper.

With a grimace of self-disgust Lilly pushed back from the kitchen table, grabbed her coat, and went out the back door. The morning air smelled sweet. To her surprise, the Corvette sat at the end of the drive, and Lilly found the keys above the visor when she opened the door and got in. Lilly pocketed them thoughtfully and crossed the quiet street, ducked down the embankment, and followed the creek as she'd done the other day.

Wednesday Lilly had no classes, but on Tuesdays and Thursdays she was busy nearly all day long. Normally she would have used this time to work on various projects and papers she had ideas for, but she wanted to give herself a few weeks to adjust to life in Fielding before pushing herself too hard. Knowing academic life as she did, Lilly knew that days like this would soon become rare as she was asked to sit on committees and review boards; she would have few large blocks of free time left.

From a dessicated, tangled bush Lilly plucked a twisted stick and dragged it around the outline of water-smoothed pebbles as she walked, deliberately in the opposite direction of Alec's house. Clouds bunched along the horizon like determined shoppers at the door of a sale. Cottonwoods and elms arched over the lip of the creek and behind them long grass sighed in the wind. Lilly couldn't remember the last time she'd been somewhere so utterly quiet, so devoid of evidence of human beings. Was this what she wanted? Lilly asked herself, face turning up to the sun. All her life Lilly had lived in cities or citylike settings. She enjoyed this now, but was it only because it was a novelty? The change in her goals and her surroundings had left Lilly on an emotional roller coaster. One minute she felt confident, sure of her choice to go against her family and the security of an assured, high-salaried career at Burns Electronics. The next minute she'd feel depressed and ready to give it all up and take off in the Corvette for home. At least that's how it had felt for the first weeks after she made the decision, but now it was beginning to get better.

Lilly stopped, the stick falling from her surprised hand. Ahead of her sat Jonathan Thomas, head resting in his hands. The wind had turned his dark hair this way and that, revealing far more gray in it than Lilly remembered from their first meeting. Today Lilly didn't see the dogs. Today he was alone and something in his manner made Lilly hesitate to intrude. About to turn around and head back the way she'd come, Jonathan turned and saw her.

"Hello," Lilly offered hesitantly.

"Good morning." Jonathan stood, smoothed his hair and with that gesture banished that lost expression Lilly had caught on his face earlier.

"Sorry to intrude—"

"Not at all, Lilly," he said with a wry smile. "Although I'm sure my expression when you arrived wouldn't encourage you to stay and keep me company."

Lilly laughed. "Not forbidding, just sort of lost in thought. And as the newcomer on the block, I didn't like to seem too pushy. You look like a man with a lot on his mind, Jonathan.

"I'm planning to open a checking account with you soon, so I hope this pensive mood doesn't mean the bank is running out of money," Lilly teased.

"Not yet." But his smile was strained. "If grain prices don't start going up, I may be forced into some foreclosures that I'm not looking forward to."

"That must be hard, especially in a small town where none of your clients are strangers to you," Lilly said softly. In strong daylight she caught in bright relief the lines running from the corners of his eyes and deeply etched grooves along either side of his nose. "I'm sure you must give them every allowance you can, though."

"I do, but I also have a board of directors to report to, and that hampers me from giving more time to people. I'm allowed to use my own discretion, but only to a point." Jonathan smiled and bent to pick up a stone that he skipped expertly along the shallow amber surface of the creek. "Don't get me started on business, or I'll talk your ear off."

"I don't mind."

"I do. I'm glad you showed up today. I have something I wanted to ask you."

Lilly stiffened, thinking it was something to do with Alec.

"I've got theater tickets for this Saturday. I realize it's short notice, but would you be interested in going to a play with me?"

"Is it at the college?" Lilly asked mostly to give herself time to think about this new development. The idea of dating Jonathan wasn't unpleasant, but it was surprising.

"Oh, no. It's in the Cities. A rather experimental play being put on by the Arlo II theater. Do you know it?"

"Yes, of course. I've taken students there, and even have one friend whose play was produced there."

"Terrific! Then you'll come?"

"I'd like that very much."

"Good. I'll pick you up around six on Saturday and we'll eat in Minneapolis, then go on to the play. How does that sound?"

"Sounds wonderful to me." A night of uncomplicated entertainment in the company of a man she liked and respected sounded like heaven on earth to Lilly just then, and there was the added stroke to her ego that he must find her attractive to invite her.

"I'll look forward to it," Jonathan told her as Lilly walked off, and she waved back over her shoulder.

The phone was ringing when she entered the house,

and Lilly made a dive for the hallway and the phone when she realized Mrs. Jordan wasn't back yet. "Hello?" It was Hilda. She'd been out to visit her uncle and if Lilly was interested in seeing the cottage she could pick up the keys from her today at the office.

Lilly was in the Corvette and on her way to the College within minutes. "I really appreciate this, Hilda," Lilly told the secretary. "You really don't waste time on things, do you?"

"Oh, I owed Uncle a visit," Hilda said, dismissing her promptness.

Lilly felt excitement rising in her as she finally located the narrow, grassed-in lane leading to the cottage. Two-storied, the house clung to the cliff above the creek, reminding Lilly of that lone maple she and Jonathan had seen that first day.

She stopped the Corvette and got out. That driveway would definitely need fixing, she thought, and rubbed her rear end ruefully. The low-slung Corvette just couldn't handle the small clearance.

The cottage was surrounded by overgrown flower beds, and a few sunflowers bobbed in the direction of the midday sun in the backyard. The garage was large, but in poor shape, and Lilly could hear her father's scathing comments on that in the back of her mind, but she didn't care. She was going through all the motions of looking the property over, but she'd known the minute she drove up and saw it that she was going to buy this house.

The key scratched in the lock and finally turned. Lilly felt her heart accelerate as she stepped into the musty hall. To her right, sunlight spilled in through filthy French windows that were encrusted with years of dust and dirt. Several mystery pieces of furniture were covered with ancient dustcovers, and the rug looked like horsehair. The fireplace was very attractive, though. It was made from large fieldstones of slate blue and gray, with two large grilled vents to allow the heat to come into the room. Lilly could imagine that Mongo would be stretched out there most of the winter. Cats had a way of finding the most comfortable spots, Lilly knew.

She tried to move the heavy dark oak doors that closed the living room off from the hall, but they were warped into the floor.

Love was an inscrutable force, Lilly thought as she paced off the room, because the place wasn't in good shape and would need a great deal of work. It would be much simpler to move into a newer place and not have all the inconvenience of workmen under foot and all the mess remodeling created. But no matter how bad things were, she was going to buy this place. Of course she'd try to hide that from Hilda's uncle, and try to use the faults to lower the price, but she'd buy it in the end whatever price he wanted for it.

This house had life. Lilly could just imagine the families that had happily grown up along this creek, with acres of land to roam free on. Now it held only the skittering shadows of mice and the smell of slow rot in the corners, but Lilly knew she could bring it back to life.

The kitchen and baths were the worst, but that was to be expected in a house of this age. The roof, on the other hand, was in surprisingly good condition, and most of the dampness in the house seemed to come from its proximity to the creek, not from a leaky roof.

From the bedroom windows, Lilly could see Fielding College up on the bluffs and could just make out the pointed roof of the chapel in the middle of the campus. Then, when she went to check on the heating, Lilly found the source of the dampness. The basement was not concrete but dirt. Good, Lilly thought happily, once that was taken care of, the dampness should disappear.

"How much does he want for the place, and how many acres does the property cover?" Lilly was back in the office of the Department Chairman within an hour and half. Hilda looked slightly taken aback by Lilly's rapid-fire questions and the speed with which she was moving on this.

"You're interested in buying it, then?" Hilda seemed to need a minute to take that in. She removed her glasses and neatly ordered a pile of papers she'd been going over, then closed the folder over them. "But you just saw it. Don't you want to think about it, or look—"

"No. It's exactly what I want. I fell in love with the house on sight," Lilly said, knowing her father would groan to hear her put herself totally in the seller's hand. In the end, though, it didn't matter. Hilda called her uncle and the price he'd set was more than reasonable. He was old, but obviously knew how to evaluate a house. Hilda handed over the telephone to Lilly. "He wants to speak to you."

"Hello, Mr. Peterson," Lilly said excitedly.

"I hear you're innerested in my little cottage," he said slowly, his voice cracking with age.

"Oh, yes, I am very much. I just loved it. There must have been so many happy memories in that house. I could feel them when I went inside." Lilly flushed a bit, worried that she sounded corny, or worse, that the old man might think she was trying to butter him up in hopes of lowering the price.

But she needn't have worried. "That's just the way I feel, my girl! And you're right. There's many a happy time I had in that house as a boy, and in the fields around that creek."

"Alec could have taken a few lessons from you in dealing with someone tactfully," Hilda said with a jerk of her head toward the chairman's door when Lilly hung up. "My uncle might have sold to him, if Alec hadn't put his back up at every turn."

"I just told the truth," Lilly said with a shrug. Until this moment she'd honestly forgotten Alec's interest in what she was already considering "her" house. Well, she couldn't do anything about it if this made him angrier at her.

"I suppose this means a trip to see Jonathan Thomas?" Hilda asked with a smile.

"What?" Lilly gazed blankly at her, then said, "Oh, no. I'll pay cash. In fact I need to get in touch with my bank and see about transferring funds. And I'll need a lawyer, too."

She left the office knowing Hilda still had an astounded look on her face. Cash wasn't the smartest way to obtain the property, but it was the fastest. And Lilly was in a hurry.

"So do you think you could take care of this for me, Harry?" Lilly asked, fingers tracing the straight lines of the phone as she spoke. Harry was one of her father's few personal friends. He was a crack lawyer, and Lilly considered him her own special friend.

"If the title's clear and there are no liens, I should be able to handle it," Harry assured her. "But since you're in a hurry, we'll need to use what's called a Move-In Agreement. Insurance, maintenance and improvements, et cetera, become your legal responsibility in the interim while the title is cleared."

"That sounds like just what I need!" Lilly said excitedly. "The bathrooms and kitchen need work, and I'd like to get started on that right away."

"Now, as your legal counsel, I have to advise you that paying cash isn't the smartest—"

"I know that, but it doesn't matter to me, so let it drop." Lilly's voice became softer. "And I have just one other favor to ask."

"What's that?" A note of caution had crept into Harry Idle's voice.

"Don't tell my father about this just yet."

"He won't appreciate me keeping something like this from him, you know, and I can't blame him."

"It's only for a short while. I want to surprise him," Lilly argued. "I don't expect you to lie; just don't volunteer anything at the Friday luncheon. That's all I ask."

"All right. But just this once!" Harry growled. "I'll get back to you as soon as I can."

He hung up before Lilly could express her thanks. But Lilly knew she was safe from Harry spilling the beans at the weekly luncheon with her father and a few others that had been a tradition for years. She was sure there would be no problems, and by the end of the week she could be a homeowner.

Chapter Five

By Thursday afternoon everything was set. Harry had
called Lilly back promptly the day before with the good
news that the property was indeed free and clear, all
three and a half acres of it. "Say, what price are you
getting for this, dear?" he'd asked in a casual tone that
didn't fool Lilly one bit. She told him and listened to
the respect grow in his voice. What she didn't tell him
was that that was Mr. Peterson's offering price! "Of
course, the house does need repair work, especially in
the basement and kitchen areas," Lilly had added in an
effort to dilute her triumph a little. But Harry had dis-
agreed, saying that any property that old was bound to
need repairs, and that even if they ran to twenty or
thirty thousand she was still getting a good deal.
"There are no assessments pending, either. So that's
good."

"What are those?" Lilly had asked.

"It means that there are no plans to build, say, a
large road near the property." Harry had explained.

"Why should I worry about that, except for the noise
perhaps?"

"Because they'd charge you to connect up with it—
something from a few thousand up to tens of thou-
sands of dollars. Or if they decided to run the city sewer
system out your way. There are so few houses in your
area the costs could be prohibitive, or—"

"I get the idea, Harry. Pending assessments are to be avoided," Lilly had broken in, knowing once he got in full stride he'd tell her every kind of assessment there was, pending and not.

She'd reminded him of his promise not to tell her father of this, and he'd agreed. Getting through her classes today and doing a creditable job of it had been hard, but now she was ready to go out to see Mr. Peterson.

Lilly was surprised to see her hand shaking as she wrote out the check. "Now I know why they give you so much space," she said to the frail but sharp gentleman sitting opposite her in the sprawling farmhouse.

"Well, you know Ellie Thomas's boy was after me to sell a few years back. Looking for a piece of property along the creek, he was." Mr. Peterson seemed lost in rumination on that one, but Lilly wanted to hear more.

"So what happened?"

"Young pup got my dander up's what happened," he snapped, and slapped a hand on his bony thigh. "Throwing offers at me, telling me I'd never see that good of a price again.... I didn't like his attitude, girlie, and that's a fact!" A kind of soundless laugh shook through him, and he curled his weathered hands into the straps of his overalls.

"But now you're ready to sell, is that it?"

"Nope. Was ready to sell then. Good price that damned pup offered, too."

"Then what was the problem?" Lilly asked in puzzled tones as she handed him the check. He looked at it slowly, taking his time. Then he folded it and stuck it behind him between the sugar and flour jars on the counter. Lilly wanted to tell him that wasn't a smart place for a large check like that, but decided it was none of her business. From the same place he plucked the title and handed it to her.

"You got somethin' wrong with your ears?" he demanded, and Lilly shook her head. "Like I told you before, I just didn't like his attitude."

"Mr. Peterson," Lilly said with dawning comprehension of the way the old man was having the last word. "Neither do I."

All the way back to Fielding Lilly kept chuckling over that cunning old man. The money didn't matter to him as much as teaching a young pup a lesson, she realized. And Lilly vowed that she would see that the young pup had a chance to hear about it too!

Her next stop was the hardware store, where she opened a charge account. She picked up hammers, measuring tapes, and an assortment of things she'd need for getting the house into shape. The hardware store owner recommended a few contractors in the area, but cautioned that they might be booked up for a while. He proved to be correct. There were only three reputable contractors in Fielding, and Lilly was forced to go further afield to find one. Eventually she settled on a Mr. Mattson from St. Peter, that city of wide, majestic avenues once slated to become the capitol of the state. Only another Saint got the call, and St. Peter was left all dressed up with nowhere to go.

Lilly was able to go to bed happily on Thursday night. She'd gotten a lot accomplished in less than forty-eight hours. Mrs. Jordan, back from her frequent visits to Mankato, was amazed and kept clucking away about moving too fast. But Lilly was serene. She knew exactly what she was doing. She couldn't wait for Friday morning to come so that she could spend the whole day out at the house. At first she'd thought of spending the night out there; then she remembered the Holmes's party and decided she'd better save that for later.

On top of the brown paper sack with Lilly's hammers and measuring tapes lay a packet of sandwiches and some of Mrs. Jordan's justly famous chocolate cake, with the note that she wasn't to forget to eat while she was out there working.

The sun was just peaking over the edge of the sky when Lilly bumped along the grassy lane to the house. For a moment she just sat in the car and stared at it. This is mine, she thought, and felt a thrill of satisfaction. Then from back behind the house came a doe and a buck, slowly cropping grass. They were outlined against the dawn for a moment, and Lilly stared in awe at the sight. Then they sensed something and bounded off into the fields beyond. Lilly got out of the car, unloaded her bags of stuff, and closed the door quietly. She opened her purse and scribbled in the notebook she'd started for the house: *Buy corn to feed deer.*

Then she went into her house. The morning passed swiftly. Mr. Mattson rattled up the lane in a rusting El Camino, looked over the work she wanted, and gave her an estimate. Lilly told him she wanted the work done quickly and that there was a bonus in it for him. He told her he couldn't start on it until Monday, but that he'd try to start ordering material and check on such things as permits and such, since he wasn't familiar with the Fielding area.

"You're lucky being out in the country this way," he told her, a cigarette, unlit, flopping up and down in his mouth as he talked. "Cause there's usually fewer restrictions on getting stuff approved."

Lilly watched him drive off. She didn't like him much, but then she didn't see any real need for her to like him. As long as she kept an eye on him and he did a good job, that was all that mattered.

Lilly left the front door open to allow air to circulate through the house and went into the living room. Late afternoon sunlight streamed through the dirty windows as she sat on the floor to eat the lunch that Mrs. Jordan had so kindly provided. It tasted good after working so hard all morning, and it didn't take Lilly long to down it all. No shortage of things to do, Lilly thought as she pulled out her notebook and wrote: *Bring window cleaner and lots of toweling!*

"Not really your sort of place, is it?" a male voice said from the living room doorway. Lilly had been poking around in the chimney trying to see what was blocking it, but was a little afraid to find out. She dusted her palms on the front of her jeans and stood up.

"That's just where you're wrong," Lilly told him crisply. "How in the world did you know where I was?"

Alec shrugged. "As my brother pointed out to you on your first day here, nothing in Fielding is very far from anything else. Since this is your free day, I thought you might be looking for housing. You can't stay in that rooming house forever."

"Hilda told you I might be out here, you mean," Lilly translated with a shrewd glint in her hazel eyes. The wind was picking up, and it sighed down the chimney, dislodging a few chunks of dirt and debris that landed with a puff of dust in the grate. Lilly exhaled in a gusty cough. "Shut that front door, will you?"

Lilly smiled at his back as he complied. She had an excellent idea why he was here, and she decided to make him sweat it out first. "What makes you say this isn't my kind of house? I think it has a lot of atmosphere and potential," Lilly said when he came back in, pointing to the fieldstone fireplace and the attractive French windows.

Alec pointed to the warped doors leading into the living room and said, "And I happen to know the kitchen is nothing like what you're used to."

"How do you know what I'm used to, or what I'm like, for that matter?" Lilly asked him in a reasonable tone. "You've ferreted out the fact that my father is wealthy and then extrapolated from that all kinds of conclusions about the type of person I am. Most of them are wrong, too.''

''Maybe.'' Alec settled himself on one of the dust-covered pieces of furniture, dropping one cowboy-booted foot onto the knee of the opposite leg as if he were settling in for a long chat. ''But as far as this place is concerned, it doesn't matter. Old man Peterson will never sell.''

''He just did. To me. Yesterday afternoon.''

''What? He couldn't have! But I worked on him for months! I even offered him twice what the place is worth.'' Alec leaped up and began to pace with thudding fury. ''You're lying!'' He stopped in front of Lilly, his blue eyes furious.

''I'm not.''

''But—Hilda told me he was interested. I just thought he was looking for a new victim.''

''We didn't seem to have any problem dealing with each other,'' Lilly commented.

''Well,'' Alec said with a snort, ''if you're rich, I guess everything is easy. You could pay him three times the actual value and never miss it.''

Lilly quietly told him the price she'd paid and watched the color drain from his face. ''But that's less than half my offer of five years ago.''

''So Mr. Peterson told me. He just didn't like your attitude.''

''My *attitude*?''

''Yes. I think he felt you were throwing your weight around by offering twice what the place is worth, and he simply dug his heels in and refused to sell to you.'' Lilly found she wasn't enjoying this as much as she'd thought she would. They seemed to have returned full circle in terms of their relationship, too. Relationship? Lilly asked herself, who am I kidding? This seems more like a contest than a relationship most of the time.

"Well, congratulations. This can be a terrific property. It has a lot of potential, as you pointed out." Alec was obviously making an effort to pull himself together. He thrust his shirttails into his snug jeans and straightened his sweater, a bulky knit dark blue one that looked very attractive on him.

Shoulders slightly hunched, hands balled in the pockets of his jeans, Alec shot Lilly a look and said, "Once more, I only have to get near you to lose my temper. And the thing is, I didn't come here to pick a fight with you."

Lilly found her eyes drawn to the taut pull of fabric and the flex of hard muscles beneath as Alec pivoted slightly away from her. His snug jeans were a uniform faded blue except in the spots on his back pocket where the sharp edges of the notebook he was never without had worn it white and threadbare. Somehow that endeared him to her; it seemed like a sign of vulnerability in his usually impenetrable defenses. "What did you want, then?" she asked, sensing he was waiting for some encouragement from her.

He came and sat next to Lilly on the hearth. Immediately she felt smaller, less sure of herself than when he kept his distance. She looked at their two knees, side by side, yet separate. His legs weren't much longer than hers, but very differently shaped. Lilly found she liked the difference; hers were all curves, while Alec's seemed to jut and angle, his knees square and hard.

Lifting her eyes, Lilly saw that Alec was studying her intently.

"We started off badly, Lilly. And that's my fault. But I'd like to make it up to you." Alec spoke softly, his intense eyes unwavering.

Lilly felt she couldn't pull her glance away. "How?" she whispered.

"I have to fly out to New York this afternoon on some business. It's to do with the new play. Most of this is in the planning stage for Off-Off Broadway—or maybe Cherry Lane, I don't know. Anyway, I won't be involved in business the whole time, and I'd like you to come along. We could stay at the Plaza Hotel, or—"

"No."

"Why not? Do you already have plans?"

"Yes, I do." Lilly seized on that, and it was true. But not the whole truth.

"What? That slow-witted gathering at David's? Forget it," Alec said dismissively with a wave of his hand.

"It's not just the party tonight at David's. I have a date on Saturday night, too."

"With whom?"

"With your brother, Jonathan."

A short silence fell following that remark. "I thought I told you that first night to stay away from my brother. You're not his type."

"I think your brother is old enough to decide who is or isn't his type, if he even thinks of women in those terms," Lilly said, and felt a protective anger flaring inside. "At least he respects me."

"Respects you?" Alec sputtered. "Sounds like pretty cold comfort to me."

"It's not. Respect is everything in an equal relationship," Lilly said defensively, tucking her fingers into the soft warmth of her cashmere sweater.

"Ahhhh, now we're talking about equality," Alec said softly, with a sage nod of his head. "Feel free to pay your own way to New York. Hell, I'll even meet you more than halfway on this one, and let you pay for the whole thing, since you're the richer of us two."

"You know, I sometimes think your social development got arrested somewhere around age fourteen." Lilly ruefully took in the teasing glint in his blue eyes as he rocked back and forth on his heels.

"I'm just trying to play by your rules," Alec insisted innocently.

"Liar," Lilly said, and her smile got away from her and became a grin. Alec charmed her, made her laugh at herself. She turned away in a last-ditch effort to keep him from seeing it.

Lilly heard him take the few steps necessary to reach her, his boots loud on the uncarpeted floor. "Why is that serendipitous call of one body to another never enough, Lilly?" He spoke right behind her left ear in a warm, moist exhalation that curled down inside her and round itself into her insides. "When I'm near you my blood sings. I wish I could just describe what that tender bend in your neck, or that fragile gold down on your arms does to me." His fingers followed the path of his words.

"Oh, I think you're doing just fine," Lilly murmured shakily. She unfolded her arms to stare at them as if she might see something new. "No one's ever admired my forearms before," she added, and gave a husky laugh.

"Then it's time someone started." Alec lightly ran his index finger over one of her extended arms, the gesture sending a sensual shock wave up Lilly's spine. She half turned, and her shoulder bumped his chest. Alec inhaled sharply but didn't move.

Tension wound around them in the musty, silent house. Dust motes floated around them and whispered to the floor. He touched her face and her eyes glided shut, her mouth turning eagerly into his palm where it opened and she ran her tongue along the outline of each finger. The taste of him filled her nostrils, but she was greedy for more and inhaled him into her until she felt each cell bursting with his imprint, his indelible mark. She belonged with him; that gnawing sense of constant loneliness was gone. Her mind cried, Why this man? But there was no answer, only his free hand closing in her thick hair and their mouths meeting with a pleasure that shook them both.

With arms wrapped around each other, they kissed, deepening the passion between them each time their tongues twined, released and repeated the pleasurable motion with increasing moist pressure. Her finger slid up his neck to curl and lock in his black hair and the heat of his scalp burned along her nerves. Sensation, heavy and insistent, surged through her belly, and Lilly pulled Alec's hips against her own. She arched into him, needing the press of his hard masculine length as surely as she needed the thrusting beat of her heart. From the murmured sounds that came from Alec's throat, she sensed that he needed that, too. He opened her legs and she clasped them to his as Alec lifted and held her against him. She made the surrender willingly and reveled in his murmured words of need and desire.

Just as suddenly they slowed, and like the orchestrated movements of a dance their lovemaking grew softer, more delicate. But it was no less impassioned. Lilly felt herself turning like a sunflower following the sun as Alec moved his heated mouth along the outline of her face and into the curve of her ear, then down her throat.

She sent eager fingers beneath his sweater to open the buttons of his shirt. Hot, hard flesh met her touch, and she curled her fingers into him, leaving her mark. Then her hand slid down the front of his thigh and then rose in slow massaging motions in between them until they reached the loops of his belt, where they stopped. She hooked her fingers in his belt loops and just held on as he stilled her hands against him.

Alec dropped his head to her shoulder, his breath rising faster and faster. With one hand he pressed her to him, turning them both to the dustcover-draped sofa that sat in the middle of the room facing the fireplace. He sat and pulled her into his lap, hands seeking and finding the clasp to her bra and moments later the smooth and tender flesh of her breasts.

Lilly shifted to straddle him, a knee poking into the dusty sofa on either side of his waist as she pulled his sweater off, and then, more slowly, his shirt. His chest was hard under her caressing hands and felt like satin to her flattened palms. Then they kissed again with flirting tongues that surged against one another eagerly. Their jeans proved to be more of an exercise in erotic play. Lilly knelt at Alec's feet and with smooth sure tugs removed his boots and socks, taking his toes into her mouth just to taste him and was surprised at the strong response this evoked in him as he lifted her against his chest, before standing them both up and after quickly shucking his own jeans, took a much more lingering approach to the removal of Lilly's.

First he unzipped them, peeling back the sides and kissing a straight line of sensation between them. Then he took them, one in each hand, and peeled her jeans down to her ankles where Lilly stepped out of them. She looked up with a shadow of something that wasn't quite apprehension in her eyes.

"Your body is beautiful, Lilly. Your skin is so soft and smooth to the touch." And a bit of the doubt Martin had instilled in her about her own attractiveness faded in the glow coming from Alec's eyes and the irrefutable evidence of his body.

"Yours too," she said shyly, liking the narrow lines of his hips that so differed from the broader planes of her own. She drew a finger along the ridged muscles just above his navel.

"I'm glad. I need to know you find me desirable too." His voice had a rough, vulnerable edge to it that caught at Lilly's heart as he drew Lilly to his lap, their bodies sliding together like the two last missing pieces of a puzzle.

Then he turned her beneath him and the smells of musk and must became desire, the feeling thickening her tongue and filling her senses with only Alec. His square, strong fingers spread beneath her shoulders. Sensation wound them tighter and tighter together until the final moment loosened Lilly's tongue and she cried his name, straining toward that impossible oneness with Alec that she craved with her whole being.

Sensation ebbed slowly, erratically, and it was a while before Lilly felt the convulsive stroking of Alec's hand along her side. "Come to New York with me, Lilly. It could be like this every night, better even, when I learn everything I need to know to please you."

"You pleased me very much," Lilly told him softly, an inexplicable sadness coming over her momentarily at the pleading note in his voice. He sounded so unlike his usual brash self at this moment.

"I can't," Lilly answered, and saw a look of pain in his eyes. Overhead two squirrels chased each other over the roof, and they sounded like elephants in the intense quiet lying between Lilly and Alec. Their activity shook something else loose in the choked chimney and it fell into the grate. Lilly lifted her head to look. A dead and dusty starling lay eagle-spread in the dirt and debris.

"Why not?" Alec demanded, raising himself on one elbow, black brows descending like storm clouds. "Why the hell not?"

"Nothing has changed," Lilly pointed out quietly. "I still have commitments and obligations that can't just be tossed aside." She shivered and tugged gently at her sweater where it lay pinned beneath his thigh. Alec sat up and yanked her sweater down around her waist as Lilly fitted it over her head, and his face reminded her of a small boy who sees a treat he thought was his snatched away by bigger kids.

"Look. I'll talk to Jonathan. He'll understand." Alec's expression brightened. "And I've already told you that a party at David's is never any big deal."

"It's you who doesn't understand, Alec." Lilly stood

and pulled on her jeans. "I have a life of my own, and I won't drop plans I consider important on a moment's notice."

"Didn't this afternoon make a difference to you?" Alec asked.

"Should it have?" Lilly's head tilted to the side, her hazel eyes guarded. She felt tired, chilled, and uncertain. This wasn't a situation she'd found herself in before. In some ways he was still very much a stranger to her.

"Of course it makes a difference! We're certainly not total strangers anymore," he said in an odd echo of Lilly's own thoughts. "I want you. I want you with me, and I think this weekend in New York would be a great opportunity to get to know each other better." Alec stamped down to get his heel into the cowboy boots and made an obvious effort to control his temper at Lilly's continued refusal to agree with him.

"Won't you miss your plane if you don't hurry?" Lilly asked him.

Alec left without another word. Lilly felt him go, and knew that even now, if she just gave in, she could be on her way to the airport with him within an hour. But she said and did nothing until she heard the roar of his car starting up and then quickly fading. She felt emotionally battered, even stunned by the events of the past few hours. She needed to think, and she wanted to be alone to do it. Instead she had to go home and shower and get ready for a business function.

Lilly picked up a pair of gloves Alec had left behind, drawing their leather scent past her nostrils, before resolutely shoving them into her purse. She didn't want to leave anything of value here until she'd gotten rid of the mouse problem.

She locked up and went out to the car. The sun was going down and she shielded her eyes against its hurtful power, tears coming into her eyes and squeezing out of the corners as she drove.

As she got ready Lilly talked to herself, convincing herself that she could get through this party tonight. A warm bath of scented English bath salts helped to ease the tension and begin the process. Lilly was discovering new things about herself; and like all change it was unsettling. She'd never known she was a passionate woman. Martin's lovemaking had been tepid, filled more with embarrassment and fears that she didn't look, smell, or act like some mythical ideal woman. That was how he'd made her feel. Alec's lovemaking had been completely different. With him she'd felt bold and capable of anything! For the first time Lilly knew what sexual passion was like. But far from clarifying things, it only muddied them up. Part of her longed to be with Alec right now, but the other, larger part knew she'd done the right thing. She didn't want to be too heavily invested in anyone. She'd trusted Martin totally, and the devastation he'd left in his wake when he betrayed Lilly still hadn't all healed. For months she'd felt bruised and battered. She'd lashed herself over her foolish, blind faith in a man, and vowed then never to let it happen that way again.

"I'm so glad you could make it, Lilly!" David Holmes exclaimed as he opened the door of his modest rambler-style home. "You look gorgeous. Come in and meet everyone."

The evening progressed pleasantly enough, and Lilly only found her thoughts gravitating toward Central Park and the Plaza Hotel once or twice when things got really dull. Rita, David's wife, wasn't what she'd expected, and that always interested Lilly.

"I hear you're looking for housing in the area. If so, I'm the best real estate agent around, and I'll be glad to help you out," Rita assured her forcefully.

"I'm sorry, but I've already bought something," Lilly said with a smile as she surveyed the small, plump woman, whose dark hair fell in a fringe over her high forehead, then absolutely straight to her shoulders. She reminded Lilly a bit of Cleopatra, which didn't suit David's personality at all. It seemed obvious that Rita had the lion's share of personality in the Holmes family.

"Oh, may I ask where you bought? Is it here in Fielding?" Interest sharpened her green eyes. "Somebody surely works fast in these parts. David only told me on Tuesday night that you were looking for a place."

"I wasn't in that much of a hurry until I saw this place. It belongs to the department secretary's uncle. The Peterson place on the creek, just about opposite the Thomas brothers' home."

"That old thing must be in terrible shape, surely?" Rita asked with a frown. "It's been empty for the best part of five years to my recollection.... Ahh, fallen in love with it, have you? Well, then there's nothing more to be said in the matter." Rita Holmes was brisk in defeat, and Lilly found she liked that.

"It is in bad shape, but the roof is sound, and I got a good price," Lilly said, knowing the other woman had read her expression of disagreement when she'd criticized Lilly's new home. She could see Rita was dying to ask how good, but politeness held her in check. "Just ask Alec. He was out there today with me, and I explained the whole transaction to him. He seemed quite fascinated by it." Lilly's voice was bland as cream.

That gave Rita pause for a moment as she tried and failed to see into that remark. "Well, I have a brother in Mankato who's a contractor and electrician. So if you need—"

"That's the spirit, Rita. Never say die!" Todd Godwin wandered over and cast an arm over the small woman's shoulders. Rita tried to appear unaffected, but Lilly saw that Todd's little arrow had gotten under her skin.

"Loyalty, whether to family or employer, is always a charming trait," Lilly said pointedly. "Don't you agree, Todd?"

"My, oh, my, aren't we tart!" he answered with a smirk that irritated Lilly. She caught a glimpse of herself in the windows that opened onto the Holmes's deck. She looked angry, with bright pink cheeks and a hostile stance that worked to the advantage of someone like Todd. Lilly was coming to distrust him. Unpleasantness seemed to follow him like a cloud, Lilly thought as she remembered Tuesday's incident in the bar. Lilly disliked anyone who seemed to take such joy in making others uncomfortable.

"Excuse me," she said coolly and pushed past into the living room, knowing if Todd lost his audience he'd subside quite a bit.

"That's a lovely dress you have on," Margaret Schwartz said admiringly. Like her husband, Al, Margaret spoke with a heavy German accent. About fifty-five, she had a chic that was more French than German, and Lilly felt genuinely complimented by the older woman's approval of her simple black sheath dress. With it Lilly wore the pearls her father had given her for a twenty-first birthday present, and shoes that were a mere confection of straps and the thinnest of soles to keep her feet off the earth.

"Thank you," Lilly said as she moved forward, gracefully excluding Todd, who had just emerged from the kitchen, from the group without problem. "I hear you're quite the painter."

"Only the words of a fond husband could so describe me," she said with a rich chuckle as her eyes sought her husband affectionately. He stood in a huddled group, and paused to raise his glass when he saw his wife looking over. "Al speaks highly of you, Lilly. Your methods are of the unorthodox, I believe. Nonetheless, you get the job done, right?"

Put that way, Lilly had to laugh as she imagined the consternation her "unorthodox methods" had caused at that first staff meeting.

"Have some of this punch," Todd broke in, thrusting a glass of pink liquid at Lilly. "It's something this party has lacked so far. But I have this psychic feeling things are going to pick up very soon."

Lilly had seen Todd go to the phone when she'd moved to keep him from this group earlier. She accepted the punch with a sense of uneasiness. How did the Holmeses come to invite him anyway? Lilly wondered to herself, forgetting how difficult it was to keep a party a secret in an English department. And once Todd knew about it, he could quite easily invite himself.

A commotion just a few minutes later caught Lilly's attention, but she couldn't see what was going on. Then she heard a clear, piercing female voice say, "Where is he, then? I've come here to have it out with him once and for all!"

A red-headed woman exploded into the room, her sherry-brown eyes making a wild sweep of the room. "Just calm down, please," Lilly heard David sputter as he tried to catch the redhead's arm. "As you can see for yourself, I didn't lie. Alec isn't here, but you're welcome to stay and have a drink. No one here is deliberately ostracizing you, no matter what nonsense someone may have poured in your ear."

"I want to see Alec!" She spoke as though David were just hiding him somewhere to annoy her. The folds of her emerald green cloak swung around her in a dramatic gesture that nearly cleared the hors d'oeuvres table behind her. "He's the only man I've ever truly wanted!"

Everyone had huddled into small groups where they pretended to ignore the woman. Lilly stared quite frankly at her. She was beautiful enough to command attention in her own right, but her theatrical entrance made ignoring her ludicrously impossible.

"Ahh, Toddy boy is right again," he crowed, and Lilly felt her hackles rising.

"You've had too much of your own punch, Todd," Lilly shot back, and it was true. He smelled heavily of alcohol, although his tone was more offensive than his breath.

"I see you still have no idea who our mystery guest is, do you?" Todd was absolutely in his glory. He preened himself, stroking his thin chest, too much of which was visible. He tended toward lots of gold chains that he clinked together constantly. Lilly was sure the aftershave companies would never go out of business while Toddy was around.

"I don't have any idea who that is, but I feel certain that you're eager to tell me," Lilly said in a bored tone and turned to examine a particularly ugly porcelain dog. She knew if she displayed interest Todd would drag this game on for ten minutes, but this way she hoped to sting him into talking.

But the woman was teasingly familiar, as though Lilly didn't really know her, but had seen her in a movie or in an entirely different setting than the present one.

"She's Karen Willis, and you've got her to thank for the way you've been treated in this department so far. Thanks to her suit, the whole staff is leary about you now." Todd's hand shot out to close on Lilly's icy fingers when she didn't seem to respond to his bombshell.

All the blood in her body drained away to some hidden place, and Lilly felt the room receding. Now she realized where she'd seen the redhead before. It had been in that photograph on top of Alec's piano. Karen

Willis was the mysterious flame-haired woman! Suddenly the relationship between the Thomas brothers and Karen Willis was as clear to Lilly as the sluggish black waters of the Mississippi on a dark winter's day.

Chapter Six

"Aren't you listening to me?" Todd persisted. He shook Lilly's cold hand and leaned in closely so that his alcoholic breath made her eyes sting. Lilly steadied the porcelain statue with her free hand before stepping back. "Karen and Alec had quite a thing going. Everyone in the department knew. Hell, everyone in this whole lousy little town must have known about it for years!"

Lilly could see the warmth and laughter bubbling around her, but inside she went cold and dark. Her hands felt like ice sculptures of the real thing, lifelike but lifeless. Well, what did you expect? She asked herself harshly. Were you given promises of undying love and a rose-covered cottage by the sea? Alec made himself clear, didn't he? Lilly demanded of herself, prodding at the wound.

She raised hazel eyes to stare across the room as Karen tossed her red hair, laughing excitedly at something one of the circle of men around her had said. Even across the room the exquisite quality of her skin was apparent, and Lilly felt drab, ordinary, and totally foolish in comparison. Alec and Karen were two of a kind, she realized. Oh, God, what have I done to my life now? Lilly thought of the painful nights she'd spent over Martin, and it felt like comparing a hangnail to the gnawing pain of a cancer deep within. No matter how you twist and turn you can't escape or ease the pain, nor can you cut it out without dying yourself.

"Hey, Lilly! Are you okay?" Todd tried to put his arm around her but Lilly jerked away. She found his phony sympathy unbearable at that moment. She sat down abruptly and picked a chair that hit her in exactly the wrong place and left her feet an inch off the floor. Pure physical discomfort brought her back to reality.

Lilly looked around for her drink and tried to arrange her expression into polite interest, but a feeling of complete misery swept over her as she listened to Karen's carrying tones.

"Oh, God!" she said, then realized she'd spoken aloud. The sort of self-doubt she'd created in herself by succumbing to her growing passion for him and going to bed with Alec had never plagued Lilly before. She knew she wasn't handling it well. But Martin had been her only serious relationship; her family's wealth had made theirs a rather closed environment in which outsiders were rarely welcome. Lilly had dated carefully approved boys and men only.

Then there had been Martin. He wasn't a passionate man, which had been all right with Lilly, since she hadn't until today considered herself a passionate woman. Alec had changed her. He'd taken her mental landscape and turned it into a storm zone where all the usual posted warnings and speed signs were obscured.

Rita Holmes was bending over her with a concerned look and Lilly tried to pull herself together. "Would you like to come into the kitchen for a breather? It's getting really warm in here."

Lilly nodded gratefully and stood up to follow her hostess as she wove through the knots of people. In Lilly's sensitive state it seemed to her that all eyes followed her. All of them except Karen Willis, who was giving an animated account of her latest "work-in-progress" to anyone who would listen.

"I appreciate the rescue job," Lilly said with a grimace as the kitchen door swung shut behind them. Lilly felt herself reviving a bit in the cool, relatively quiet kitchen. Yet inwardly Lilly had to acknowledge that it was her actions this afternoon with Alec that were making her queasy, not Todd's little games or even the possible thoughts of the other staff members.

For Lilly was usually honest with herself, or tried to be, and she knew that most of the people out in that living room didn't notice or care about her reaction to Karen Willis. But the Todd Godwins of the world were a special case, and Lilly knew she needed to be more careful around him if she didn't want him to find out about her relationship with Alec.

"Well, this is probably none of my business," Rita began, and Lilly froze, then relaxed when she went on. "I noticed Todd's been hanging around you a lot tonight. David thinks the department is lucky to have him. And for all I know he may well be a professional whiz kid, but on a personal level he makes me sick. Be careful what you say around him, Lilly. He enjoys making trouble." While she talked Rita had been busy loading dirty glassware into the dishwasher. Now she shut it with a bang and turned it on. Lilly could see that she never allowed time to go to waste. "... and that's what makes me think it could only have been Todd."

"What?" Lilly filled a plastic cup with water and ice and took a long gulp to ease her parched throat. "What could only have been Todd? You mean he called Karen and told her about this party?" Lilly remembered Todd using the phone, now that she thought about it.

"Well, Alec would have been here if he hadn't had to go to New York, and Todd might have thought he was coming late." Rita sounded a bit defensive. "David claims I see things, but I think Todd is out to get Alec. He's just plain jealous of him."

"Honey, are there more of those bacon things?"

David asked, coming in as if on cue. He looked around vaguely as if the hors d'oeuvres might be floating around in midair somewhere.

Rita gave him an indulgent look and whisked a cookie sheet full of bacon-wrapped water chestnuts from the oven, arranging them on the tray David held out with her quick, efficient fingers. A sprig of parsley at the corners and she sent him off again.

The pause gave Lilly time to think and gather her thoughts, but just as she was about to launch into a discussion about Karen and hopefully get some much-needed information, they were interrupted again.

"We've come to relieve you galley slaves," Hilda announced cheerfully. "And it's about time you stopped hogging the guest of honor, Rita. Whatever needs doing, you just point us in the right direction and stand back!"

Lilly and Rita laughed, allowing themselves to be ousted from the kitchen, even as Rita protested that there wasn't that much to do. "All the more reason to get out and mingle," Hilda pointed out.

But when they stepped into the living room, the laughter died away. Rita gave Lilly a knowing look. Across the room, Karen and Todd had their heads together, and Todd was plying his punch insistently.

About to say something, Rita was prevented from doing so as David called her over to confirm something, his encircling arm closing Rita in and Lilly out.

For a moment Lilly stood alone in the noisy room. She felt very lonely and sorry for herself. This was the first party she'd attended in a long time, and for one crazy second she actually missed Martin's assured social self. Then she caught Karen's eyes, which held a surprisingly wry expression. Todd seemed to have wandered off, and before she knew it, Lilly had walked over and was introducing herself.

"I'm Lilly Burns. I don't believe we've met."

"Ahh, but I'll bet you've heard of me. I'm Karen Willis, the village bad seed." Her voice was deep, brushed with the harsh quality of a heavy smoker.

Lilly laughed. "Actually I have heard of you. We have a mutual acquaintance, Mike Durrell. At the University of Iowa?" Lilly added at Karen's blank look.

"I'm sorry I don't recall the name." She lit up, pulling the smoke in deeply. Then with half-closed eyes she carefully exhaled to the side. "See, I've already noted that you don't smoke," she said lightly, but Lilly noticed a tremor in her long, thin fingers as Karen replaced her lighter in the side of her leather cigarette case.

"Well, you'd remember Mike if you saw him. He's a big bear of a guy, and really outgoing. Odd though, he remembers you vividly, but then"—Lilly smiled as she spoke—"Mike always had perfect recall for an attractive woman's face!"

"You've spoken to him recently? Why? About what?"

"We're friends. I talk to him often." Lilly was at a loss to understand Karen's almost angry attitude. As far as she knew, Mike didn't have an enemy in the world, and when she'd mentioned Karen Willis to him Mike had recalled the flamboyant redhead with relish. Lilly supposed it was possible, although not probable, that Karen didn't remember him and decided to let the topic drop for now.

Up close, the long oval of Karen's face had a strangely vulnerable quality to it, a sadness in repose that added, in Lilly's opinion to the beauty of her features. Lilly found herself wanting to know this woman. There seemed to be several Karen Willises, and Lilly wondered which was the true one. For this vulnerable, sad woman wasn't the same as the vivacious person who'd made such a dramatic entrance only a short time ago.

"Why do you call yourself a bad seed?" Lilly asked curiously. She reached for one of the fresh bacon hors d'oeuvres, more for something to do with her hands than because she really wanted it, she realized as she crunched into the water chestnut inside.

"Oh, you know," Karen said with a careless shrug. "The village troublemaker. The kid from the bad family everyone always *knew* would come to a bad end." She spoke lightly, but her words were edged. She pushed her thick, vibrant hair behind her ears and strode to the window. She thrust it open and stood with the soft night air rippling the curtain she held tightly in her hand. The nails of that hand beat an impatient tattoo on the frame.

"That's the sort of stuff that comes true only if you believe it," Lilly said quietly. She felt an unwanted sympathy for this restless woman. Something was driving her, making her unhappy. That in turn changed her from a caricature to a human being. Lilly couldn't just think of her as "that woman bringing the suit" anymore. With those few words she'd become a person with feelings just as real as Lilly's own.

"Oh, come on. Have you ever had a whole town despise you and your family?" she asked, and when Lilly shook her head mutely, she went on. "Then spare me the platitudes, please!" She flicked a chunk of plaster from the edge of the window frame. "These kids could have used a good plasterer when they moved in."

"I do this sort of work now that I'm unemployed," Karen explained when Lilly looked nonplussed. "Don't you think painting and plastering and cleaning up after workmen is a good use of my writing degrees from the University of Iowa?"

"I'd like to hear your side of this suit. You don't know me, but I think we have a lot in common."

"Oh, sure!" Karen gave a hacking laugh. "Like you

have my job and my man. I guess that does give us something in common, at that!"

"Alec Thomas and I have a purely professional relationship!" Lilly said heatedly, answering the accusation that bit closest to the bone. The crack about having taken Karen's job didn't merit an answer as far as Lilly was concerned.

"And what about your relationship with Jonathan? Or are romantic walks along the creek with your banker just a usual part of opening a checking account for you rich types?" Karen demanded sarcastically. A blotch of color appeared along either side of her prominent collarbones.

"What?" Lilly said loudly, forgetting where she was for the moment. "What in the world does Jonathan Thomas have to do with this?"

"Nothing! Just forget it," Karen ordered. "So you think you can handle Alec and the gang?" she changed the subjects abruptly with a big gesture towards the room at large. Lilly followed her gesture and noticed that there were fewer people in the room now. They'd been leaving regularly since about midnight, and looking down at her watch, Lilly saw how late it was getting. She tried to think of how best to answer Karen.

"Are you still going to need a ride home, Karen?" Rita asked pointedly. She and David were cleaning up napkins and other litter. Lilly noted that Todd had left long ago, unnoticed. Not enough dirt in the making for him, Lilly guessed shrewdly.

"David is leaving now to drop the Schwartzes, and they're sort of out your way," Rita added.

"I'll drive you home, if you like," Lilly heard herself offer.

"I think the party's over," Karen said with a shrug.

"No, no. Stay as long as you like," Rita said firmly. "I just wanted to let Karen know that David was leaving and headed in her direction." Rita evidently thought she might have sounded a bit rude and was doing all she could to soft-pedal it. But Karen and Lilly were already to the door.

"Thank you for a very pleasant evening. It was good to meet you, Rita," Lilly said as they went out the door.

"Such nice manners. Your mama raised you right, I see," Karen mocked as they went down the drive to the street where Lilly had parked the Corvette under a street light. Lilly let that one alone and asked Karen for directions to her house.

"I just live out on Route 3," Karen said in that dismissive way those in a small town give directions. As Jonathan said, though, nothing was too far from anything else in Fielding. Lilly remembered that Route 3 was the address of the only Willis in the phone book and figured it must be the family home.

"So how do you like the thriving cultural hotspot of Fielding?" Karen asked. She'd slid into the Corvette without commenting on it, which was unusual for Lilly's passengers. The heavy throb of the engine before her calmed and soothed Lilly as they cruised out along the highway toward Route 3.

"Why do you stay here if you dislike it?" Lilly asked mildly, answering Karen's sarcastic question with one of her own.

"It's a disease," Karen said, only half-jokingly. "Once Fielding gets into your blood you never get it out."

"Sort of a variation of 'you can take the girl out of Fielding but you can't take the Fielding out of the girl,' huh?"

"Yeah, that's it. Say, would you stop at that truck stop up ahead there? I need a cup of coffee." Karen flung open the door as Lilly pulled up. "You want anything?"

Lilly shook her head and watched Karen's long legs carry her swiftly into the white light of the truck stop. She emerged moments later with a plastic-covered Styrofoam cup.

She jumped back into the car, cracking the plastic cover at tiny intervals all the way around before taking it off and dumping several packets of sugar inside. A small silence fell. Lilly didn't want to drive off right away because Karen would probably spill the hot coffee.

"You know, it's weird. I like you, Lilly." Karen broke the silence. "I hope my bringing this suit doesn't make things too hard for you at the college."

"I'm not officially supposed to know about it," Lilly admitted. Her hazel eyes went dark, and she stared straight ahead at the white lights of the truck stop as she spoke. "But I overheard David and Alec arguing about it my first day in the department. It made me feel pretty lousy to hear I was a token female hired just to take the sting out of your impending suit."

"They actually said that?" Karen asked excitedly. "That's great! How did Alec react? Was he really angry? What did he say?"

Karen sounded so eager that it made Lilly uneasy, and she paused before answering to start up the car and head back to the highway. "Look, Karen. I can tolerate feeling uncomfortable for a while, and I think I'm already beginning to turn their ideas around as far as the composition program goes. But if I'm going to be giving you information when I'm already suffering as a result of your actions, I think I have a right to know why."

Karen shrugged, and Lilly drove for about another half-mile in silence. Just as she saw the sign for Route 3, Karen indicated she should turn left. They jolted another two miles down a rutted road that ended in a farmyard. The glare of the headlights put the bleak place into high relief. It was filled with refuse, rusting farming equipment, and even in the cool fall air the stench was unmistakable. To the right a sagging building rose shakily toward the sky, and the house itself looked in little better condition.

"Well?"

"I'll tell you this much," Karen said tersely. "You're going to have to be *damned* good to hang on to your precious job at that place. Because there are different standards for male and female academics at Fielding. Have you asked yourself why there aren't other female staffers, let alone tenured women, in that department?"

"Then you were fired because you're female? Not for any other reason?" Lilly persisted.

"Yes! I was sexually harassed into quitting by Alec. He once attacked me in his office, and you can ask Todd Godwin about that!" Karen said bitterly, the long line of her throat visible as she drained the Styrofoam cup and tossed it out the car. "Alec even had one of his buddies, Gary something, lined up to take my job before the rest of them got in first with you."

Karen got out, then bent down to look Lilly in the eyes. "So just think about that before you get too involved with Alec Thomas!" The door slammed shut and once more Lilly found herself watching the swift motion of Karen's slim legs carrying her away from the Corvette. Lilly waited until she got in the door of the peeling frame house before backing out of the yard and going back into Fielding the way she had come.

As Lilly pulled into Mrs. Jordan's driveway her head bent over the steering wheel and her body shook with sobs. She sat that way for many minutes, then backed out of the driveway with a squeal of breaks, headed for the interstate leading out of Fielding. She flashed past the cut-off to Karen's farm going about ninety-five and was nearly to Minneapolis before she felt calm enough to turn around and head back.

Until the exact moment she wheeled the powerful car around and headed south, Lilly hadn't known for sure that she would go back. For a certain thought beat a constant rhythm in the back of her mind: *Daddy would take care of it for her.* If Lilly wanted to give up, she could. She wouldn't have to face any of them again. Of course, once she was on her way back Lilly didn't think she'd been serious about quitting. She'd only needed to work a few of the knots out. She didn't think she could just have gone in and gone calmly to bed. Too much had happened. Karen's warning had bitten to the bone, and even now Lilly couldn't think of it without feeling her body begin to shake. But that was no reason to quit.

Lily knew she would never give up on all the good things she'd started at Fielding College. Her projects were taking root already, and she knew she was good at her teaching. Lilly already knew she was getting to like the sense of independence having her own town and her own house gave her. She hadn't realized how claustrophobic her life would have been if she'd settled for working at her father's company. Oh, she'd have had an excellent position at nearly three times her present salary. Yet there was always the nagging sensation at the back of her mind that she'd never really tested herself.

As far as Alec went . . . well, Lilly would just have to handle that as it came. Despite Karen's warning and her own well-founded fears that he would always have a warped view of women, Lilly just couldn't give up on him. But Monday morning loomed like a precariously balanced weight ready to crush her.

Just think about one day at a time, she advised herself as she garaged the car and picked her way back to the kitchen door, where a welcoming yellow light spilled onto the black space in front of her. The brief, violent rainstorm the night before had denuded the trees and driven leaves into small, sodden mounds against any solid surface and drained them completely of their fall beauty.

The next morning a heavy frost covered most of the ground, and it had etched intricate patterns on all the windows. Lilly was glad she'd thought to put the Corvette in the garage. She spent Saturday morning engaged in a round of those mundane chores that hold life together. She did laundry and some shopping and talked to her parents on the phone for a few minutes to keep them filled in. Her father mentioned his luncheon with Harry, but nothing about the house. She was tempted to call Jonathan and cancel their date.

Then she decided it wasn't fair to him, and anyway, most of this had nothing to do with Jonathan. He was an easygoing man who would not put any demands on her. Besides, she knew from their previous conversation that he'd be hard pressed to find a use for those tickets at this late notice.

During the afternoon Lilly worked on a project she'd devised for her composition classes in the past. It worked like an old-fashioned scavenger hunt, only the students collected information instead of the traditional objects. The goal was to get these first-year students familiar with the resources of the library. For that reason, Lilly herself checked out both the college and public systems to make sure all the information she was asking the students to gather was available to them.

At the college library she spent a pleasant few minutes in the hushed atmosphere with which she was so familiar after so many years spent in libraries doing research herself. Her warning about the impending hordes of students was good-natured, but firm.

"Try to get them to do as much on their own as possible," she pleaded. "They can be very persuasive, but the whole point of this exercise is to get them to learn to find material on their own.''

"I think what you're doing is wonderful, Miss Burns. This will help these young people throughout their college careers," Fran Pelt, the head research librarian, said approvingly. She looked the very stereotype of the librarian, complete with tortoise-shell glasses, but she was one sharp lady. "I wish a few more in that English department would do the same. You're one of the few there to appreciate the importance of good library skills."

Lilly nodded, but her mind had moved on to what she would wear on her date with Jonathan, since she knew this particular speech by heart, and just waited for a suitable break-in point to say farewell politely. She left the library with Fran still beaming after her.

In the end, Lilly decided on a soft, high-collared knit dress of turquoise that flattered the dark blond highlights in her hair and raised her spirits whenever she wore it. Mrs. Jordan complimented her highly when she came downstairs, leather coat over her arm. By the time six o'clock rolled around, Lilly felt pretty good about herself.

On the drive to Minneapolis they discussed a variety of subjects amiably. *Unlike Alec and me*, Lilly couldn't help thinking, *who can't agree for more than three minutes at a time.*

"I hear you've bought the old Peterson place," Jonathan said. They had stopped for a red light in the small town of Shakopee, and he turned to her with a smile in his navy eyes. Once more, as she explained the story of her purchase, she thought how attractive he was. *Why couldn't I have fallen in love with this Thomas?* she asked herself, even as Jonathan roared with laughter at Alec's reception of the news that Peterson had sold to her.

"And to think Peterson waited five long years for his

perfect revenge!" Jonathan was still wiping his eyes as
the light changed and they began moving again. They
turned left and crossed the Minnesota River and soon
were on the freeway that ran all the way into the heart
of downtown Minneapolis.

Lilly watched Jonathan as he drove. No, the family
resemblance wasn't apparent at first, but it made itself
subtly felt the longer she knew them both. In their own
ways, each man was thoroughly at home and in control
of his environment: Jonathan through his calm, au-
thoritative approach and Alec through sheer force of
personality.

"Have you and Alec been getting along any better
lately, or are the sparks still flying?" Jonathan asked.
He stretched his legs and for a moment the only sounds
were the humming of the smooth-riding Cadillac and
the strains of Mozart playing over the stereo.

"We didn't get off to a very auspicious start, as you
might recall," Lilly said finally. "He wanted someone
else for the position, you know." Lilly answered the
question strictly in professional terms and could only
hope that was how Jonathan meant it.

"I could be way off base, Lilly. But I think Alec is a
bit in awe of you—now, don't laugh. You're a highly
qualified and capable woman. I don't think you should
shrug off the idea that you might intimidate him so
easily."

"I doubt he's intimidated by me. But if he is, that's
his problem, isn't it? What am I supposed to do,
simper and say, gee, aren't you smart, Mr. Wonderful
Playwright?" Lilly had turned toward him with hazel
eyes blazing.

"Hold on. All I'm trying to say is not that either you
or Alec is right about this. I'm just trying to get you to
see what his point of view might be. That gives you an
advantage, don't you see?"

Lilly did see. She'd overreacted, and felt the heat of

embarrassment flash over her. Could Jonathan have a point? Could part of Alec's overbearing attitude be based on feeling threatened by her? That was a hard idea for Lilly to swallow, but she forced herself to consider it, to look at things from Alec's point of view based on what she knew of him. The more she thought about it the more it fit her own insights into what made Alec tick. A woman that didn't fit his rigid formula of women as belonging either in his bed or in the kitchen ready to wait on him *would* make him feel threatened, Lilly realized.

To her surprise, Lilly saw they had entered to downtown area of Minneapolis. Jonathan headed across town until he reached the Mississippi River, where with a sharp right he turned down by the river itself. The big car bumped along the cobbled street lined with old-fashioned lamp posts that glowed orange. For a moment Lilly could almost believe she was gazing down on a street in Victorian England. Jonathan parked and led the way into a stone building that looked like an old flour mill.

The whole staff seemed to converge delightedly on them, and after a loud and long discussion in which Lilly did little but murmur yes or no when asked, the meal was decided upon. They had delicious lemon sole after an appetizer of marinated vegetables. Best of all, though, were the Potatoes Anna, layer after layer of paper-thin slices of potatoes brushed with the flavors of onion and butter and then slowly baked until they were caramel in color.

Lilly and Jonathan sat in an alcove with a crackling fire behind them that filled the space with the clean, sweet spice of applewood. Several attentive but unobtrusive waiters stood ready to fill their smallest needs. It ought to have been highly romantic, Lilly thought, remembering Alec's scathing comment yesterday. Certainly it made a great change from the salads and tuna

sandwiches Lilly had subsisted on when Mrs. Jordan
was in Mankato. Lilly appreciated good food and
service, and Jonathan was extending himself to be
charming. He even managed to make banking sound
interesting. That was no small feat as far as Lilly was
concerned, and she told him so.

But one level of her mind was constantly on Alec.
What was he thinking about that afternoon? What was
he doing right now, and with whom? Lilly kept corral-
ing her straying thoughts, but like wild steers they
seemed adept at finding holes in the fences she put
around them. Redoubling her efforts to attend to him,
Lilly told herself Alec wasn't worth the mental space
she allowed him and stirred cream vigorously into her
coffee, even though she didn't take cream. Lilly looked
up to find Jonathan's eyes twinkling.

"That's the third time you've put cream in that coffee. Is it that bad?"

"Of course not! The entire meal was superb. My
congratulations on your choice of restaurant. I'll have
to tell my parents about it. They're always on the look-
out for new places to eat. My mother isn't big on cook-
ing," Lilly said, without consciously adding the dry
note that crept into her voice. A picture of her sleek
blond mother was instantly conjured in Lilly's mind.
Her mother hadn't had time for a lot of the traditional
female graces, which was all right with Lilly. "My
mother is the unsung originator of quality time, too,"
Lilly said lightly. Then she expanded her statement at
Jonathan's puzzled expression. "It's a current buzz-
word in child care, used mostly to justify dumping kids
in daycare for ten and twelve hours a day while the
parents both have careers." The dislike came through
strongly. "I'm all for women working, but I think both
parents need to share the responsibility of children
equally, and the children should be wanted," Lilly said
passionately. Over the years she'd gained the definite

impression that her own birth had been a concession on her mother's part to family pressures. Certainly, it was a decision she'd openly regretted at times. Millicent liked a tidy balance sheet and a good cost/benefit ratio. And motherhood, as she'd once told Lilly, has no termination clause.

"If you can get your parents down to Fielding, they ought to try the Halsted House," Jonathan said gently.

"I'm trying," Lilly said, grateful to be rescued from her own inner turmoil by his good manners. "My father loves seafood, and I hear Halsted House is the best. But both of them being in the business... they're rarely able to take time off."

"Burns Electronics is an immense empire. I'm not surprised that it takes up most of your father's time," Jonathan commented as he looked up from signing the credit card voucher.

"Oh, he could never do it without my mother, and he's the first to admit it," Lilly said. Her relationship with her father caused fleeting silence but little anger. Carlisle Burns had been a shadowy figure during Lilly's childhood. He was the man who made flying visits to solve problems, and then took off again.

"Oh, what does your mother do in the company?" Jonathan asked as they strolled to the Cadillac and he saw her in.

"She's the consummate executive," Lilly told him when he came around to the driver's side. Lilly knew there were many things to be admired about her mother, but somehow, illogically perhaps, Lilly had never forgiven her mother for not being a quantity time mother. "Which is great, because she was a lousy Girl Scout Leader!"

Jonathan laughed as she'd intended, and the talk moved to theaters in general and the Arlo II in specific. Arlo II was an off-shoot of the Walter Arlo theater, one of the oldest and best known in Minneapolis, although it had surprisingly stiff competition from local theater groups.

"I think it depends on your definition of good theater," Jonathan agreed when Lilly voiced the thought that the Arlo was the best. "Because if you prefer lush productions, then the Arlo main theater is definitely the tops in the Minneapolis market."

"I think it's what the general public prefers," Lilly said. They'd descended a steep set of stairs and had been handed programs and told to find their own seating on the stark white benches once they entered the Arlo II. "And I can't say I blame them. In fact, these benches could make any evening pretty long." Before them on the open stage were only two straight-backed chairs that had seen better days. Lilly shifted on the bench and thought of the luxuriously padded seats at the main Arlo theatre. This better be good, Lilly thought. She hadn't yet looked at her program, and now she flipped through it to the section with the playwright's biography and comments. Lilly felt the world slow and stutter. Shock gripped her as she read: "To pierce the social conventions, the hypocricsy we all live by, and to reveal the real ways men and women relate to each other is why I wrote *Twilight*. The heated controversy provoked by its original Off-Broadway opening pleased me, and I hope you leave the theatre tonight moved in some way, whether it's to violent outrage or wholehearted agreement—I don't much care...."

Oh, the arrogance of the man! Lilly thought furiously. "Why?" Lilly demanded of Jonathan as the lights dimmed and a man and woman seated themselves in the back to back chairs at center stage. The room grew black except for white circles of light on the actor's faces. There was the sound of hollow footsteps and the scraping of another chair. A third spotlight lit the face of an older man, and the woman began to speak.

"Why did you bring me to this?" Lilly whispered.

"I'll tell you later," Jonathan promised. Several people shushed them, affronted looks on their faces. Lilly settled back half-reluctantly, half-excitedly, to watch the opening act of Alec Thomas's first play.

Chapter Seven

"I wanted to surprise you," Jonathan said at intermission as they stood sipping sherry at the improvised bar near the entry. The intense babble of voices was testament enough that Alec had succeeded in reaching his audience, Lilly thought. Snippets of conversation caught at her ears: "He's the worst cynic about women," one woman said breathlessly. And another man argued, "Not at all like Tennessee Williams; I see Shaw's influence!"

"Well, you did surprise me," Lilly said dryly as she watched an amber swirl of sherry in her glass, and saw the vibrant blue of Alec's eyes in her mind. "Thomas works on so many levels!" an insistent man kept repeating, and Lilly thought, doesn't he though? "But I don't know what the big secret was about seeing Alec's play." She met Jonathan's eye challengingly.

"Would you have come if you'd known?" Lilly dropped her eyes to the plastic sherry glass in Jonathan's large hand, and saw it tighten. "This play reveals a lot about things that are very personal to me. I had a very strong reason for wanting you to see this play with me tonight."

Just then the bells sounded for the beginning of the next act and ushers motioned them to hurry to their seats. Jonathan hesitated, then placed a hand at her elbow. "We'll talk later, I promise," he said, and helped

Lilly into her seat. Lilly was very curious to know what Jonathan's personal reasons were, but she could do little but comply.

At first she found it difficult to concentrate, since she knew that Jonathan wasn't the type to enjoy creating suspense just to get attention. But the drama unveiled before her soon caught Lilly up, and she forgot everything else but the gripping, passionate tale of two men and a woman. Joanna was a fascinating woman who had risen above poverty and an abuse-filled childhood to return triumphant to the small town and to the childhood sweetheart who had scorned her. Or so she felt. Daniel was the one great passion in Joanna's otherwise sterile emotional landscape, and she was determined to make him as miserable as he'd made her all those years ago. The other man, Calvin, was Daniel's father, a man whose life seemed on the verge of destruction. Attempting to intercede between his son and Joanna, Calvin falls deeply in love with this bitter, tragic woman and is torn between conflicting loyalties of love and family. At times grim, the play was nonetheless enlivened by stinging humor that reminded Lilly intensely of Alec.

The framework of *Twilight* was simple. Each character got a chance to tell the story from his or her point of view. The result was like a prism held to the light. As you turn it the colors change; something is added and something is taken away. Each time Lilly thought, Ahh, now we're getting to the bottom of this, that character's face would go dark and another one would begin to speak. Soon Lilly would begin to side with that character, and then it would change again. The tension built and built until the final speech in which Calvin made an impassioned plea for them to deal reasonably with each other. Suddenly the stage went completely dark. A shot rang out, and Joanna screamed. Moments later the house lights came back up and the stage was empty except for the three empty chairs. Lilly was stunned.

So too, it seemed, was the rest of the audience. Several long moments went by before some tentative applause thundered into whole-hearted approval and the actors returned on stage, hand in hand, to take their bows.

"I thought it was a powerful piece of work," Lilly admitted as she and Jonathan left the theater, slowly tracing their steps to the Cadillac in that hazy faraway mood that any intense movie or play left her with. "If you wanted to convince me what a talented playwright Alec is, then you succeeded."

"Yes. Alec is talented, highly so," Jonathan said absently as they waited their turn to squeeze into the line of exiting cars whose glowing red brake lights marched toward the stop-light. "Did you notice anything else about the play?"

"Alec's misogyny reared its ugly head," Lilly said promptly.

"What do you mean?" Jonathan demanded swiftly, shooting Lilly an eager look.

"I got the feeling that he *began* with a definite concept of Joanna, but she refused, as a character, to be reduced to a stereotype. In short, if it wasn't for Alec's tremendous abilities as a storyteller, he would have ruined this play by his determination to make Joanna out to be the bad guy."

"I think Alec is being made out to be the bad guy at Fielding these days, and maybe that's carried over to the play," Jonathan said, defending his brother.

"Sex discrimination is a bad guy thing to do!" Lilly retorted. "And I don't think I'm doing anything but judging this play on its own merits. I constantly felt that he was sympathetic to both of his male characters, but not to Joanna's plight."

Without seeming to move, Jonathan's whole body

tensed, and Lilly was reminded of that first morning when Alec blazed into the staff meeting and eleven people snapped to instant attention.

"Karen can be such a destructive child at times," Jonathan said sadly. "She was so angry about *Twilight*, but I thought she'd gotten over it. I'm still hoping this will pass with no damage done."

"Wait a minute," Lilly said, completely lost now. "What does Karen have to do with *Twilight*?" Enlightenment dawned on Lilly with the force of a body blow. "Joanna is based on Karen! That's why Alec tried so hard to indict her!"

"Yes." Jonathan finally managed to squeeze the big car in line, and they edged toward the stop-light. "When *Twilight* was first produced about two years ago, Karen was just beginning her career at Fielding. She threatened to sue, but was terrified that such a suit would only confirm people's suspicions and rekindle the humiliations of her childhood and she couldn't bear that. Then, when there was talk of bringing a second production here to Minneapolis, she went nuts. She went to Alec's office and they had some terrible fights over it."

"Didn't Alec care about how this would affect Karen?" Lilly remembered Todd's sly comments at the bar that Tuesday night. So this was what those fights between Karen and Alec had been about!

"There's always been tremendous animosity between them. Karen fixed her eye on Alec in high school, you see. And she lived for a time with our family. Her own family relationships were bad, and she developed this eating disorder...."

"Anorexia nervosa?" Lilly guessed.

"Yes, that's it. She was in the hospital several times as a teenager and nearly died. Both her doctor and her social worker felt environment was to blame, and recommended foster care."

"So Karen came to live with your family," Lilly said

thoughtfully. She could see that the similarity between Karen and Joanna must extend to their childhoods too. There had been a certain suppressed anger in Jonathan's tone when he spoke of Karen's family. And Lilly herself had seen where Karen's family lived and had sensed from her comment about "being a bad seed" that her family wasn't exactly an ideal one.

"She was a pathetic little chick. Just ninety pounds on her, and so scared. I'd never seen a child with less self-confidence, although she could put on a tough act at times."

Lilly heard and understood more than Jonathan thought. As a big, self-confident male, he would always have a soft spot for the underdog. Jonathan slammed his hand on the steering wheel and startled Lilly out of her thoughts.

"We all did what we could for her. Even Alec was kind, at first. But Karen became fixated on him. She followed him everywhere. Did everything he did, and no matter how cruel he was to her, Alec just couldn't shake that intense devotion she felt for him."

Lilly was shocked by the raw jealousy ripping through Jonathan's tone. The urbane, easygoing facade cracked for a moment, and Lilly got a glimpse of the suffering he held inside.

"Of course I didn't see how much I was in love with her then. I focused on Alec's bad behavior," Jonathan said wryly.

"That must have placed strains on your own family," Lilly said quietly.

"It almost ended our relationship. Luckily, Alec's the forgiving type, more so than I am," Jonathan said.

Lilly gave a snort of disbelief that she quickly turned to a cough. Perhaps Alec was more generous and open with his own family. She really couldn't judge that. All she knew was that Jonathan was hurting. Her image of the calm, emotionless banker who easily controlled not just his life, but the financial lives of many of Fielding's residents was changing. Lilly felt the urge to help Jonathan. She liked him and didn't like to see him in such pain.

"Have you told Karen how much you care for her?"

Jonathan laughed, and the sound ran over Lilly like the rasp of sandpaper. "I might as well be offering her a case of leprosy. In my own way I'm just as fixated as she is—a pity the three of us never got our fixations straightened out." Bitterness ran like corroded steel through his voice.

"I think she cares a great deal for you," Lilly said after a moment. She had hesitated to say anything, aware of how cruel it would be to encourage hope in Jonathan if Karen didn't love him.

"She seemed unusually concerned about *our* relationship, at any rate," Lilly temporized with an attempt to lighten the mood.

"When was this? What exactly did she say?" Jonathan ran the big car off the highway onto the shoulder and turned to face Lilly. They were close to Fielding now, near the turnoff to the Willis farm. Jonathan's intense interest alarmed Lilly a bit, but she had no choice but to go on.

"Well, at the party at David's last night she accused me of having romantic trysts with my banker along the creek," Lilly offered, and was a bit startled by the boyish glee that lit Jonathan's face.

"Aha! I knew she was working with her brothers on the new Amundsen house, and I just thought she might look out—"

"You devil!"

"It was only a thought," Jonathan said modestly. But the look he shot Lilly from underneath his lashes caught at her heart, and she thought that Karen Willis was a fool not to snap up this loving man.

"What are you doing tomorrow morning?"

"I don't have a class until ten o'clock, but—"

"Meet me at the creek at eight thirty. And wear that red jacket."

"Now, wait a minute," Lilly began.

"Please?"

The big car hummed contentedly beneath them, and Lilly ran an absentminded finger along the leather seat. "All right. I just hope this doesn't make things worse."

"I disavow you of all responsibility!" Jonathan said happily, and gave her a spontaneous hug that made her ribs creak in protest.

"That's what you say now," Lilly murmured, but knew she would try to help him. Weariness washed over her as she watched Jonathan back out of the driveway after dropping her at Mrs. Jordan's. She felt bombarded with images of the play, and had little to guide her as to how to put those images in order. What should she believe or not believe? Lilly wondered. Did Karen have a basis for this suit or not?

Lilly was more confused than ever. Karen was so different from the way Lilly had pictured her, so vulnerable, and yet Lilly could see the toughness Jonathan had talked of in her, too. The trouble was that Lilly could see it both ways: She could see Karen bringing the suit as an act of revenge and she could see Alec having made it so impossible for Karen to work at Fielding that she'd been forced to quit. Whose view was right?

Lilly sighed in frustration, thumped her pillows, and tried to slow her rollicking thoughts enough to allow herself to sleep, but again and again the white-lighted faces of the characters from *Twilight* came back to haunt her. Like flirtatious shadows they dipped and swayed just out of reach, promising *their* version would enlighten her but delivering nothing but further confusion.

And what of yourself, Lilly asked. Is there any future

in involvement with Alec Thomas? Lilly sat up and shoved the covers away from her irritably, pressing both palms against her temples to stem their throbbing. The battle between sleep and thought had produced a vicious headache, and Lilly reluctantly headed for the bathroom and some aspirins. She disliked taking drugs of any kind, but this pain was severe. She felt faint as she tried to stand, and clung to the doorway.

She got the aspirin down and lay back on the bed, sweating. What about you? The question returned relentlessly, refusing to let her take refuge in pain. You touched him, made love with Alec. What about that? Lilly pressed her palms flat to her eyes, and colors sparked in strange patterns. Such strange small things about Alec were crystal clear in her mind. The rough edge on the second finger of his right hand, where constant hard pressure of pen in contact with flesh had left a badge of his career. The way the planes of his face had become part of the contours of her mental landscape was another. And the smell of him as he covered her body with his own reminded Lilly of crushed clover in a freshly mown lawn. All these things would never go away, Lilly realized.

She loved Alec Thomas, and no amount of brainwashing scrubbed that reality away. But what she did about that love was at least partially under her control. Lilly knew she'd have to talk to Alec and try to get his side of this. So far she'd heard two sides of the triangle. Now it was time to hear the third, and, for Lilly, the most important side.

All her defenses screamed at the idea of opening herself to such pain. But what else was there? She could behave like an immature idiot, or she could risk being rejected. Those were the choices.

What is the worst that could happen? Lilly demanded. If he won't talk to me about it, then he won't. Life will go on, a bit dingier and discolored with regret.

But it will go on. That much Lilly had learned. She was stronger, much stronger than she gave herself credit for.

The pain began to dissolve, the edges of it less clawing, though not entirely without its hold on her. Lilly slept.

Next morning she awoke as the back door banged shut and she stumbled to the window in time to catch sight of Mrs. Jordan, white gloves snug over her freckled hands, walking briskly across the backyard toward the church a block away.

It was time to visit her parents, collect her animals, and make a firm start in Fielding, Lilly decided. She was tired of living in limbo; common sense dictated that she wait until the remodeling was done before moving into the house by the creek. Lilly wasn't in the mood for common sense. She was in the mood to make a statement to herself and to the rest of the world that she was digging in her heels. No one was going to chase her out of town, not even Alec Thomas himself!

"I'll be glad to help you out," Lilly's father assured her to Lilly's surprise. The weather was turning colder, and a fire blazed in the family room. "Although from what you say, it might make better sense to tear the place down and rebuild. Something solid, with good insulation and plumbing." He grunted with disgust as the Vikings lost the football for the fourth time that quarter. "That looks like the game, Ben." Lilly's brother didn't move. He lay on the thick rug, along with Lilly's dog, Monty, and stared straight ahead at the television.

"Maybe Kramer can pull it off. He runs a great two-minute offense," Lilly said softly, going to seat herself beside him, her hand automatically going out to stroke Monty's silky fur and was rewarded by much tail thumping and a wet kiss.

"Maybe." It was a forlorn sound.

Ben had been uncommunicative ever since Lilly showed up and announced she'd bought a house. Once more, Lilly was struck by the essential coldness of the place; despite its obvious costliness, the Burns's house remained more of a possession and proof of Carlisle's status in life than a home.

"Would you like me to leave Monty here with you for a while longer?" Lilly asked gently, noting her brother's continuing silence and guessing it had little to do with the miserable performance of his favorite football team.

"Could you?" Ben's dark curly head swung around, his brown eyes glistening with hope.

"Of course I can," Lilly said. "He'll be a lot happier here with you, anyway. Mom tells me you've been really diligent in taking care of him."

"I have, I really have. Oh, leave him here, please, Lil?" Lilly nodded, and then was shocked when her brother leaned over and gave her a short, one-armed hug. She couldn't recall much physical affection being doled out in the Burns family and was deeply touched by Ben's overture.

The game ended in a resounding defeat for the home team, and Carlisle Burns hit the button that shut off the picture on the big screen with a crack. "Let's get some of that stuff loaded into the trailer, then we can stop by the office and pick up your mother. Our dinner reservations are at six o'clock, so let's hustle."

Both Burns children jumped up. Lilly's father had agreed to drive down to Fielding with her after dinner, pulling the trailer Lilly had leased at the rental company nearby.

"This is so good of you, Dad," Lilly said when they'd loaded the last box of books into the compact rental trailer and locked the door. In truth, she'd been surprised at how easily her father took to the idea of her being a homeowner.

"I think buying this house will be a good move for you taxwise. You remember I tried to talk you into buying some real estate last year when your taxes were so high."

Lilly sighed. She knew her father was right. He was always right when it came to money. But why did his advice always have to sound like subtle criticism? Lilly wondered sadly.

"I never found anything I liked until now," Lilly explained. "And it seemed silly to buy a house back when I thought I'd be living with Martin in a few months."

They drove in silence for a few minutes.

"That twit Martin may not be long for this world," Carlisle said cryptically as they pulled into the parking lot of Burns Electronics. A single light burned in the office on the third floor, and it went out as their headlights swept the building. Millicent emerged seconds later, got in the car, and turned to her daughter.

"Darling! Hello!" Lilly leaned forward to accept her mother's kiss.

"You're looking well, Mother."

"Things went well tonight. They always do when I have the building to myself."

"The Talis contract?"

"All cleared up. They'd try to squeeze on delivery dates, but—

"Can we talk about something other than business tonight?" Lilly pleaded as the restaurant came into view. It was close to the office and the one her father liked best. Ben shot her an adult look that said, Why bother? But Lilly thought it was worth it. Her parents were a perfectly orchestrated business team, but sometimes Lilly had the feeling that was *all* they were. Ben and she were treated like fledgling branch offices that needed prodding from the parent company!

There was silence as food and drink was contemplated, then ordered.

"We saw that strange play by your boss the other night. What was the title of that again? It's at the Arlo II. Your Aunt Sylvia gave us the tickets. She thinks he's marvelous." Millicent's tone indicated she couldn't agree with her sister's opinion.

They'd worked their way, by this point, through soup and salad. This was Millicent's third attempt to introduce a non-business topic. Lilly had to give her credit for trying, since they'd already exhausted Lilly's job and Ben's dirtbike escapades.

"The title is *Twilight*," Lilly supplied in an even tone.

"He must have had a terrible mother, to be such a cynic about women," Millicent added without conscious irony.

"Not at all. He's got women nailed as far as their true natures go," Carlisle said, face bland as he chewed his steak. He was immediately attacked by his wife and daughter, as he'd known he would be. Humor was both a weapon and a form of affection in Lilly's father's hands.

They dropped off Millicent and Ben at the house around eight, and Lilly got into the Corvette, which held only the cat carrier that she'd just now brought out of the house. It just fit on the passenger seat. *Miaowwwww. Miaowwwww.* Lilly thought it might be a long drive down to Fielding, but Mongo eventually settled down to a sullen silence. Lilly chatted to him and tried to keep his Siamese spirits high, but he wasn't having any of that.

Lilly paced herself, glancing often in the rearview mirror to make sure her father was keeping up with her and that he wasn't having trouble with the trailer. Her mother had raised some protest over Lilly taking antique china and furniture into a house about to undergo major renovations, but not too much. She said it just made more room for all the new furniture she was planning to get, and Lilly's father had groaned.

Lilly guessed that the Talis merger had something to do with Martin's plight. The undertones of competition in her parent's short business discussion in the car indicated that they didn't agree, and mergers would be something Martin would handle. And her parents hadn't ever agreed on Martin.

Also, Lilly knew what the phrase "not long for this world" meant in the language of Carlisle Burns: If Martin didn't shape up drastically, he would be out on his ear. Lilly hoped for his own sake that he knew how serious his position was. Briefly, she toyed with the notion of telling him, but cast it aside. If he didn't know he was in trouble, he wouldn't last anyway, and if he did, she knew he wouldn't thank her for rubbing his nose in it.

In fact, the more she thought about it, the more she saw that Martin might even lay all his present problems at her door. After all, what more perfect revenge than to make him lose the job that was more important to him than she'd ever been? Except Lilly hadn't had a thing to do with it, and she knew her father didn't operate that way.

It took a bit over two hours to reach the outskirts of Fielding—almost double the time it usually took Lilly alone in the Vette. A lone police car waited at the blinking yellow semaphore, and Lilly slowed the car to a crawl. Now wasn't the time to impress her father with a speeding ticket.

Her spirits rose as she led the way out of town and then down the dirt and grassed-over track that led to her house. The country sky was black satin strung with rhinestone stars, with just a dying moon to guide the way. Lilly jumped out, fumbled for the set of keys, aware that she ought to have cleaned the cottage a bit more before leaving.

As she flicked at a light switch, she was thrilled to see a light bulb had been put into the socket. Had Mr.

Peterson called the electricity company for her? Lilly thought gratefully. She didn't know who the benefactor was, but she'd find and thank him, that much Lilly knew!

Carlisle Burns emerged slowly from his car, shutting the door behind him. Lilly went back to the car and turned off the headlights. Wind rustled the drying grasses behind the house, and the creek hurried along, scolding itself as it ran.

"Ground firm enough for me to swing the trailer around?" her father asked, rubbing his back slowly to ease the strain of sitting still for two hours. His voice sounded small in the immense space surrounding them, and he himself appeared less all-powerful in these vast, rolling plains.

"Uhh, I guess so," Lilly muttered, uneasily aware of her total lack of knowledge. She quelled the image of her father's Jaguar XJ6 disappearing in a sudden landslide over the cliff, followed by most of her worldly possessions.

"Keep back from this cliff, sir!"

Lilly whirled to see Jonathan and Alec coming up over the edge of the cliff, both shouting in unison as her father continued to back toward them. Jonathan kept waving a package that he held in one hand. Finally her father heard and stopped the car. It had only taken seconds, but seemed longer. He straightened the wheel and drove straight down the narrow lane; then staying well away from the edge, he backed to within inches of the door.

"You don't waste time, do you?" Alec said, coming to stand in front of her. Lilly shrugged, her senses busy drinking him in. The yardlight lit his bony face dramatically and reminded her of the play's stark lighting.

"What are you doing here, anyway?" Her voice sounded hoarse in her own ears. "I thought you were in New York."

"Obviously I'm back," he said dryly, and gently urged her out of the way as the trailer came within inches of the front door. Lilly felt his touch arrow through her in a burning arc.

"Alec, I—"

"Open the back, Lilly. I'd like to get back to Minneapolis before three in the morning."

"Maybe you'd be better to stay here overnight and drive back early—"

"I'll decide what's best," Carlisle Burns said shortly, his pale eyes sharpening in interest as he looked at the two men before him.

"Father, this is Jonathan Thomas and Alec Thomas. Gentlemen, my father, Carlisle Burns," Lilly made the introduction wryly. She'd seen her father in operation before.

"Ahh, the banker and the boss," he identified them succinctly. His eyes glinted with satisfaction when they both laughed. Jonathan was nearly as tall as Lilly's six-foot-three father, but in terms of energy Carlisle and Alec struck Lilly as more alike.

"We saw the lights go on, and Alec figured Lilly might be moving in right away. Can you use some help?" Both men were dressed in plaid wool shirts and jeans. It was the first time Lilly'd seen Alec in jeans so snug and worn and was surprised at the sensual impact he carried. Although short, his body was well proportioned and without the paunch that characterized her father. She could see the muscles of Alec's thighs through the worn material, and remembered how they felt against her own softer skin.

"We'd like the help. As you heard earlier, Daddy has to be back to Minneapolis tonight," Lilly said, in an effort to shake this sensual reverie. She saw the look of refusal forming on her father's face and hurried on. "Some of these boxes are really too heavy for just Daddy and me to manage."

"Appreciate the offer, lads," Carlisle agreed stiffly as pride and practicality warred visibly in his manner. Once the choice was made, however, he swung wide the trailer doors and began tossing boxes to the two younger men, almost catching them off balance because he deliberately made the boxes appear light when they were actually loaded with Lilly's books.

"Daddy, just take it easy, will you?" Lilly said with a sigh. She could see that this situation had instantly become a challenge to him to outdo the younger men. "Just think of what Mother might do with the company if you dropped dead of a heart attack after some adolescent contest of strength," she added, her tone sarcastic.

Behind her she heard someone's indrawn breath. And to an outsider her comments might seem cruel. But Lilly knew her father. Tender pleas for him to slow down and take care of himself never worked; reminding him what his wife might do with his precious company at his demise did, though.

He said nothing, but the next load of boxes were handed out at a reasonable pace. Alec gave Lilly a stony look that she ignored. It hurt, but her father's health was more important than Alec's erroneous opinions, or so Lilly told herself as she followed Alec's broad, stiffly held back into the house with the armload of garments her father thought her capable of carrying.

"Oh, how wonderful!" Lilly cried, and dropped her burden on the nearest chair as she went into the living room. Gone were the dust covers, the cobwebbed corners, and instead the air was redolent of window cleaner and furniture wax. Lilly flipped on another light switch and the oak floor gleamed up from beneath her feet. Only two days ago this place had looked forlorn and abandoned. Now...

"Who has done this?" Lilly asked in wonder.

"I think Hilda came by yesterday with a gaggle of her cronies. She felt badly that her uncle had let the place get into such a state." Alec spoke stiffly from the doorway, broad hands balled on his hips and his face dark with dislike. Yet his glance seemed to follow Lilly compulsively as she moved around the clean room.

"But there was no need. How incredibly good of them!" She was eager to see if they'd done anything else, and pushed past Alec. The old-fashioned bathroom under the stairs shone too. Lilly went on to the kitchen at the back of the house. The refrigerator hummed, and inside were milk, eggs, and bread. "I just can't believe her kindness," Lilly said, choking back the silly tears that crowded her eyes.

"People around here believe in kindness," Alec said pointedly. "And courtesy." He came in and shut the door behind him. "Something you seem to think you can ignore." He walked toward her. "Maybe you think your wealth, your rich daddy, will always protect you?" Lilly had backed up until she was against the refrigerator. Alec slapped a hand on either side of her and she was trapped. "Well, where is he right now?"

Lilly just looked at him, her heartbeat uneven. Until this moment she'd managed to put Friday afternoon in the back of her mind, but now the smell of him brought it back in an instant replay. Her normally quick mind stumbled under the drugging sensation of his nearness; the spicy tang of his skin filled her head and made her hands shake with desire.

"If you're referring to the remark you overheard," Lilly began, "you just don't know—"

"I don't care," Alec said roughly, and lowered his mouth the necessary quarter-inch. Their kiss held an aching sweetness that absorbed them both. "God, why wouldn't you come to New York with me?"

"Oh, here you are. Your father—" Jonathan's head dipped into the room for a moment.

"I'm coming," Lilly answered breathlessly. Alec

stared at her, his blue eyes blazing. "Stay here," he said, and his voice was so low she barely heard him.

Lilly shook her head and ducked under his bent arms.

"I can wait."

She heard the words drifting after her as she hurried to see what her father wanted.

"This isn't a bad little place," Carlisle Burns commented when she came into the entry and glanced at him questioningly. That was as near to a compliment as she was likely to get, and Lilly, shaky as she felt, responded in kind as she followed him into the living room.

"Thanks. I'm glad you approve."

"It'll need improvements, of course. The water pressure is only middling, and the upstairs looks like it's got no insulation at all. Have you had the boiler and heating system checked?" He paced the nearly empty living room, spitting questions at her as though he were in a board meeting, and strangely, Lilly's heart swelled with love for him. It was as though for the first time she saw him as an adult would, not as a child looking for something he just couldn't give. This was his way of expressing affection, the only way he knew, which unfortunately took the form of criticism, but which Lilly was finding easier to take now that she'd moved out of his daily orbit. Somehow the decision to take the job at Fielding College had helped to dissolve a few of the old resentments for Lilly.

"Oh, Daddy, I love you!" Lilly exclaimed, and hugged a shocked Carlisle Burns around the middle before walking swiftly out to the trailer where Jonathan handed her a box marked Fragile—Handle with Care. Not me, Lilly thought as she picked it up. I'm strong, and getting stronger all the time!

Chapter Eight

It seemed to take a long, long time to get all the furniture unloaded, but around midnight they could see the rough plywood back of the trailer, and things picked up from there.

"Sure you won't spend the night?" Lilly asked softly as she followed her father out to the trailer one last time. She could feel his weariness as he knelt to snap the lock shut, but knew better than to push.

"Yup. Just wanted to help you get that bed set up before I headed back. I've got a board meeting at eight thirty tomorrow, and there are going to be a few surprised faces that I don't want to miss." Carlisle thrust back a shock of silver-gray hair from his sweaty forehead as he stood up, but his grin was almost boyish. Somehow Lilly knew the surprises wouldn't be pleasant ones.

"Is there trouble in the company?" Lilly asked, wanting to ask directly about Martin, but realizing she might just make her father clam up completely. He was highly selective in what information he divulged to Lilly.

"Could have been if I hadn't caught it in time," Carlisle replied complacently. "But young Stone has had his last chance, and when he didn't catch that Talis error—"

"Dad, you're not going to fire him? At the board meeting?" Lilly winced. "You can't!"

"No. Not until after his presentation of the Talis offer," he agreed, rocking back and forth on his heels, all trace of tiredness gone. Then his pale eyes sharpened and he said, "Anyway, why the hell are you interested in protecting that twit? Are you still—"

"No. I'm not still in love with Martin. But he's worked hard for Burns, and aside from what he did to me, he's always been an asset."

"Not anymore."

"Does Mother agree?"

Carlisle shrugged irritably, partway through the motion of getting into the Jaguar. "Not at first," he admitted. "She talked me into letting one other mistake go by, but when this Talis thing cropped up, I—"

"You decided it would be great to nail Martin to the wall and show Mother up," Lilly interrupted with a shake of her head. "Oh, Dad," Lilly said, and gave him an exasperated look as she saw a mulish expression descend over his face.

"I'll return the trailer for you. Good night, Lilly."

"Good night, and thanks again!" Lilly said, her wave a bit forlorn as the Jaguar bumped slowly down the lane and out of sight. She disliked it so when her parents got into these power struggles at work, but she knew she couldn't stop them. Hard as it was for her to believe, Lilly was beginning to think they loved them, too.

"Who's this Martin character?" Alec asked, his voice startling Lilly out of her reverie. "Sounds like you're still in love with him to me the way you were protecting him."

"What are you doing listening to my conversations with my father? Are you making an occupation of it?"

"Jonathan made some coffee. I thought he might like a cup before he drove back. But that conversation seemed a touch personal to interrupt for a cup of coffee."

"So you eavesdropped instead. How mannerly! What

a gentleman you are, Alec." Lilly felt her temper smoking, ready to burst into flames. "Just let me get my purse and I'll pay you what I owe you for helping with this move." She stalked past him into the entry where her purse sat on top of the cat carrier. Mongo saw her and began complaining, loudly, that he'd been in this hideous place for hours. "Just a minute!" Lilly shouted at him, and he subsided. He was not used to being yelled at, his baby blue eyes said, and she'd hurt his feelings. Lilly yanked her wallet out of her purse, riffling through the cash. "How dare you listen to a private conversation like that?" Lilly demanded of him, thrusting a fistful of money at him.

"Well, who is he?" Alec asked, ignoring the money. Lilly anticipated, wanted even, an angry reaction from Alec over the money. When she didn't get it, Lilly's mood collapsed without his matching one to hold it up. What was worse, she even felt a bit cheap.

"He was my fiancé."

"Was?"

"Yes. It ended a few months ago." Lilly bent to pick up the spilled money, then released the cat from his carrier and watched her indignant cat slink out. He surveyed these new surroundings with suspicion, glancing frequently at Lilly as if to say, Are you kidding?

"Why?"

"What?"

"Why did you and Martin break up?"

"I discovered we had different sets of priorities," Lilly said stiffly. And that was putting it politely, Lilly thought, as she remembered the painful way she'd discovered Martin was more in love with being married to Burns Electronics than Lilly Burns.

"Did you try to work things out?"

"They couldn't be worked out."

"How do you know? Did you try, or did you just run

away to Fielding, the way you've tried to run out on me?"

"You're the one who ran off to New York!"

"You're the one who refused to come with me," Alec roared back, as angry now as Lilly could have wished for earlier.

"I don't trail around after any man," Lilly said, ignoring the way her thoughts had trailed Alec all weekend long. "But neither do I run away."

"The hell you don't! Women! Not a one of you is honest until it's dragged out of your throat."

"Oh, swell. I was wondering how long it would take you to get to that argument," Lilly said acidly. "The truth is that you're so damned prejudiced when it comes to women that you can't recognize honesty!"

"I'm sorry. That remark was uncalled for." Alec moved with jerky steps into the living room. Lilly's heart stopped, then started thudding rapidly again as Alec ran one broad, powerful hand over the back of the sofa that faced the fireplace. Lilly inhaled and felt the biting rise of excitement hit her with a force that almost hurt as she remembered their lovemaking.

"I've had bad experiences with women in the past. But you're right, Lilly. I have no right to a knee-jerk reaction because I didn't get the response I wanted." His expression was wry, and his hand continued to stroke the sofa.

"And what response was that?" Lilly asked, her throat dry. She felt mesmerized by the play of muscles along his stroking arm. Underneath his plaid work shirt, which had been discarded when he worked, Alec wore a thin black T-shirt, and she watched him hungrily, eyes tracing the path her hands longed to traverse. "Alec?"

Lilly scarched his face eagerly, her whole body tuned to the movements of his.

"That you missed me as much as I missed you. That you thought about me all weekend." Alec's voice was low. "Instead I came back to hear you talking about a fiancé I didn't know existed and hear you not too convincingly denying that you're no longer in love with him!" He vaulted lightly over the sofa and came toward her.

"I guess we all can misinterpret things we overhear," she said thoughtfully, thinking of that overheard conversation that first day at Fielding that had resulted, for Lilly, in so much doubt and soul-searching.

"I didn't deliberately eavesdrop on you and your father, either," Alec added. "It just happened—"

"I really didn't think you did." Lilly stopped for a breath and then plunged on. "My first morning at Fielding I felt something odd was going on. Then I overheard you and David discussing Karen's suit."

"Yes, that was the first I'd heard of it," Alec said bitterly. Then comprehension dawned. "Do you mean you've known about that damned suit from the beginning?" He started to laugh, then laughed harder. "To think of all the trouble they went to—" He gasped for breath. "David nearly stood on his head to keep it from you!"

"I didn't deliberately eavesdrop, either," Lilly pointed out. "You were shouting. I heard you through the door of my office. Alec, I need to know. Does Karen have—"

"What in heaven's name is going on in here?" Jonathan asked. He stopped in the doorway with a steaming container of rich brown coffee, and in his other hand was a coffeecake. "You may have to do something about that oven, Lilly. It takes forever to heat up."

Lilly could have screamed her frustration as she watched him placidly putting the coffee and food on the hearth. "It sounded like the two of you could use a break from all this shouting."

"Yeah, and that coffee smells so good that I think I'll get a beer," Alec said, and rolled to his feet with a grunt, already at a trot as he left the room.

"Does he ever slow down?" Lilly asked tartly. "He seems to be in perpetual motion." Lilly wandered over and picked up a mug of steaming coffee. While she was there, the coffeecake looked good, and she sank her teeth into a piece and felt the raspberry spreading over her tongue and filling her mouth with flavor. "This is great. Do you make it yourself?"

Lilly gulped down her piece completely while Jonathan was still buttering his first one. She knew it wasn't his fault, but did he have to apply butter to every damned centimeter of the thing? she wondered. He'd come into the room at just the wrong moment.

"It's my mother's recipe. I'm glad you like it." Jonathan, finally having finished his buttering, now began the slow, savored process of eating his coffeecake, spaced with sips of hot brew.

"Ugh. Don't you ever tire of that glutinous stuff?"

"Do you ever tire of beer and hot chilis?" Jonathan countered, and took another small sip of coffee.

"Oh, but that's different!" Alec said with a grin and raised his can of beer to his mouth. Lilly sensed the exchange was a ritual of sorts between the two brothers.

When Alec burst into the room, Lilly had felt the world grow brighter, sharper and more in focus. It was almost as though Alec were a new pair of glasses through which she saw the world as a clearer and brighter place. She watched him prowl around, flipping open cartons to remove books or even the indignant cat, who gave him a sharp slap with his clawless paw before scooting out of the room. Alec was never still.

"Feel free to look through anything you want," Lilly offered wryly, as he fanned the pages of one book after another, then slammed them down in a haphazard heap. His restless energy failed to speed up his brother, however, who placidly began another piece of coffee-cake.

"Getting late, brother." Alec drummed his fingers on a stack of precariously piled books.

"Are you hinting I'm in the way?" Jonathan looked up, his navy eyes calm, but with a distinct twinkle.

"Nope. I'm telling you." Both men laughed.

"That wasn't too nice," Lilly said when Jonathan had packed and gone.

"He knows I'd do the same for him, though," Alec said with a totally unrepentant expression. "Now, where were we?"

Lilly saw him coming up behind her in the window. She'd gone to see that Jonathan made it safely across to the other side. Alec's arms crossed over her collarbones and slid slowly down. Fingers caressed the sides of her breasts and the crease where her tightly held arms pinned the flesh to her sides. His palms were a hot pressure over her nipples, and Lilly angrily shrugged her shoulders against the excitement he raised in her. Alec allowed his hand to fall away, but even his warm, moist breath on her neck was an invasion of her self-control Lilly could barely withstand, and she turned jerkily away, saying, "This isn't where we left off, at all." Her mind filled with bitter, unwanted, relentless desire.

"Lilly," he whispered, and she closed her eyes and ears against him. He frightened her with the powerful emotions he called up, and she tried to keep him out, but it was as though her skin could hear and feel him. She swallowed painfully, and her breathing grew ragged.

"No." She shook her head, not knowing how she even got the word out. What frightened her most was that after she moved away, Alec didn't come after her. He stayed where he was, yet Lilly felt the pull of him so strongly, it was as though he stood inside her own skin, something she couldn't ignore or escape.

She reached out and grasped his forearms and his hands turned up to take hold of her elbows in a warm clasp. "I need some answers, Alec," she said hoarsely.

"About what? About how much I desire you? About how you turn my insides hot with longing every time you arch your neck or touch your mouth? Are those the questions you have, Lilly?" Alec's voice grew as hoarse as her own. His blue eyes moved feature by feature over her face, his expression one of raw emotion so different from his usual polished attitude that Lilly couldn't doubt him.

When his mouth descended, Lilly's reached to meet it. Arms locked together, they kissed with a force that shook them and left them breathless. "I want to make love to you, Lilly. I thought about nothing but you the whole time I was in New York."

Alec moved his hands feverishly over her, as though he couldn't get enough of her skin and the feel of it against his hands. Lilly knew what that was like, since she moved her hands over him the same way, drinking in his words with the eagerness of a dying man hearing the news of a miracle cure.

Lilly wanted to enfold him into herself; she wanted to forget about everything else. She wanted to forget about her own doubts, Karen's warnings, and anything remotely connected with the reality that existed outside this pulsing cocoon of passion she and Alec created for themselves in this empty house. But she couldn't.

"Does Karen have any grounds for her suit, Alec?" Lilly asked. She hated the way he withdrew from her, both physically and emotionally, as the sense of her question hit home to him. Alec not only pulled away from her, he walked savagely to the opposite side of the room. Lilly felt her emotions teetering on a cliff, then crashing to the rocks below. The silence grew as Lilly waited for Alec to say something—anything—in his own defense.

"What do you want me to say?" he asked finally. His face was bleak, shadowed by thoughts and memories that Lilly could only guess at. "To tell you the truth, I haven't the vaguest idea what stories she's putting out about what I'm supposed to have done to her. But you, of all people, I would have thought would give me the benefit of the doubt."

"Maybe so. But I want to do more than that. I want to hear your side of this thing. I've heard enough rumors and second-hand information. Are you in love with Karen, Alec?" Lilly found those words stuck to the roof of her mouth, but they did come out after a struggle. After all, if he was, then they could both be spared a lot of time and grief. Because if Alec was in love with Karen, then none of the rest of it mattered a damn to Lilly.

"No! God forbid. If she said I was, she's a damned liar!" Alec said explosively. He thrust both hands into the wildness of his hair and left it standing on end. The result ought to have been comical; instead, Lilly felt desire rise in her again, and she had to work hard to keep herself from running to him to soothe away the pain his face held. "Lilly, you've got to believe me. I had no idea this was worrying you."

"Karen didn't actually say you were in *love* with her," Lilly admitted, "when I talked to her at David's party, but..." Lilly stopped, aware that what she'd been about to say might keep Alec from answering her honestly.

"I'm sure she made a pretty good case for the poor Karen routine. I'm not surprised she got you running with it. She's got half my own family against me, so one more ought to have been no trouble for her."

"I'm not against you. Far from it! Neither did I blindly accept everything Karen told me—"

"Can we drop the topic of Karen Willis?" Alec came to Lilly and took her hands in a pleading gesture. "She's haunted my life for years, and I'd like to keep just one area of my life free of her." They were of a height, but Alec was built along tensile strength lines and Lilly felt the leashed power in him now. Needing to think clearly, she attempted to pull back from him, but his grip only tightened. A shadow of alarm must have shown in her face, for Alec released her immediately, saying, "Please don't look at me like that. I'd never hurt you, Lilly!"

And Lilly felt instant shame, both for her doubts and for letting them show. She brushed her heavy hair back from her face in a confused gesture.

"I can understand that you aren't crazy about discussing Karen Willis," Lilly said slowly, one slender hand massaging the nape of her neck, which ached with tension. "But you still haven't answered my original question."

Alec sighed, then flung himself into a large black chair Lilly had brought with her. The chair clashed violently in style with the rest of the furnishings, and Lilly couldn't wait to move it to another room. She'd grown to be fond of the Victorian sofa, and would try to work a design plan around it—something she wouldn't even have considered a few days ago. Alec was staring moodily around the room.

"I guess you're entitled to some sort of explanation, but don't blame me if it doesn't dovetail with whatever poison Karen poured in your ears last night." He spoke with weary assent.

Lilly slid quickly onto the sofa, her hazel eyes intent on Alec just a few feet away. She said, "All I wanted to hear from you was your side of things, Alec."

Blue eyes raised to the beamed ceiling, Alec was lost in thought. For several minutes the silence held, and Lilly's momentary sense of expectation began to fade.

Was he just killing time in order to think up some convincing lies? she wondered as the silence went on. Then he spoke, and his tone was cool, emotionless.

"Here's the deal. I met Karen in high school. She tells me she noticed me from way back, but that's when I first knew of her existence. As you saw last night, Karen's great to look at. Not many women have that combination of looks, brains, and that certain indecipherable something..."

"Charisma?" Lilly supplied quietly, trying to ignore the sense of foreboding Alec's words gave her. After all, Karen was exactly as he described her, and if he'd said anything else, Lilly knew she would have been suspicious, too. But it's one thing to think something and another to hear the deep, attractive voice of the man you love describing the competition.

"Yeah. Charisma's one of those buzzwords I never liked, but in this case it applies, I guess. Anyway, Karen had a pretty rough time of it as a teenager—I'll give her that much. But somehow she got the crazy notion I was her savior from all that," Alec said with a heavy sigh. His eyes had gone slate gray with memory.

"She just wouldn't give up. No matter what I did, she kept following me around. I got hell from my buddies about it, and I guess I was immature enough to want to pass some on to her."

Lilly shivered and prayed Alec never had occasion to do the same to her, for she suspected he'd be all too good at it. "She not only took every class I took, but then followed me to college, too. That was the first and last time any woman harassed me into making love to her," Alec said softly, but with total conviction.

Lilly winced again, then raised her brows in delicate disbelief. Alec flashed her a glance out of the corner of his eyes.

"Think it can't be done, eh?"

"Sounds just a touch impossible to me, although I've heard it does happen the other way around," Lilly said with a small smile as she smoothed an invisible thread along her thigh. "But I'm sure—"

"Hah! That shows all you know about it. Well, she's a gorgeous woman, or she was before she smoked so much and got so thin. And I was a susceptible young male. The deadly combination." Alec's voice dropped, and Lilly strained to hear it. "But let me tell you I paid, in full, for any few moments of pleasure I had with that woman's body."

Lilly felt shock ripple through her at the absolute bitterness in Alec's voice. He rolled to his feet and began pacing before the long windows as if his energy was too much to contain.

"Then she disappeared," he went on, voice back to the neutral tone of someone telling a story to a friend. "Only to turn up here in Fielding a few years later. She applied for a position, and I was forcibly against it. But she'd just had her little burst of success with her first volume of poetry coming out. The department was desperate, and I was overruled. But she was only in an untenured instructor position, and I told myself she'd never last the year."

"But she did," Lilly murmured when he stopped.

"Yes. The clever little witch came out with a second volume of poems, and they were well received, too. She was not only rehired but put on a tenure track, and I saw an unremitting sentence stretching out before me."

"So you decided to help her get the desire to go somewhere else?" Karen's husky voice echoed in Lilly's ears: *He had one of his buddies lined up for the job.*

"No. At least I never thought it out like that. There was no organized campaign against her. I admit I wasn't thrilled when she came into my office with transparent

ploys for my attention. But I never had to go out of my
way to make life difficult for her at Fielding. She did
that for herself.''

"How?''

She desperately wanted to believe Alec, and so far
his story bore an eerie resemblance to the one told by
both Karen and Jonathan. Alec just gave the same
events a slightly different twist; they gave Lilly another
angle through the prism.

''By not meeting with her classes. By refusing to
come to mandatory staffings. By substituting readings
of her works-in-progress for actual composition work
in the classroom.'' Alec fired off his answers in a crisp,
staccato voice, as though he found this recital of
Karen's failings distasteful. ''These things aren't a fig-
ment of my writer's imagination, but a matter of record. Other staff members can corroborate them.''

''And you're positive you didn't have anything personally to do with her resignation?'' Lilly persisted.
''You didn't harass her verbally or sexually?''

''No! I learned my lesson the first time on that score.
She resigned to save face. Her dismissal was already in
the works when she did. Her claims of harassment,
sexual or otherwise, are pure wishful thinking...al-
though she's certainly trying to make it look that way.
In fact, now that I look back on it, some of the en-
counters in my office *could* have been staged for the
benefit of other staff members once she'd seen the
writing on the wall.'' Alec's voice had slowed and
grown more thoughtful. He rubbed a hand over his
dark, stubbled chin.

''What do you mean?'' Lilly felt a sense of sureness
that had been totally absent minutes ago.

''Well, Todd came in at what turned out to be a very
opportune moment....''

Lilly got up and went over to him. ''Don't leave me
hanging, you tease! What happened?''

"Karen had come in with her usual list of complaints. I was in the midst of revisions on *Twilight*, and the words just weren't coming right. I was, in short, in no mood for her brand of nonsense. So I assisted her back to the door—"

"You didn't hit her, did you?"

"Not quite," Alec said with a wicked grin. "I grabbed her arm, she pulled it away, and she was wearing one of those off-the-shoulder blouses. Anyway, I swear the thing sort of pulled free of her skirt and rolled up like a window shade." Alec was obviously enjoying this memory. "I think she was as surprised as I was. But Godwin chose that exact moment to burst in, which seems highly suspect now."

"So Todd came in and caught you with your hands on a half-naked Karen," Lilly murmured. *He attacked me in his office. Ask Todd Godwin.* Lilly could hear Karen's warning echoing in her tired mind right now.

"And, boy, was she mad!" His head tilted back as he drained the last drop of the cold coffee left in Lilly's mug and set it on the hearth with a crack.

Lilly thought about what he'd said, and tried to weigh all the stories against one another. Her head was swimming. This incident in his office worried her. Alec might laugh it off, but Lilly wasn't so sure. "You realize how that incident might appear to the Human Rights Commission, don't you?"

"I guess you could make it look bad," Alec said with a dismissive shrug.

"Bad? You could end up in a courtroom, maybe prison!" Lilly told him bluntly. He stared at her in total surprise.

"That's exaggerating things, isn't it?" he offered kindly. "After all, even taking the worst case. Let's say Karen's suit is considered worth investigating and that eventually, after about five years, she actually wins. She's only filed with the State Human Rights Commission. They'll give me a slap on the wrist and, worst of all, in my opinion, reinstate her."

Lilly just stared at Alec. He was playing with his empty beer can, juggling it lightly back and forth, back and forth, between his strong hands.

"Listen to me, you fool!" Lilly exclaimed, and snatched the can from midair. She flung it across the room and it ended up rolling against the far wall. "This is no joke. Haven't you heard of the word *eyewitness*? That's what Todd is, to a possible assault case, which means if Karen wants to get nasty she can skip Human Rights Commissions and head right for criminal court. She's got a damned good case, as far as I can see, and you're potentially in a lot of trouble."

At last Lilly could see she was getting through to Alec. He seemed sobered by what she'd said, as well he might be. Lilly didn't know everything about the law, but her father had had a nasty discrimination case against the firm a few years ago, and Lilly knew they were no joke. Her father's suit had eventually been settled out of court, but there had been some tense and unpleasant months at the Burns house while it went on, Lilly remembered.

"She wouldn't."

"She could; that's the point. You know her better than I do, of course," Lilly said ironically. She watched Alec shoot upright and stalk to the window, pacing back and forth like a leopard in a cage, filled with that kind of rage that knows there's no way out, but it can't give up.

"I could kill her," Alec muttered. He rubbed his face as he paced.

"Oh, that would really help," Lilly agreed, and folded her hands in her lap.

"To pull this just now, when things are beginning to jell on the new play...." His blue eyes blazed, and the words left his mouth with quiet menace. "Damn it, I haven't got *time* to deal with her the way she deserves."

"Well, that certainly leaves out poison," Lilly said. "But you could always shoot, stab, or strangle her. I hear they're fast and effective."

"What are you talking about?" Alec demanded irritably. "You just spent an hour convincing me to take this thing seriously, and now you're making jokes?"

Lilly fidgeted, stood up, and then raised her arms in a tired gesture. "I'm sorry. All I wanted was for you to see things the way they are, but I didn't want you to go overboard, either." But didn't you? the question popped into Lilly's mind. Didn't you try to prod him into reacting over this just to see for yourself whether or not he was really in love with Karen? Lilly tried to tell herself that line of reasoning was ridiculous.

"I'm going to have it out with Karen. Tonight."

"You can't do that," Lilly said, alarmed. She held out her wrist and pointed to the time. "It's after two o'clock in the morning. Let it wait until tomorrow."

Alec halted.

"All right. That will give me time to decide if I play my final card. I tried to wait her out, but Karen has just pushed me to the limit on this one."

"What's that supposed to mean?" Lilly said, not much reassured by his rather cryptic utterances.

"Never mind," Alec said. His face was set, his mouth a thin uncompromising line that made Lilly very uneasy. "I'll see you tomorrow."

He brushed past Lilly and went out the door. Lilly stood in the doorway watching him stride away, and she wondered whether or not she'd done the right thing to make him see that Karen's threats could mean serious trouble for him. One thing was for sure. Lilly wouldn't like to be in Karen Willis's place and see Alec coming toward her with that set, ugly look on his face. With a shiver, Lilly shut the door and trudged upstairs, where she lay fully clothed on her own bed for the first time in weeks and fell into an instant, exhausted sleep.

Chapter Nine

Lilly awoke early, with a vague sense of unease that faded once she was up and about. She'd found that, on the whole, she woke earlier in the country, although the shopkeepers and people of Fielding always referred to her house as being "in town." That amused Lilly, since the creek and surrounding cliffs seemed wild to someone used to the manicured greenery of suburban life.

As she showered, Lilly planned her day. She would introduce the scavenger hunt in composition class today, and wondered how Susan Thomas's class would do with it. They were without question her best group, and Susan herself had such a marked talent for description that Lilly seriously hoped she might reconsider brain surgery as the only field in which to use her talents.

The warm sunshine felt good to her naked skin as Lilly went back into the bedroom to dress. She chose a pale blue work shirt and worn blue jeans for the moment, and decided to worry about what to wear to class later. Right now she was hungry.

But once seated in front of her yellow-faced egg and toast, Lilly found herself frowning. Something tugged at the edges of her mind. There was something she needed to do today, but for the life of her Lilly couldn't remember what it was. Lilly stood up and took her dishes to the sink. One of her requisite changes, she noted mentally, will be to get a dishwasher. She rinsed the dishes and set them on the ancient tin drainboard, and as she did so someone knocked at the back door.

That gave Lilly a start, and to give herself time to calm down, she carefully dried her hands on a clean white dish towel before answering the door.

"Good morning!" Jonathan stood there, cheeks reddened in the crisp morning air that eddied in and made Lilly's bare toes curl. "Come in," Lilly motioned, and quickly shut the door.

"Alec not here?" Jonathan asked. He looked behind her, puzzled as he looked at the single fork, plate, and cup on the drainboard. He looked big in the bright hunter's jacket he wore, and not much like a bank president.

"He lives with you. Why should he be here?" Lilly was embarrassed by Jonathan's assumption that Alec had spent the night, and as a result her voice was sharper than she realized.

"Er, never mind," Jonathan said hastily. "Still game for our walk by the creek?"

"Of course!" Lilly exclaimed. "That's what I've been trying to remember since I got up! All I need are shoes and I'll be ready to go. How did you know I'd forget?"

Jonathan lifted his big, heavy shoulders in a cautious shrug. "The excitement of moving in and..."

"Look, I'm sorry I snapped at you," Lilly interrupted; seeing him try to be diplomatic made her see the funny side of it. She lay a hand on his arm. "Alec's probably still asleep at home."

"It was presumptuous of me to assume he was here," Jonathan said ruefully. "But you're wrong. He hasn't been home all night."

Lilly suddenly remembered that feeling of uneasiness that she'd awakened with. "Are you sure?"

"Yes. Of course, sometimes he sleeps in the office. If he's working on a new idea, he sometimes stays there all night. And they've been holding readings on the new play with advanced drama students at the college, so I'm sure there were things he wanted changed once he saw the play in action." Jonathan seemed unconcerned, now that the discomfort of having almost insulted her had faded.

But Lilly was not. She desperately hoped Alec had gone back to the college when he left her last night, but somehow she doubted it. That left the question of where he went. And what he did when he got there.

"He's certainly lucky to have a built-in place to develop his plays," Lilly murmured as she filled two cups with the still hot coffee and brought them to the table. The feeling of uneasiness was growing heavier. God help me, if I've only made things worse, Lilly thought as she sipped strong black coffee, her mind going over the events of last night.

She came back to the present when she heard Jonathan's deep, full laughter. In front of him sat her cat, and that unyielding stare of Mongo's had unnerved people in the past. Martin was one, Lilly remembered. He always wanted to put the cat in another room when he came over.

Jonathan bent to stroke Mongo's raised head, saying "Aren't you a handsome kitty!" Mongo's eyes squeezed shut in silent agreement, neck arching under his large hand.

"You certainly know how to talk to cats!" Lilly said admiringly as she opened a tin of cat food and put it into a dish. "I don't know why, but many people find cats alarming, and even Martin—"

"Who's Martin?" Jonathan asked. "Is that your brother's name?"

"No. Martin is, or was, my fiancé," Lilly explained. She averted her head, searching under the kitchen table for her shoes, the bright green socks she planned to wear clutched tightly in her hands.

"Oh, I see." Jonathan's voice was calm, and he rose as the cat headed for the dish with deceptive speed. He handed Lilly her red jacket off the peg near the door and smiled at her. "Shall we go?"

Lilly nodded, grateful for his understanding in not questioning her further about Martin. Each time she told people of their terminated relationship, it got easier, she thought as she pulled the door shut behind them both and followed Jonathan to the cliff's edge.

He helped her down the edge, but here, near her house, the incline was relatively mild. Further along, where the Amundsen house was being built, it was a different story.

"How come you didn't bring the dogs with you?"

"They might just get in the way," Jonathan said cryptically, his eyes squinted up as he looked up the creek to the Amundsens'.

Near the Amundsen house the cliffs grew wild and steep, with the outcroppings of limestone that characterized the area. In places the grass still held the dew, and more than once Lilly felt her feet slip beneath her.

Try as she might, Lilly could not rid herself of that heavy feeling she'd first felt when she woke up. Had Alec gone out to see Karen last night? In the mood he was in, Lilly shivered to think what he would have been like to deal with. Don't think about it, she advised herself. Lilly knew that was the sensible thing to do, since she wasn't even sure what had occurred when Alec left her last night.

"What a gorgeous morning!" Lilly said as she impulsively raised her head skyward to the blue innocence of the sky above for a moment before walking on. Lilly was slowly coming to love the wide openness of southern Minnesota's landscape, and so to see its subtle beauties.

She was startled out of her musing when Jonathan threw an arm around her shoulder and bent his head in what looked very like an impending kiss. "What are you doing?" Lilly asked.

"Karen's seen us," he whispered.

"Don't you think this might be overdoing it a bit?" Lilly whispered back as he bent her in a dramatically impressive embrace, his nose inches from her neck in what must have looked like a passionate clench from Karen's perspective.

"Just go along with me, please, Lilly?" Jonathan pleaded, and Lilly capitulated.

"All right, but I absolve myself from any further responsibility if this jealousy bit backfires."

"Great. You're a lifesaver." Jonathan took a deep breath of relief and moved his head so that his mouth neared her cheek.

"Er, where did you learn this great art of stage kissing?"

"I was the villain in the community theater melodrama last Christmas," Jonathan admitted modestly, and Lilly couldn't help herself. She burst into giggles that became painful hiccups as she tried to force the laughter back. The image of Jonathan's large form complete with drooping black mustache was more than she could stand.

"I was actually very good," Jonathan said in defense of himself as he brought her upright, managing to make his back-patting look sensuous as he asked, "I hope you're going to be all right."

"I'm fine," Lilly said weakly, trying to glance up and see if her painful hiccups had been in good cause.

Something caught her about the way Karen stood staring out at them from the cliff. Even at this distance, her beauty caught the eye, and Lilly suddenly wasn't surprised that a usually dignified man like Jonathan was willing to go to such lengths to win her. Her red hair flew from her face like streaming amber light and her stance seemed to typify the kind of vulnerable defiance with which Karen faced the world.

"Does Alec have something on Karen?" Lilly asked thoughtfully, unable to get last night out of her mind as the two began to walk slowly, hand-in-hand, once more.

"You mean 'have something' as in blackmail?" Jonathan asked in a puzzled voice. "Not that I know of, but that doesn't mean much. Between those two anything is possible." His tone was amused, but Lilly stopped, rent by a stab of pain that made hiccups seem a welcome respite. Images crowded fast and unwanted into her mind at Jonathan's words, and he stumbled on, obviously aware that that hadn't been the most tactful of remarks.

"That isn't what I meant—I really—"

"Forget it. You haven't told me anything I hadn't already figured out for myself." Lilly interrupted gently. "I sensed the pull between them, and sometimes dislike, hatred, or whatever, can be as powerful in binding people to each other as love." She swallowed hard as the blue skyline blurred with the yellow line of corn rustling wildly in the wind.

"Oh, my God!" Jonathan said, his grip tightening until Lilly shook to break free, then followed his glance up the cliff. Alec was striding through the long grass toward Karen, the wind bringing stray snatches of his tone, if not his actual words, to the two standing statue-still on the creek bank below.

Karen was actually taller than Alec, Lilly thought irrelevantly as she watched them, but all the energy was Alec's as he gestured with forceful jabs of his forearms, and all his energy seemed angry energy.

With a sagging feeling of relief Lilly saw Alec turn away from Karen and begin to walk away, but something Karen said stopped him, and he came back to stand with both hands planted on his hips, so close that Karen's hair blew into his face and he impatiently pushed it away as he listened. His shoulders raised and lowered, as if saying it was up to her. Just when Lilly thought it was over, Karen swung out wildly toward Alec's face, and he stepped quickly back. Karen flailed as her own weight threw her off balance and her feet slid in the tall grass. But it wasn't enough, and she went tumbling over and over down the steep and rocky face of the cliff.

For one second all Lilly could hear was Jonathan's agonized breathing as they watched Alec try to come down from above, but the cliff crumbled, and he was forced back. Jonathan lurched forward, scrambling up the rock to reach Karen's ominously still figure only a few hundred feet from the bottom, where the creek was lapping happily along.

If she lived to be one hundred years old, Lilly was sure she would never forget the look on Jonathan's face as he brought Karen's awkward, limp length the final hundred yards down the cliff. The only sign of life was Karen's slow, erratic breathing and flame-red hair.

"We're closer to your car. Can you make it up there?" Lilly demanded, finding her voice as she watched the slow drip of crimson from Karen's head, arms, and face. From long practice at dealing with her brother's injuries and those of his friends, Lilly searched Karen's form for severe bleeding and saw none. She tried not to think about internal injuries as she followed Jonathan up the steep path and over the crunching drive to his car. "Keys in back pocket!" he gasped. As she pulled them out, Lilly felt the damp sweat of fear and exertion clinging to him. But her hands were steady as she shut the door behind Jonathan and Karen and ran around to the driver's side.

Jonathan spoke softly to Karen as Lilly drove, but the one glance Lilly shot over them didn't reassure her.

"Keep talking to her, Jonathan," Lilly urged as they pulled into the emergency entrance to the hospital. She had the vague idea that one shouldn't allow concussion patients to go to sleep, but much stronger was the idea that if Jonathan didn't feel he was doing something positive, he'd lose control altogether. An ambulance roared in just behind them, and Lilly jumped violently. Blindly she followed Jonathan in, and almost missed Alec's still body pressed against the cool gray enameled wall of the emergency room.

Jonathan went right past him without a word. Then the professionals took over, and Jonathan gave the story as best he could. Lilly could hear his deep voice droning on and on from behind the green privacy curtain that only partially concealed Karen from the rest of the room.

The other victim was wheeled in, and Lilly left when she saw his mangled arm. "Tractor accident," a nurse said briskly, and shooed her out. "We get far too many of those here."

Lilly looked at the clock directly in front of her. It was nine thirty-six. Less than an hour after Jonathan picked her up.

"How is she?" Alec said in a dry, husky voice.

Lilly shrugged. "At a guess I'd say she's got broken bones and possibly a concussion," she told him bluntly and saw him whiten. "But the doctors will tell us how severe it is."

She watched Alec's eyes train themselves on the door marked Emergency. He seemed to have forgotten her existence the minute she stopped speaking, Lilly thought wearily, and closed her eyes. She wanted to offer him coffee or solace of some kind, but the words couldn't get past the lump in her throat. For whatever he said to the contrary, Lilly was sure he was deeply attached to Karen Willis, and whether it was love or hate, it really didn't matter much in the long run—at least as far as she was concerned.

With longing she thought of running her car out along the freeway, the town of Fielding growing farther and farther behind her. Instead she stood near Alec, feeling the cool wall behind her and listening to the babble of voices. Alec's eyes never left the door, but to her surprise his hand swept out to capture hers in a snug, warm grasp.

They waited. Sometime later the double doors banged open and they wheeled a white and bandaged Karen away, with Jonathan close behind. "I called her father, but he won't come down. Said he's too busy. Her brother says he can't leave the job site." Jonathan looked only at Lilly.

"Is she going to be all right?" Lilly asked.

"If she isn't, we know whose fault it is," Jonathan said, and looked at his brother for the first time.

"It was an accident!" Alec exclaimed. "She swung at me. If you weren't so busy—"

"That kiss wasn't—" Lilly began.

"I know what that kiss was! I know all about theatrical gestures."

"Alec," Lilly warned softly, and grasped his forearm, tight with tension, with her free hand.

"You make me sick," Jonathan said, his tone low and viciously cutting. "I can't even look at you. If she doesn't fully recover, I never want to see you again." He pushed past them and strode off in the direction they'd taken Karen.

Alec stared after his brother, shock and anger flickering emotions in his strong face. "She tried to nail me. All I did was move out of the way. How was I to know how soft the edge was?" he demanded of Lilly.

"Alec, think about it. He's upset. Don't take anything he says now too seriously."

But Alec shook his head, shoulders sagging suddenly. "Jonathan isn't one to say things he doesn't mean."

"None of us really knows how we'll react in a severe crisis like this," Lilly reminded him. "Just give him a bit of time."

Alec turned and smacked a crack on the wall with his hand. "I swear I *will* do her in if she's cost me my brother," he said tightly, and Lilly felt all over again the heavy feeling of dread with which she'd awakened that morning.

"Please. Don't even talk like that, Alec." Lilly bit down on her own lip to maintain control. She felt so damned responsible for this, although she knew it wasn't really her fault and guessed that Alec felt the same, despite his strong words. "It was an unfortunate accident. But I'm sure Karen will be fine, and Jonathan will apologize for words spoken in the heat of the moment."

She sounded ridiculously like a Pollyanna to her own ears, but it seemed to calm Alec somewhat.

"Are you going up to the college?" he asked. He ran the spread fingers on one hand through his hair before turning his intense eyes to her.

"My classes," Lilly murmured in dismay as she looked down at her jeans and the blue work shirt that showed beneath her red jacket. "I have to go home and change first—if I have time."

"Well, take my car. And if you could get Hilda to let my classes know that I won't be in today, I'd appreciate it," Alec said a bit gruffly. He held out his keys, and Lilly could do little but take them.

"Sure, Alec. I—I suppose you're going to hang around here until you hear some solid news?" Lilly so wanted to comfort him somehow. Alec looked as grim as she'd ever seen him, his eyes black with emotion and his skin grainy with strain, but she didn't know what to do. Alec solved that for her by pulling her roughly to him, one finger sliding along her jaw to raise her head toward his. "Don't look so anxious, sweetheart," he muttered forcefully. "None of this is your fault."

"But I hammered away at you last night! I feel so responsible, almost as if I pushed Karen off that cliff." Lilly's voice grew shaky as she once more saw the horrible vision of Karen tumbling over and over down that cliff, her arms and legs boneless as a rag doll discarded carelessly by a child.

Alec held her close, murmuring, "I know, just stop thinking about it. You can't change what's past. As you said, it was just an unfortunate accident."

The hard feel of his body comforted her, while his words were just a mumbling stream flowing over her head. Lilly snuggled closer, and Alec's keys clanged against the wall as she wrapped her arm around him. A fraction's move and their mouths met in a kiss that mixed pleasure and comfort in a way Lilly had never experienced before.

"I'd better go," Lilly said shakily and pulled back. "I'll tell Hilda about your classes." She walked backward a few paces and raised a shy hand in farewell before turning toward the exit to the parking lot.

For the past few minutes, Lilly realized as she found the silver Omega and got in, fumbling for the switch to move the seat up to accommodate her shorter height, she hadn't thought of Karen's accident once. That brought a rueful smile to her lips.

The Omega handled easily. It was no Corvette, but Lilly had to admit it took the rutted drive to the house with better grace than the low-slung sports car. I'll have to get this driveway repaired, Lilly thought absently, as she did each time she bumped along its length.

She rushed into the house and up the stairs, causing a mild interest in the cat, who was asleep in the middle of her bed. Mongo raised a lazy head to watch her as she tore her clothes off, leaving them where they fell, her feet fighting their way into pumps and her arms struggling to do too many things at once. But Lilly nonetheless got dressed in a record four mintues, and the cat's head lowered to resume napping as she rushed away again and the door banged shut behind her.

Lilly gave some thought as to how she could return Alec's car to him and decided to take it back to the college and try to pick Alec up or have him pick the car up at the Fielding college later. She sat in the staff parking lot for a few further precious seconds to comb her hair and put on a few brushes of makeup.

"Hilda, could you please go in and excuse Alec's first class? He isn't going to make it in." Lilly tried to steady her voice, but the climb up the three flights of stairs to the English building, plus the extra one to Hilda's office, was too much for Lilly, and she was totally out of breath when she reached the secretary's office.

Lilly went to her office and picked up her notes, thanking her lucky stars that she'd left everything in such good order on Friday. Of course she was experienced enough to wing it for an hour, a prospect that had immobilized her as an apprentice instructor. Now it was often the case that an hour wasn't enough time to get across everything she wanted the class to know! As a beginning teacher, however, she had often been terrorized by how a seemingly endless stack of lecture notes could disappear in less than fifteen minutes.

The trick was learning to pace the lecture to the speed of her student's understanding, Lilly had come to see. "Good morning, everyone. Are there any questions about the paper assignment I gave you last week?"

All information had to be repeated and rephrased several times before the students absorbed it, Lilly had learned, and today was no exception, as several hands went up to ask questions about information she'd already given. Lilly answered patiently, trying to give fresh examples of what she was looking for in this paper, and soon many of the puzzled expressions gave way to understanding. Only then did she move on to the new material of the scavenger hunt, and the hour passed quickly.

After class Lilly went back to her office, followed by two or three students who wanted to discuss possible paper topics in further detail. Lilly dealt with them patiently, although she was aware of how tired she was. Adrenaline had carried her through what had to be done, but now that a few unfilled hours stretched ahead of her, Lilly felt her energy plummeting. She knew she should work on her presentation for the Composition Conference. That was what she had planned to do originally with the time between her classes. Instead, she went slowly to the window, reminded of the first time she'd stood looking out at the valley below, and what her feelings had been then.

Hard to believe I've known the Thomases so short a time, Lilly mused, so intertwined have our lives become. Lilly kept her mind off whether this was a good or a bad thing, since she could do little about it at this point. Emotional involvement is such a risk at the best of times, she reminded herself, and refused to mull that over any further.

With a decisive look on her face, Lilly turned away from the window, her hand reaching for the phone.

"Hello, Mr. Mattson? When are you going to get out to my place? I thought you promised me nine thirty on Monday morning?" Lilly made her requests in a voice that was soft, but one her mother would have recognized in surprise as being close to her own.

Lilly listened to Mattson's rambling list of excuses with a cynicism that surprised her. "Well, I'm quite

willing to pay a very handsome bonus, if the work is
done in the time you assured me it could be, so whatever delays, whether they're labor- or material-related,
don't specifically concern me, Mr. Mattson. But I am
making it clear that I want top-quality work done."
Lilly listened, and felt from his reply that she'd made
her point strongly enough for the moment. "Good day,
Mr. Mattson," said Lilly, and hung up. There was a
fine line between helpful and non-helpful pressure,
and when it came to applying pressure, Lilly had an
example in her mother of the best there was.

When she hung up, Lilly felt better. Action does
help, she admitted in silent apology to her absent
mother. This distance from her parents was helping
Lilly see that they'd given her many valuable lessons
over the years, lessons that, although she'd refused to
follow their careers blindly, could well be applied to
problems in her own life.

For she'd been worried and a bit irritated when she
came back to the house to find no contractor and no
workmen. Mr. Mattson had promised they'd be there on
Monday morning to start work on the kitchen, and she
had tentative agreements with electrical and plumbing
subcontractors that would be voided if Mattson failed to
make good on his promise to get the work done quickly.
Mattson had sounded surprised to have a woman deal
with him so firmly. Lilly tried to make her femininity
work for her, but sometimes it was a distinct disadvan-
tage that had to be overcome with effort.

Lilly was deep into a pile of exercises when Hilda
spoke. Lilly jumped and said, "Oh, I didn't hear you."

"Alec would like to see you. He's in his office."

"Thank you, Hilda," Lilly said as she stood up. She
paused only to pick up her purse before following Hilda
back down the hall to Alec's office.

He stood at the window. "Shut the door, will you?"
he asked politely, and Lilly reached behind her and
brought the frosted-glass door shut with a click.

"How is she?" Lilly asked, and moved forward, unsure of his mood. He turned toward her, and his face shocked Lilly. If she'd thought he was white and tired at the hospital, he now looked ashen.

"She's not dead, is she?"

"No."

"Well, what is it, then? You look like death," Lilly exclaimed, emotions churning inside her.

"Karen is going to be all right."

Lilly felt a giant weight go off her.

"But she didn't escape unscathed. As you predicted, she's got broken limbs and a concussion. They're keeping her in the hospital for a few days' observation."

"That's good news, isn't it?" Lilly asked tentatively. It hadn't seemed to lighten Alec's mood any to tell her this, and Lilly was at a loss to figure it out.

"Did Jonathan—"

"My brother is no longer communicating with me," Alec said with heavy sarcasm. "My information was extracted, after much waiting around, from the doctor in charge of her case."

"He's probably still upset. People look strange and frightening in casts and—"

"Give it up, Lilly!" Alec ordered harshly. "You're way off base. He means it. Jonathan is no longer speaking to me. Which makes it difficult, if not impossible, to explain things to him," he went on as he saw Lilly open her mouth and guessed what she was about to say. Lilly shrugged and fingered a pile of official-looking papers scattered across Alec's desk.

There was a distance between them that made a mockery of their closeness at the hospital. Lilly sensed that this and Alec's sarcastic attitude were his way of protecting himself against the obvious hurt Jonathan's attitude had inflicted.

Lilly found herself growing irritated with the absent Jonathan. What right did he have to blame Alec for this? she wondered. She'd been there too, and to any rational person the whole thing had been an accident. It was Karen's fault, if fault had to be assigned to anyone, she thought angrily as she stood helpless to ease Alec's pain. She'd have a few choice things to say to Jonathan the next time she saw him, Lilly thought.

"And the irony of it is that none of it matters all that much to me anymore," Alec went on with a dry snort of laughter.

"What do you mean by that?" Lilly demanded.

"Take a look at all that," Alec commanded with a jerk of his head toward the papers Lilly had been unconsciously fiddling with since she'd come into his office.

Lilly picked up a few pieces of it. The top piece was an acknowledgment that the Barron Foundation was willing to extend funding for the production of Alec's work-in-progress as long as the federal grant matched or exceeded the amount they supplied.

"What's wrong with this?" Lilly asked, feeling that all sorts of things were going on that she knew nothing about. "This all looks pretty positive to me."

"Read on, Macduff." Again, Alec gave that dry, ghostlike laughter.

Lilly turned to the next sheet and it was a long, complicated-sounding letter. The gist of it was that the government was rescinding its grants, and wished Alec to pay back any amount he'd already received until the suit against him was cleared up.

"But how can they do this? How can they get you to pay back funding already spent?"

Alec gave her a look that said it all. "Very easily."

"So this invalidated the Barron Foundation letter?" Lilly surmised, and Alec nodded curtly.

"I just got that great missive this morning when I came back from the hospital. Poetic justice, don't you think Jonathan would call it?"

"I don't give a damn what he'd call it!" Lilly said

sharply. "I think he's behaving childishly, and you shouldn't let it get you down. He'll come around, I know he's not normally stupid."

For the first time Alec's laughter held genuine amusement. "I don't think intelligence has anything to do with this, do you?"

Reluctantly Lilly had to shake her head. "But that doesn't mean you have to join him in it, Alec."

"Once more Karen has won. That's what's so ironic about the whole thing. I mean the whole reason she brought this suit in the first place was as an act of revenge against me. And I'm sure she will consider her physical pain worthwhile once she realizes how she's managed to come between Jonathan and me."

Lilly tried to maintain her calm. Around her everyone seemed to be losing theirs, she thought, to paraphrase someone famous. But she'd never been in such a swirling tide of emotions in her life. All her life Lilly had striven to avoid emotions. They got out of hand and were painful and hard to control once she did give in to them. Besides, both her parents discouraged emotional outbursts. Now Lilly felt she went through more emotions each day than she used to feel in a month, and with no end in sight.

Alec's mood was black, and she could make no impression on it right now, Lilly realized as she left his office. She was surprised at how much she wanted to, surprised and more than a little uneasy as she admitted how deeply this intense and somehow dangerous man had embedded himself into her thoughts and into her life.

Chapter Ten

After her second composition class Lilly went home. Al Schwartz was on his way out and offered her a ride, which she gratefully accepted. "Just drop me at the end of the drive" was her only stipulation. "I wouldn't want to be responsible for tearing out the bottom of your car!"

She was pleased to hear the sounds of hammering and rending of wood as she walked down the rutted drive to the house. Two cars, a white van, and an old Chevy El Camino stacked with Sheetrock, sat on the grass.

"Hello!" Lilly called as she went in. Mongo glared at her from the safety of the hall closet as she went past. The old cabinets had already been ripped out and the old sink lay sadly on its side in the backyard.

"Afternoon, Miss Burns." Earl Mattson eased himself upright from his leaning position against the doorframe. "I managed to find some help to get started this afternoon."

"I thought you would," Lilly said dryly. One of the two muscled young men looked somewhat familiar to her, but she couldn't place him. Probably related to one of her students, Lilly thought briefly, and then dismissed it. She listened with only half of her attention as Mattson listed the various complaints and impending disasters facing this project.

"Just do the best you can to get it done, that's all I ask," Lilly said finally, noting that both young men seemed to be doing competent, if not sterling, work. Earl seemed to be doing nothing but talking, but so long as the work all got done Lilly would refrain from commenting on that. She wasn't an expert on construction, although her parents had done quite a bit of work on their lake home themselves, mostly because Lilly's father found it relaxing. Lately they'd spent less and less time there, and last year they sold the place. Lilly missed it. Up on that lake she'd learned something about electricity and carpentry, and even plumbing. So she knew Earl and his gang could go faster than they were without hurting the quality of their work.

She nimbly got around them, and went out to the backyard. Across the field she saw a combine at work in the rustling tan corn husks, and she shivered as she remembered the young boy's mangled arm. Lilly had always thought of farms as sort of idyllic spots with placid cows and room for all the cats a person could want. This morning had dramatically destroyed that notion, she thought as she came around the house to the front and slid into the Corvette. She backed carefully around the other two cars and left.

Lilly stopped at the local drive-in hamburger place and ate a thick burger and fries. She enjoyed sitting in the sun in her car. The car soothed her, and the motion had the effect of calming her.

Since she learned to drive, Lilly had always used it as a way to vent emotions that weren't acceptable at home. Today was no exception. She took the long way back to the college, and by the time she pulled up for her three o'clock class in the parking lot behind the English building, she felt much better able to cope. The events of the morning weren't erased from her mind by any means, but Lilly knew she was calm enough now to put her teaching in the front of her mind and thoughts.

Luckily it was one of those class days all teachers love, in which the discussion flows easily, and the argument is stimulating and to the point. This was easily her best class. They faced the prospect of the scavenger hunt with curiosity, if not exactly relish. That was far better than the morning section's reaction, Lilly thought.

"How long do we have for this assignment?" That was Susan Thomas, the future brain surgeon, her yellow pencil tapping. In class she displayed an often impatient concentration on the "facts" that would gain her a good grade in the course; her papers, however, showed a thoughtful, sensitive observer of life that Lilly liked much better. Lilly wasn't sure what battle the young girl was waging but knew enough about eighteen-year-olds to know she'd have to wait until Susan herself offered more clues. Lilly guessed it might have something to do with the scenario she'd laid out for herself in that first essay. Coming from a family of high-achievers, she seemed determined to out-achieve them all, and that could be putting a lot of stress on Susan.

"You have until the end of this week to complete the assignment. You can share information, or do it completely on your own." Lilly saw the exchanged looks of quickly concealed glee in the faces of some of the less enterprising students. But Lilly knew they would get together on it, and the explicit permission might just make them do a better job of it. The object was to make them better at using the library, and if they helped each other out in that, so much the better.

"I want to remind you that there will be no class this Wednesday or Friday. I'll be in Minneapolis attending a Composition Conference. But this assignment will keep you busy until we meet again on Monday." Lilly smiled at the groans that met distribution of the five-page scavenger hunt. "The information you'll need for this exercise is scattered among the various libraries of the college. Some of it is available through the public system, too. Quite quickly, you will see how good your detective skills are, and if the most deeply you've gone into research before has been to crack the cover of an encyclopedia, I'll tell you right now you'll need to allot generous time for completing this assignment."

Several hands shot up, waving violently.

"Yes?" Lilly asked, hiding amusement at the horror in some of those faces.

"But if it's not in the card catalogue, or the encyclopedia, where do you look?"

"Anyone have an answer for that?" Lilly asked, and looked around the room. "Where else can you find information in a library?"

"The *Readers' Guide*, for one," a bearded young man answered. "And I think there are other, er—"

"Indexes, yes. That's an excellent source. But what if you don't know which index to look in for, say, the third question on page one about the campaign slogan of a former president?"

Silence met her. Lilly waited patiently, hoping wheels were turning in some of those suddenly bent heads. She hoped they weren't just thinking about a late lunch and waiting for her to tell them the answer.

"What do you do when you get lost, or confused in a strange city?" Lilly asked softly.

Suspicion flitted across the faces of some students. They clearly thought this was a trick question.

"You ask someone for directions," Susan Thomas said wearily. "In a library, you ask the research librarian where to look for the information you need."

"Exactly. And once you've asked, you listen carefully and write down the source. Any more questions? On either this assignment or the first paper?" No hands went up, and Lilly dismissed the class.

"Miss Burns, Lilly!" Cries of her name chased Lilly back to her office as the slower and shyer students, who never got the nerve to talk in class, followed behind her like ducklings.

Lilly dealt with them patiently, wondering as she did so how Alec ever handled the repetitive nature of teaching, even on a college level. Listening to information seemed to be a skill that didn't necessarily improve with age. But finally they'd all been satisfied and had left Lilly in peace.

The phone rang, and Lilly grabbed it off the hook. "Hello?" She thought it might be Jonathan with news of Karen's condition, but it was Mattson telling her in his gruff voice that he'd managed to get a hold of some materials he'd told her at noon would take weeks to arrive.

"Oh, and I've hired another lad, local this time. We'll need all the hands when it comes to installing them custom cabinets you wanted." Reluctance dragged at his voice, and Lilly smiled. She guessed she hated to dilute his profits in any way, but he was caught between a rock and a hard place, because in order to get the bonus he had to get the work done on time, and that meant another man.

"Sounds like you've got things under control," Lilly said mildly.

"Things are never under control in the construction business," Mattson said sourly, and hung up. Lilly laughed, and replaced the receiver in its spot.

When she got home, she was impressed with the progress, although she knew the ripping out was more dramatic and swifter than the putting in of new materials. She was a bit concerned about the amount of cigarette ash everywhere, and made a note in her little notebook to install smoke detectors. No need to have all these gorgeous improvements go up in smoke.

Sheetrock dust had even managed to find its way into the living room and, as Lilly found out after dinner, upstairs into the bedrooms, too. Throughout the evening she unconsciously stayed within earshot of her new telephone, which sat in the middle of the hallway floor. She was half expecting a phone call from one of the Thomas brothers at any time. But she went to bed, finally, disappointed that neither of them had kept her informed of Karen's progress.

As far as Jonathan's ridiculous vendetta against Alec was concerned, Lilly was hoping that might quickly dissipate. Right now Alec didn't need anyone in his family against him. Of course, even under ideal circumstances Jonathan couldn't have just loaned Alec the money he needed, for as Jonathan himself had said, he had a board of directors to report to. And theatrical loans must be of the riskiest sort there was, Lilly thought reluctantly. She knew he'd never take the money from her, either. So that left Alec in a rough spot.

Lilly sighed and rolled over. She kneaded the pillow and hunched her shoulder into it. Sleep was evasive. The image of Karen tumbling over and over down that cliff haunted her each time she closed her lids. Lilly felt alone in this dusty, torn-up house. Did the workmen shut the back door? she wondered suddenly. She thought she'd locked it before she came to bed. But maybe she'd forgotten, and since she couldn't sleep anyway, Lilly went down to check the doors.

She stubbed her toes on a hidden piece of wood, and limped to the back door muttering vicious things about construction workers. It was shut and locked. The shadows of Mongo playing hide-and-seek in the piles of debris and materials danced across the wall. At least someone was thoroughly enjoying this mess, Lilly thought, and went back to bed.

The next morning she realized she hadn't yet warned the theater department of the impending cannibalization of their small library. Several questions on the scavenger hunt dealt with theater facts, and in order to prevent ruffled feelings when her students began to descend on them, Lilly thought she ought to stop by and warn them.

Classes were in session when she walked onto the sidewalks of Fielding College that Tuesday morning, and thus the campus was deathly quiet. Her shoes made a distinct clicking on the cement as she crossed the tree-lined green of the campus. The theater building was attached to the main library by a long, glassed-in walkway that made winter life much more bearable, as Lilly'd been told. Just now that walkway was empty. She pushed open the theater doors and walked briskly toward the chairman's office. Somewhere someone was reciting Shakespeare loudly, if not well. Lilly heard the phone ringing in the chairman's office before she got there, which meant everyone was out or at classes. On the off chance that he might be somewhere in the building, she tried first the theater itself.

Built along the lines of the Arlo theater in Minneapolis, the Fielding College theater had a very impressive and new thrust stage. Since the audience sat on three sides of the actors, instead of the usual one, there was a much greater sense of intimacy and involvement with the play. Lilly had opened the door quietly, since she didn't know if a rehearsal or class of some sort might be in progress inside.

"I don't care what you say. I've never let anyone use me, and I won't start now." A strikingly attractive girl with dark hair stood on the bottom step that led up the left side of the stage. Alec sat on the arm of the front-row seat, his expression one of sardonic amusement.

"I don't see what you can do about it, my dear." His voice was low but carried well in the empty theater. He made a small wry gesture with an upturned palm.

"That just shows your lack of imagination, Ted," the dark-haired girl replied. "Even you aren't invincible." She made a big, expansive gesture that brought Alec screaming down on top of her.

"No, no! Haven't you listened to anything I've said, Jill?" His voice grew hoarse in his struggle to tone it down as Jill shrank back. He put an arm around her shoulders and turned away from Lilly. She knew this was just technique, but Lilly felt a pang of jealousy shoot through her. Lilly knew only too well how good Alec could be at soothing the female spirit. Alec's wiry, muscled back seemed to accentuate the girl's fragile beauty. Lilly let the dark murmur of Alec's voice flow over her and luxuriated for a moment in her passion for him that seemed to grow with each encounter between them.

"Okay. Shall we try it again?" Alec asked pleasantly. To Lilly's surprise, a languid young man unfolded himself from his slumped position in the second row and took a position near Jill on the stage.

They made an attractive pair, but Lilly's attention was all for the man poised below them. Each grimace or fleeting smile on his face interested her. For the first time Lilly thought she was seeing Alec in the environment that suited him best.

She'd never realized what a difference that would make. But in this place Alec's almost manic energy was perfectly in tune with his surroundings. The stiffer, more structured world of the academic must be smothering to him, Lilly thought, and had the fleeting notion that perhaps holding in his natural energies was what made him so hard to deal with in the more conventional world of the classroom.

"Much better. Thank you both for your time. Thursday we'll tackle the kitchen scene, so try to look that over," Alec said crisply, and clapped a hand on their shoulders as he guided them down the aisle toward the main doors.

Alec stayed in the theater, flexing his shoulders in an impatient gesture as he hurried back to pick up his script, make a few notes on it, and close its red plastic cover. Then he stepped up on the echoing stage. The central spotlight that was on showed the lines that time and experience had put on his face. Hands on hips, Alec slowly revolved, staring out into the darkened theater. Lilly noticed that he looked neither embittered nor discouraged. Yet considering the news and Karen's accident, he had every right to be. Instead he looked invigorated, and very alive standing alone center stage.

"Lilly?" his deep voice echoed hesitantly.

"Yes, that's right." She was more than a little amazed that he'd seen her, for not only was the theater dark, but Alec appeared to be in a world of his own, and Lilly was sure he'd been looking out with his inner eyes only.

She went to him, steps muffled by the rubber mats that ran down the aisles. "Was that the new play?"

Alec nodded, and motioned for her to come up on the stage with him. "Jill and Oscar have been good enough to read for me. It helps," Alec said ruefully, with a smile that crinkled the corners of his blue eyes, "to hear the words somewhere besides echoing and re-echoing inside my own head."

"I think it's a pretty rare opportunity for them to work with a playwright of your ability, too," Lilly said tartly, then felt her face warm at the obvious bias in her voice. But Alec just laughed easily and shrugged.

"I'm not sure Jill saw it that way when I yelled at her today. I just get carried away, and forget these are just read-throughs with college students, not Broadway rehearsals." Now Lilly thought she detected a tinge of bitterness.

"I'm really sorry about your funding. Perhaps this brush with death will bring Karen to her senses."

"You've said that before, and I, for one, don't see it happening," Alec said with a brisk shake of his head as he walked to the edge of the stage. "I've had my orders to stay away from Karen—relayed through Mother, of course. Since my brother no longer speaks to me."

Lilly sighed, but said nothing. Nothing was the most constructive thing to say in the circumstances, Lilly thought. If she criticized Jonathan, who was behaving like a total idiot in this, it only forced Alec to rise to his brother's defense.

The unfortunate part was that Karen now had such a firm defender in Jonathan. Before this accident, Jonathan had thought Karen was acting out of spite. Now he seemed to have lost all sense of perspective where Karen Willis was concerned. With Jonathan behind her, Karen was more likely than ever to keep pushing on the suit, with results that could be tragic for everyone.

"Has anyone tried to reason with Karen, I mean someone other than you?" Lilly added hastily as she saw the glowering expression draw Alec's bushy brows together. "Perhaps if she could be offered a face-saving way to compromise on this she might settle—"

"Don't you think I'm thinking of all the reasonable things that might have been possible before this accident?" Alec demanded harshly. "God, the only time I'm not thinking about ways is when I'm asleep in bed. And even then I dream about it!"

Alec picked up the script and slapped it into the open palm of his other hand. "Timing is so important. And now it's all going against me."

Lilly took a few agitated turns across the stage. All that came into her mind were useless platitudes that Alec would reject with a scornful jerk of his head.

"Then this exercise with Jill and Oscar that I witnessed was pretty pointless, wasn't it?" Lilly asked, her soft voice holding a note of challenge. "That is, if everything is as hopeless as you say."

"I beg your pardon," Alec muttered, and stiffened. He swept Lilly with a cold blue gaze, then tossed the script into the front row, where it landed on his jacket with a thwack.

"I'm glad to hear you know so much about working on a play," he said in silky tones. "Otherwise a comment like that might sound a bit...er, audacious."

He bit off that final word with a snapping of white teeth.

Lilly tilted her head, her heavy dark blond hair sliding across her shoulders in an attractive fall that she quickly pushed back. "Well, I never found I got anywhere in life by being a...er, milksop," she said, deliberately mocking his delivery.

Alec came at her and wrapped strong arms around her. "You don't have to worry about being wishy-washy. Underneath that hair a computer ticks day and night."

Lilly freed a hand and touched his head. "And what's under that hair? Cotton candy?"

Alec lowered his head until his face lay against her neck. Lilly could feel the ridge of his nose and the tantalizing brush of his lashes. They were stubby and as unyielding as the rest of him, she thought ruefully as they scratched her skin.

"Point made," he said in a warm exhalation that sent a wave of sensation like the sharp sting of an electrical shock down her spine. It seemed to get short-circuited at her waist, though, and diffused into a warm, spreading heat that never quite reached Lilly's legs.

"You taste good," he murmured with the pointed tip of his tongue on her skin like a sensor, reading her reaction to him in the quickening beat of her heart and the unconscious catch in her breath.

"Alec." Lilly said his name back to him, feeling its echo inside her, her hazel eyes darkening like the summer sky when the rain-heavy clouds cover it. Her hands shaped his face, tracing the broad flare of his nostrils and the lines from them to his mouth. "You have a wonderful mouth."

Alec pulled back. They looked at each other. Each wore a serious expression, and Lilly felt the power of the attraction between them, felt that this moment was crucially important without being able to say exactly why.

A mixture of fear and eagerness blossomed in Lilly. Alec attracted her like no other man; he also had a strange and powerful relationship with another woman, a relationship so tightly entwined in his life that Lilly feared he couldn't free himself—even if he wanted to.

But all that faded beneath the look of passion sparkling in Alec's eyes. "Do you know that in some lights, when you hold your head that way, you look about twelve years old?" he asked.

"Is that good?" Lilly asked lightly.

"It makes me want to hold you and protect you from every harm," Alec answered, his deep voice grave.

Lilly felt her heart thump to a stop and then start up with an uneven rhythm. She wanted Alec to crush her close and kiss her, but he stayed where he was. So Lilly raised her hands and flattened her palms on the hard curve of his biceps, savoring the feel of her soft flesh against the firmness of his. The springy hairs under her fingers tickled, and she moved her palms in a slow, circular caress.

"I want to make love to you, Lilly."

Lilly's lids shut as she tasted his words. The fact that they were spoken without Alec touching or kissing her made them all the more powerful. Firm ground was slipping from under her. Lilly felt herself sliding into the sea of emotion that Alec always tugged her toward, leaving Lilly exhilarated and afraid for her life. What if she couldn't swim it alone and Alec left her to drown? one small part of Lilly's mind worried.

Just then Alec leaned forward and touched his mouth

to hers. Lilly's breath stopped as she absorbed the outline of his lips and opened to the hot edge of his tongue. Their mouths clung and she mingled his breath, his scent, the brand of his being, in each breath she took.

This time their mouths met more surely, and Lilly explored the glossy barrier of his teeth before penetrating the secret heated recesses of tender flesh his mouth offered hers.

Lilly's hands dropped away and they were connected only by the moist warm eagerness of their mouths for many moments before simultaneously raising their arms to cocoon their passion from the world.

"Come on," Alec said, and led her offstage. Lilly followed him warily into a small, stuffy room that had a careless cascade of cushions in the far end of it. Wigs on Styrofoam heads, swords, and a rack of stick horses with dusty black manes lined the walls and spilled onto the floor of what was obviously some storage room. Alec wedged a chair under the door and came to hold her in his strong arms, moving his face gently over her neck and face. Desire rose again in her, even though Lilly had felt an instant of apprehension when they entered the room.

"I want you so much, Lilly. The smell of your skin, those secret, distant-looking eyes of yours—they drive me crazy, did you know that?" Alec asked, his fingers busy on the efficient removal of her clothes. Then his breath caught sharply as he slid her simple sheath dress off her shoulders and let it go. Underneath Lilly wore only a silk teddy that cupped her small breasts in lace and rose high on her rounded hips.

"Like it?" she asked somewhat shyly. Lilly always felt wicked when she put this teddy on. It was a French import her mother had uncharacteristically picked out as a Christmas present last year. Lilly reveled in the feel of it on her skin, the slither of silk between her thighs.

Alec's chest rose with a ghost of laughter, but his

eyes shimmered like flames of blue heat that warmed Lilly and made her feel totally desirable. "It's not bad," he said dryly.

"Of course the back's a bit risqué, don't you think?" Lilly asked innocently, and turned. She bent from the waist, head tilted and eyes fixed on Alec's expression intently, as though she really needed his opinion. "Here, I mean," she insisted, and saw the flame burn brighter as his blue eyes followed the arc of lace riding up her hip.

"Mmmm. It's hard to tell from here. I think this requires some hands-on experience," Alec said, and his voice had a rough edge that made Lilly's heart quicken.

"When you say hands-on experience you don't fool around, do you?" Lilly teased, but she felt curiously out of breath as Alec's warm hands cupped her flesh and pulled her close until they were hip to hip.

"Only with you, darling," he murmured, and Lilly caught that wicked flash of white teeth as he bent to kiss her.

Love for Alec exploded inside her, and Lilly reached to hold him close. With Alec's mouth on her, his skin against hers, the rest of the world faded to some far distant, out-of-focus place. And the former Lilly who would have been afraid to make love on a bed with the doors locked, let alone in a dusty props room, faded too. Now it was Lilly's fingers that eagerly removed Alec's clothes, making the most of smoothing the material slowly down his arms, fingers hooking in to free the buttons of his cuffs and caressing his wrists. She paused to nip the flesh from wrist to elbow in a rapid, playful attack that ended at his armpit. He smelled clean and excitingly male, and Lilly changed abruptly to a gentle exploration with her tongue as she followed the line of shoulder to neck to jaw. Alec's breathing told her that she was pleasing him as much as it pleased her to know every inch of him.

"You make me feel so special, Alec," she said huskily, the words stumbling out of her as she neared his mouth, the journey almost ended. Her boldness surprised Lilly, but she spoke only the truth. Alec did make her feel wonderfully alive and wanted.

Alec took the initiative back from her, and sloughed his pants to stand naked in front of her. Lilly felt excited as she looked at Alec's body. What she was doing went so much against the ingrained need to protect herself from emotional hurt that Lilly couldn't totally suppress the faint urge to flee, and it must have showed in her face.

"I'd never hurt you, Lilly. Stay with me. I need you," Alec whispered, and Lilly gave a start.

"How did you know that's what I was thinking?"

"I love you," he said simply, and brushed the straps of her teddy from her shoulders. With slow, sensuous tugs he took it down over her hardening nipples, down over the heated surfaces of her stomach and thighs until the silky material lay in a creamy pool at her feet.

"Alec, oh, Alec, I love you, too," Lilly murmured as they lay length to length on the faded sea-green cushions, and she knew she'd never wanted anything, longed for anything, the way she longed for Alec Thomas.

Every pore reached for him, and Lilly gave a moan of pure pleasure and satisfaction when he rolled her beneath him and she felt his weight on her. Her mouth opened demandingly, and Alec brought his own down to answer that demand. His fingers locked in her hair on that edge between pain and pleasure that excited her, and she moaned again as they moved slowly together. He was rock and she water, and Lilly enveloped Alec in her, holding him in hands and legs that grew tighter and tighter.

Lilly arched up into Alec, trying to reach a higher and higher peak. But Alec resisted her. He kept the same exquisite, tantalizing rhythm until Lilly thought she couldn't take it a second longer. "Alec," she pleaded with him in a thin voice, and he seemed to explode into the powerful driving rhythm Lilly craved. Sounds of pleasure tore from her throat, mingling with the cry of his name. Alec's ragged breathing filled her ears as the rest of his body filled all her senses until nothing existed but Alec, Alec, Alec.

They disentangled slowly, and filled the process with caresses and tender kisses on knees and elbows. Lilly looked up into Alec's relaxed, happy face and knew her own must look the same.

"That was quite a performance, Mr. Director," Lilly teased, drawing a finger down his strong nose and tapping gently on his lips.

"Ahh, but I can't take full credit for it," Alec countered with a modest duck of his head. Then he raised his wicked blue eyes and said, "It's called an ensemble performance, you know."

Lilly laughed and hugged him. "I guess we were about as 'together' as it gets."

Alec reached to hold her face between his hands. "Ensemble acting means more than that, Lilly. It means working as a team, with no prima donna, no stars of the show, and that's how I want it to be with us—in all ways."

"That's how I want it, too." Lilly said, hazel eyes bright with happiness. Until this moment Lilly had had doubts about just how much Alec thought about their relationship. But this seemed to her to be proof that Alec cared; that he'd spent time thinking about how he wanted things to be between them meant as much or more to Lilly than his declaration of love.

"Oh, Alec, I do love you so!" Lilly said, and she refused to let any creeping shadows of doubt crowd the bright light of her happiness, not even the large, dark shadow of Karen Willis.

Chapter Eleven

Footsteps sounding in the hallway outside broke into their privacy, and Lilly jumped violently when someone rattled on the doorknob as they went past. But the chair held easily, and Alec laughed at the horrified expression on Lilly's face as she instinctively clutched some clothing to her.

"Come on. We'd better clear out of here. One o'clock is when they have full cast rehearsals for the latest play, and there may be people pounding on the doors to get at these cushions in a few minutes."

Lilly rushed into her clothes as he talked. "How in the world do you know what props they'll be needing?" she asked, stopping to wonder at the pleasure she got from just watching him do the simplest things like tucking in his shirt. Alec looked up and caught her expression. His face darkened, and he moved close enough to snatch her to him. "Stop looking at me like that, or the students will have to direct themselves," he said as he kissed her.

"You're directing the Sam Shepard play? How do you find time for all this?" Lilly asked in genuine admiration. Alec shrugged dismissively in that way he had when someone asked him a question that irritated him, and too late Lilly remembered just how much he was involved in at the moment. Her remark might well sound like criticism, Lilly knew.

While Alec unhooked the chair from beneath the doorknob, Lilly glanced around the dusty room to make sure they had everything. Half-hidden by a cushion lay Alec's script, and she swooped it up as he turned back from the door. About to ask him about it, she halted.

"Will I see you tonight?" Alec spoke first as he stepped aside to allow Lilly to go in front of him. His tone sounded more polite than eager to Lilly's sensitive ears.

"It would have to be late. The Composition Conference starts on Thursday morning, and—"

Alec swore under his breath. "I forgot all about that damned thing. And I'm slated to attend. I can't get out of it, either." Alec rumpled his hair in exasperation. "I just don't have time for that nonsense."

"That's a fine way to talk about a conference at which I'll be presenting a very important paper," Lilly teased. "Maybe my original judgment about you was right. You probably don't consider my career as important as your work," Lilly went on in a musing tone, catching the fulminating look on Alec's face out of the corner of her eyes.

Just then three young men came around the corner and strutted past Lilly curiously. They went into the props room. Lilly forgot all about her teasing in a moment of pure panic. Had they left some kind of incriminating evidence behind? Or maybe the young men had seen her and Alec leaving there, and had put two and two together?

"Lilly? Is something wrong?"

"No, nothing."

"Liar. You've got a strange look on your face."

"It's just those boys. They looked at me oddly. Do you suppose—"

"No. I don't," Alec interrupted firmly. He took her hand, and, just as at the hospital when they waited to hear about Karen, Lilly felt strength flow into her from him. "You're forgetting that you're worth a second glance, or two, from any red-blooded male. And they're also students of mine. Since they've never seen me with a woman before, they're naturally curious... and jealous." Alec added that last word with an appreciative survey of Lilly's attractive figure. "So don't look for problems where they don't exist."

"Okay," Lilly agreed, touched by his kind explanation. He hadn't laughed at her panic, and she felt warmed by his compliments, even though she thought deep down that they were exaggerated.

"How about dinner tomorrow? I know a great place. One of my cousins owns it, actually. Tonight is starting to look kind of complicated."

"Is it the Halsted House? Jonathan mentioned it to me as a potential spot to take my parents if they make it down for the evening sometime." Lilly wondered if she should have mentioned Jonathan's name when she saw Alec's puzzled glance.

"Don't worry about it," Alec said brusquely. "I can't afford to go into spasms at the mere mention of his name."

They had paused near the glass walkway leading into the library.

"Well, will you have dinner with me?"

"Of course," Lilly said, her eyes shining at his urgent tone.

"Great! I have to run." He swept her close in a warm and sudden hug, and Lilly inhaled his sweet scent deep into her lungs. "I can't wait for tomorrow. We have a lot to discuss," Alec said, and held her eyes with his for an intense moment. "Gotta go," he muttered reluctantly, and was gone with that loping stride eating up the distance.

Lilly just watched him for a minute, then with a start

realized she still had that copy of his script. But when she looked at the cover she saw Alec had penciled in "student copy" under the title, and decided he could wait until tomorrow to get it back.

She stopped in the chairman's office and completed her original errand, then went back to the English offices. This time as she crossed the campus she wasn't alone, but part of a boisterous crowd of laughing and talking students on their way to classes. As she squeezed up the steps into her building, Lilly caught a glimpse of her car in the lot, and thought longingly of a fast drive on the highway to clear her head. Instead she forced herself to go to her office where she attacked a pile of linguistics project proposals.

"Care to take a break for lunch?" David poked his head around the door about two hours later.

"I'd love to. I'm really starved," Lilly answered as she paid attention for the first time that day to her growling stomach. "I didn't have much breakfast, come to think of it."

"That isn't good for you. Rita always insists that I eat a good breakfast."

"Say, I wanted to thank you and Rita for the party on Friday," Lilly said warmly. Inwardly she was amazed that it was only a few days ago. It seemed like ages to Lilly because of what had happened since then.

"It was our pleasure. I hope Karen didn't give you any problems on the way home?" David phrased it delicately.

"No, I find her very interesting, don't you?" Lilly said innocently. She wasn't giving him any clues as to what Karen said to her. She thought he deserved to squirm a bit for his part in attempting to keep her in the dark about Karen's suit.

"Interesting...." David turned that around this way and that, trying to shake some meaning out of it. "I guess she's a talented poet, but a dangerous sort of individual to be around on a personal level.''

"Oh, how so?" Lilly asked with keen interest.

"Oh, well. Falling off cliffs and things like that aren't exactly what happen to regular folks like you and me," David said and looked uncomfortable. "I just think she's a bit unbalanced."

Lilly smiled at his unintended pun. If only he knew what caused her to fall, he'd probably be convinced she was unbalanced, Lilly thought, since he'd be the sort to think each move out. He would never be impulsive like Karen and strike out at someone.

"Are you two going to lunch by any chance?" Todd Godwin slid languidly into Lilly's office. Lilly felt an intense flash of dislike crawl over her at the sight of him.

"Yes, we were," David said politely, and shot Lilly an apologetic look that Lilly answered with a shrug that said, What else could you say?

"That's a tidy coincidence, because I'm starved," Todd drawled, and settled a haunch on the corner of Lilly's desk.

"I'm sorry, Todd. But we're going in my car and there just isn't room for three," Lilly told him without noticeable regret in her voice.

"We could go in my car."

"That's kind of you, but I have some other errands. Some other day, okay?" Lilly said in a firm way that made it a statement he couldn't argue with rather than a question.

"Well, then, darling, maybe you can solve a mystery for me before you go." His green eyes glittered as he leaned over Lilly's seated form. In the background Lilly could sense David shifting uneasily, but Lilly was not about to be intimidated by the likes of Todd Godwin.

She stood up, hands folded calmly in front of her.

"Of course, if I can," she said mildly when the silence had lengthened just enough.

"Is it true that Alec pushed Karen off that cliff?" His eyes razored in on her face, alert to the slightest twitch or change.

"What? Where in the world did you get that particular piece of nonsense, or did you just make it up yourself?" Lilly asked with just the right degree of sarcasm. But inwardly she jumped. Had Karen, or perhaps even Jonathan, begun spreading such a lie?

"A little birdy told me," Todd murmured with an unattractive pursing of his full, pouty mouth.

"That's ridiculous, Godwin. Karen was working with her brother on a construction job, and she wandered a bit too close to the edge of the cliff, which as we all know can be notoriously deceptive in places," David said heatedly. "No one pushed her!"

"If you say so," Todd said, and stood with a shrug. He gave Lilly one more look and seemed to decide he would get nothing more from her. But like the aftermath of a bad smell, there was a lingering staleness in the air even after Todd left.

"Could we make the lunch another time?" Lilly asked softly. "There's something I have to take care of right away."

David watched as Lilly snatched up the phone receiver. "Anytime," he said quietly, and left.

Lilly didn't even see him go. "Yes. May I have the number for the Fielding Hospital? Thank you." She hung up and redialed almost before the operator finished giving her the number.

"I'd like to speak to Karen Willis. I don't know her room number." An expression of disbelief crossed her face. "Are you sure? But she was rather badly hurt.... Yes, of course. Good-bye."

Karen had been released from the hospital already!

She must be falling behind on how quickly they let people go these days, Lilly thought, then called information again for the number of Fielding National Bank. "Mr. Jonathan Thomas's office," a pleasant-voiced woman answered.

"Mr. Thomas, please," Lilly said tersely.

"May I take your name and number? Mr. Thomas is not in the office yet."

Lilly rang off with a brief "No, thank you." Now what? she asked herself. Karen wasn't in the hospital, and Jonathan wasn't in the office. Something said they had to be together, but where? Fielding wasn't a large town, but a house-to-house search for the pair would still be a considerable undertaking, Lilly thought with a touch of humor. She got up and went to the room where Hilda kept the coffee, and was glad to see someone had left her a sweet roll. Munching that, she walked slowly back up the stairs to her office. A phone was ringing when she reached the second floor, and Lilly automatically hurried in case it was her phone. It was.

"Lilly? This is Mike."

"Mike! How good to hear from you! How are things in Iowa City?" Lilly closed her eyes and imagined her husky, ebullient friend. Probably still tilted back to a dangerous angle in that ancient chair of his, Lilly thought fondly as she heard a creaking sound. She listened as he told her friendly gossip about joint acquaintances. "Say, you know Janet is coming up for that Comp. Conference this weekend," he added casually.

"No, I didn't know that. Anything new there?" Lilly asked just as casually, knowing that Mike had had an enormous crush on Janet Cruse as an undergraduate.

"Not much. Except that we're getting married at Christmas break," Mike said quietly, and Lilly let out a whoop of joy.

"Oh, Mike, you tease! How wonderful! When?

You'd better invite me. Have you told your folks?''
Questions and comments flew back and forth. "That is
so wonderful!" Lilly said again when things had calmed
down a bit. "I hope you two will be very happy."

"How about you and this Alec?" Mike demanded.
"Are you still interested in him, and is Karen Willis
still causing you trouble?"

"Yes to both questions," Lilly said in much more
subdued tones than she'd used before.

"Got it bad for the guy, huh?" Mike guessed
shrewdly. "Well, as the voice of experience, all I can
tell you is to hang in there."

Lilly had to laugh. "I'm trying."

"Say, you know what? Something has been nagging
at the back of my mind since the first time you told me
about this suit Karen Willis is bringing." Mike creaked
even farther back in his chair.

"Be careful!" Lilly couldn't help shouting, and then
heaved a sigh of resignation at the crash that came
from the other end of the phone, followed by loud
complaints of intense pain from her friend.

"What were you saying?" he asked when he'd re-
gained an upright position.

"Never mind. Get back to Karen," Lilly ordered
good-naturedly.

"I don't know if this will be helpful to you, but I
suggest you check into whether Karen Willis actually
finished the degrees she claims to have earned."

"What?" Lilly was shocked. She'd thought Karen
was many things in the past few weeks, but a con artist
hadn't been one of them until this minute. "Where do
you get this idea?" Lilly wanted to know. "They check
people out pretty thoroughly these days, with so many
qualified candidates for each post."

"Look, all I know is that my memory tells me she
left without finishing her degree."

"And what does your records department tell you?"

Lilly asked dryly, refusing to get too excited about this enticing prospect. "Or haven't you checked this out with them?"

"I thought you might do that. I'm just an idea man," Mike said mildly.

"A lazy man, more like," Lilly countered, but without malice.

"I resent that! Actually, I tried to check it out before I called you, but we've got this dragon in the records department. She doesn't like me," Mike said in a wounded tone.

"Ahh, which probably means you harassed her unmercifully on some other topic, and now she won't give you the time of day," Lilly guessed shrewdly, and was rewarded by a gusty sigh from the other end of the phone. "You were always so cruelly attached to the truth," Mike lamented.

Lilly laughed, thanked him, and told him not to forget her wedding invitation. Mike told her to be kind to his fiancée at the conference, and they said good-bye. When Lilly got off the phone, she sat tapping a pencil thoughtfully on the top of her desk. What have I got to lose? she asked herself, and pushed away from the desk in a brisk motion.

All the way downstairs she tried to rein her rising hopefulness. There are a lot of possibilities, she warned herself. Don't get too excited about this. Maybe she finished her degree at another school. Maybe Mike has a faulty memory. Back down the stairs she went and into the coffee room. Al Schwartz sat sipping coffee at the long conference table. Lilly greeted him and tried to be casual about her search for the last year's *Fielding Bulletin*. Luckily, just when she found it, Al got up and wandered out, saying vaguely that he thought he had an appointment with a student today, or maybe it was yesterday?

Lilly spared a smile for his stooped retreating back.

Al Schwartz was the stereotypical absentminded professor, she thought, whose mind was always on his research and rarely on everyday reality. She thumbed to the back of the bulletin where the biographies of the staff were given.

Bingo. Right there in black and white it said Master of Fine Arts, and Doctorate from the University of Iowa. So far, so good, Mike, Lilly thought. But I need something more before I go to Alec with this, and Hilda's the person to help me now, Lilly realized, still trying to keep her growing excitement down. Because if Mike is right, Lilly thought, Karen had taken this job under false pretenses, and certainly that should weaken her case a great deal, if it didn't invalidate it completely.

"Could I see the minutes from the hiring committee on Karen Willis, Hilda?" Lilly asked moments later, and was surprised to hear a slight shake in her voice as she spoke.

Hilda looked at her for a moment. "Don't know what you expect to get out of that, but they're not top secret or anything, so I don't see why not." Hilda stood and pulled open a file drawer. She paged slowly through, and then yanked out a slim swatch of mimeographed pages. "Here you go. And may they prove helpful to you, my dear."

"Thank you," Lilly said, and ran up to her office, shutting the door behind her. For no logical reason, she didn't want anyone to see her examining this stuff. After all, as Hilda pointed out, it wasn't top secret, but she wouldn't put it past Todd, for example, to warn Karen that something was going on.

What struck her immediately was the sense of urgency in the notes. The department needed a woman, and they needed her soon. The irony of that wasn't wasted on Lilly as she thought of her own hiring. They didn't learn much, she thought cynically, and read on.

An important point seemed to be whether or not Karen could take Stanton's place immediately. Her record was entered into the minutes and Lilly looked at it.

In the next paragraph Alec's name caught her eye. He'd confirmed orally that Karen had indeed been at the University of Iowa Writers' Workshop with him. A motion was made to confirm this. Al Schwartz was supposed to take care of it. But again, the emphasis shifted to her immediate availability and the fact that she was published and could take over Stanton's composition courses.

"Al Schwartz," Lilly murmured aloud, and knew he'd forgotten to call as surely as she knew her own name. The implications of this knowledge flooded Lilly with excitement. This would free Alec from so much, Lilly thought, to have Karen exposed. He could get the funding for his new play back. He wouldn't have to worry about the job at Fielding. Lilly's mind reeled at the possibilities. But that voice of honesty at the back of her mind said, *isn't it that you really want Karen out of his life? Of course I do. I love Alec,* Lilly answered defensively, *and I want to help him.*

She ached to share her discovery with Alec, but just then someone tapped hesitantly on her door. "Come in," she said impatiently, then tried to soften her manner as a shy, young man, obviously ill at ease, edged into her office needing help with his first college composition paper. For Lilly the next half hour was an exercise in patience as she critiqued his draft, and gave him pointers on where his writing needed the most help. He left happier and more confident, but Lilly swore she was about ready to climb the walls.

She couldn't find Alec anywhere.

"He's out of town on business until tomorrow afternoon," Hilda told her calmly, when, in a fit of desperation, Lilly asked the secretary where their department chairman was.

"Were the papers of any help to you?" Hilda asked curiously as Lilly handed them back to her.

Gritting her teeth, Lilly murmured something non-committal and rushed out of the building. She was coming to the conclusion that she'd have to wait until their dinner date tomorrow to tell Alec of her discovery, and attempted to convince herself that anticipation was great, too.

Further irritation lay just around the corner for Lilly. For as she bumped down the drive, thinking for the hundredth time that she would have to get it fixed, she saw an ominously familiar car. Lilly maneuvered the Corvette in next to it and got out.

"Hello, Aunt Sylvia!" she called as she opened the front door. The house was a bit too quiet.

"Darling!" Sylvia rushed up the hall to envelop Lilly in a perfumed hug, her enormous handbag bobbling against Lilly's back. "It's so wonderful to see you!"

As they moved into the relative tidiness of the living room, Lilly said, "It's good to see you. What brings you down to this neck of the woods?" She tossed the red-covered copy of Alec's play that she'd brought in from the car on the coffee table.

"Oh, I was in the neighborhood," Sylvia said disingenuously, "but what does it matter? Can't I visit my favorite niece without a special reason?" Perching on the sofa's edge, she picked up Alec's script.

"Of course you can," Lilly said with dry emphasis as she looked into her aunt's innocent brown eyes. "Can I get you some iced coffee?"

"I hate to put you to any trouble, but I'd love some," Sylvia said, tossing the script back on the table in a casual gesture and looked around her with bright-eyed interest. Nearly seventy, her aunt had an indecent amount of energy, Lilly thought as she stopped by the dining room to pick up two glasses from under a plastic drape. She pushed open the kitchen door.

"Miz Burns, you must keep that woman out of here, or I won't be responsible!" Mr. Mattson growled at Lilly as she dipped the two glasses into the bag of crushed ice she kept in the freezer. There was enough coffee left from the morning for two cups, and Lilly was thankful for her unusual frugality in sticking the remains in the refrigerator instead of throwing it away as she usually did.

"What's the problem?" Lilly asked coolly as she put the glasses on a tray and placed a few thin mints on a plate, along with some napkins—paper—she didn't want her aunt to feel too welcome, since she had arrived totally uninvited.

"She's interfering with the work," he said importantly.

"How?" Lilly asked in blunt disbelief, although in actuality she could think of a thousand ways Aunt Sylvia could get in the way. But she couldn't allow Mattson to get the upper hand by giving his complaints credence.

"Asking what we charge for this and that—implying she'd call the law on us if we did bad work." Mattson puffed out his chest, obviously aware that the two young males were watching him now, and he had his image to protect.

"Since you work for me, I'm the only person whose opinion you need worry about," Lilly said dismissively. She picked up the tray and left the room. She heard pounding resume before she reached the living room, and heaved a silent sigh of relief. That was one difficulty dealt with, she thought.

"This is a delightful property," Sylvia exclaimed from the French windows when Lilly entered the room. "I think you made a wise choice."

"I'm glad you approve," Lilly said gravely.

"I'm sure you think I came down to spy on you, my dear. But I can assure you it's no such thing." She sipped her coffee and bit into a mint before continuing. "Because I think this move away from your family is the best thing you ever did."

"You do?" To say that those sentiments surprised Lilly was putting it mildly. "I always thought you were a hundred percent behind my throwing my lot in with Burns Electronics."

"Not in the least. And I never liked that Martin fellow, either, while we're being candid. You're well rid of him, my dear. On that subject your mother and I could never agree, and it's the greatest relief to me that he's no longer with the company."

"Ahh, then Daddy went ahead and fired him," Lilly murmured. "I was afraid he would."

"Yes. But I think he considered your advice before he did so, or at least that's what Millie said."

Lilly smiled. Her mother loathed being called Millie, and Sylvia knew it. The rivalry between her mother and her aunt had grown more intense, instead of fading over the years. When Sylvia wanted to get to her sister, all she had to do was call her Millie, and it sent Lilly's mother into an absolute fury, bringing with it all the memories of being the youngest and striving to "catch up" with her big sister. Yet Lilly could see now that the two sisters' lives would lose a lot of spice if they ceased to compete. Both of them enjoyed it; although conflict left Lilly tired and unhappy, it merely served to invigorate her mother and Sylvia.

"Now, this boss of yours, what's his name again?"

"Alec Thomas."

"Yes, that's it. A playwright, isn't he?"

"You know he is, Aunt Sylvia. More coffee?"

"No, thank you. Single, isn't he?"

"Yes."

"Are you seriously interested in him?"

"Far too early to tell," Lilly lied. "He's not rich, though," she added in an effort to distract her aunt without being downright rude, and set her glass down carefully on the empty coffee table.

"The family's well thought of here in Fielding, though, isn't it?" Sylvia replied promptly.

"I thought you said you hadn't come to interrogate me," Lilly said plaintively, raising both hands in a shielding movement in front of her.

"Oh, no. I said I hadn't come to spy, and I haven't. But surely that doesn't cover direct questions."

"I think it does," Lilly countered firmly. "Would you like to see the rest of the house and the grounds before you go?"

"If you answer just one more question. Your mother says you haven't been keeping in touch with her. That hurts her, you know, even if she doesn't say so." Sylvia patted Lilly's cool hands with her own plump, warm ones.

"What's the question?" Lilly didn't like to believe her aunt's view. It had always seemed to Lilly that her mother was highly unaffected by whatever she and Ben did. But maybe she was wrong.

"Do you think this Thomas is going places with his talent, or is he just a dabbling academic?" Sylvia said, suddenly quite serious. Her plump hands tapped on her bulging handbag as she spoke.

"Do you mean is he ambitious, or is he good?" Lilly countered with a question of her own, suddenly quite interested in the discussion.

"Both."

"Yes to both questions, then," Lilly said without an instant's hesitation. "He's a very powerful, evocative user of the language, and he wants his work to be seen and heard."

"Thank you, my dear. That's all I needed to know."

Lilly could have quite easily talked about Alec for hours, but realized that wouldn't fit with her image of not being sure about caring for him, so she allowed the subject to drop and talked of her work and the upcoming conference in Minneapolis.

"So you see, you could have caught me some time this weekend and spared yourself the trip down here," Lilly teased as she saw her aunt into her old Bentley.

"I've missed you," Sylvia said simply. "We all have."

Lilly watched the huge steel-gray car disappear onto the main road with a lump in her throat. It was true that she'd been so caught up lately in her new life that she hadn't given much thought to the positive aspects of her family's life. And they were close, closer than most, despite the struggle for dominance that went on.

It occurred to Lilly that this move might be good for them all, not just for her own sense of independence, because it seemed to her that they were beginning to appreciate each other much more now that they weren't together all the time. Lilly resolved to squeeze a visit with her parents into this long conference weekend coming up.

She went back inside and began to organize the clothes that she wanted to take to the conference. It was important to Lilly that she look businesslike and cool at all times, as she knew she had a tendency to look far younger than her twenty-eight years. That meant her navy pin-stripe suit and silk blouse, pumps and light stockings. The process took her longer than she'd thought, and it was with a feeling of surprise that she heard the workmen's cars start up, and checked her watch to find that it was already four thirty.

With the garment bag zipped up and ready to go, Lilly was free to contemplate a very important decision: What should she wear to have dinner with Alec tomorrow? A pile of discards formed on the bed with alarming speed. Finally she decided on a black dress and a snow-white jacket. The combination was both sexy and yet not obvious, Lilly thought as she tried it on and twirled a bit in front of the full-length mirror hanging from one of the closet doors. Shoes that were a confection of straps and the thinnest Italian leather added the illusion of height.

Satisfied with her choice, Lilly carefully hung the dress away and went downstairs to find something to eat. She returned with a salad and sandwich and sat in the middle of the bed, with the bits and pieces of her conference presentation about her. Mrs. Jordan's tangy dressing tasted great on the crisp green romaine and deep red tomatoes. Lilly crunched hungrily into it, realizing she'd never gotten lunch.

Thoughts of Alec's surprise and gratitude at the results of her sleuthing bubbled pleasantly inside her, and she smiled, her fingers stroking absently along the rim of her salad bowl. In a way, Lilly had to admire Karen's guts. She'd gambled on the department's need for speed in hiring her, plus her own publishing record, to cover her deception. Until now it had worked.... This certainly explained her reaction to the mention of Iowa City and Mike's name, though, Lilly realized. And it was easy to see now that her reaction to the information that Lilly was in regular contact with him hadn't been anger, as Lilly'd thought at the time, but fear of discovery.

Oh, Alec, just hurry back and hear the news! Lilly thought happily and hugged her knees to her chest, her enthusiasm nearly upsetting her half-eaten salad all over her presentation. Lilly hoped Alec's parting remark had been about discussing their future together, and she knew the news of Karen's deception could only brighten their prospects.

Chapter Twelve

Lilly awoke with a great sense of anticipation, and a lightness of heart she hadn't felt in a long time. Today she would be with Alec and what made it even better was that she would have great news for him.

She cleaned up the remains of her feast of the night before and carried them downstairs to the kitchen, washed them, and slid them under the plastic cover on the dining room table to join the rest of the kitchen cabinet contents. A clean pine smell filled the now quiet kitchen, and Lilly gazed appreciatively at the new cabinets. They gave a much lighter, airier feel to the kitchen already, even though the mess still filled the place. Lilly was pleased with her choices and was eager to show them off to Alec when he came to pick her up.

Because she'd originally planned to travel to Minneapolis early in the afternoon, Lilly had canceled her classes for the day. Dinner with Alec would now make the schedule a bit tight, since she was presenting her paper to the conference at ten o'clock the next morning, but Lilly didn't care. *Alec, Alec, Alec.* His name ran along her blood, singing through her body as she went lightly up the stairs to dress in jeans and a shirt before the workmen arrived.

Morning sunlight washed the room with a golden glow that perfectly matched Lilly's mood. Mongo chased a beam of sunlight across the rumpled bedspread, pounced, and flipped head first over the end of the bed to land with a solid thud on the floor. There was a long moment of silence, and Lilly hurried around the bed to make sure he was all right. Even though they'd gone through this routine many times before, Lilly always thought it sounded like he might have hurt himself. But no, he sat washing himself vigorously as if to cover for his embarrassing lack of catlike grace.

Lilly, who had owned cats all her life, knew the supposedly inherent grace and agility of cats was vastly overrated, more of a discretionary virtue that most cats chose to exercise only when they felt like it.

"Are you ready for a car ride to see the folks?" she asked Mongo. Having finished with his bath, he was lapping delicately from the water glass Lilly kept on the nightstand—even though he had a perfectly good dish of his own water on the floor in the corner. That was cat water, though, and inferior to the human stuff, seemed to be his conclusion. He didn't seem impressed with Lilly's offer.

She'd usually have left him at home, but with all the workmen, and all the open doorways, she'd reluctantly concluded that she had to bring him along, even though he wasn't a good car passenger.

"Miz Burns!" Lilly heard the bellowing of Mattson at the backdoor and hurried down, wondering what new disaster this cry heralded. But her luck held.

"We got lucky. They managed to get that washer and the new sink on the train that come in last night. I'm gonna head down to the depot and pick 'em up."

"That's great!"

"They say they got the right color and that fancy model dishwasher you wanted and everything," he muttered with a disbelieving shake of his head.

"Does that mean you could get the kitchen completed this weekend?" Lilly pressed.

"I reckon so," Mattson grunted in reluctant agreement. "But we don't do work on Sunday," he warned. An unlit cigarette flapped up and down at the corner of his mouth, seeming to stay there by magic. "Anyhow, we'll try."

Lilly swallowed a smile as he stalked off to the dusty El Camino. Good news was evidently suspect with Mr. Mattson, she had come to see. Bad news, delays, and disasters were the fare of everyday life, and the more things that went well, the more worried Mattson seemed to get.

The phone rang; the caller was a student. The main gist of the conversation seemed to be that he couldn't turn his already late essay in because of a complicated series of events. "Never mind," Lilly interrupted gently. "Just have it in my box by Monday morning at the latest. If you'd come to class this week you would have known that I'm going out of town for the weekend, Joel. So in the future, even if you can't get the work done, come to class so you don't get even further behind." He was relieved to have gotten off so lightly.

Next Lilly decided she needed some breakfast before the rest of the work team arrived, and fixed herself a light meal of toast, coffee, and grapefruit juice, which she carried out into the living room. Unable to resist the lure of the day, she swung open the French doors that creaked back on their hinges and stepped out onto the chipped flagstone patio. The patio was badly in need of repairs, but flanked as it was by the creek and sheltered in the curve of the house, it was attractive nonetheless on this unusually warm fall morning.

Lilly dragged a chair out and put her breakfast on the flagstone nearby. She told herself that she wasn't just using this as an excuse to stare at Alec's house, barely visible through the brush and trees that lined the cliff at the point.

She cast a brief glance around for Alec's script, but she must have taken it upstairs, because it wasn't on the coffee table where she'd left it yesterday, she thought. As she settled into the chair, Lilly listened to the wind sighing through the long grass along the creek, and watched an uneven patch of burnt umber, gold, and rust chrysanthemums dip and sway in an acquiescent wind dance.

A bright-eyed chipmunk popped its head over the edge of the flagstone, and Lilly threw it a small crumb of toast that was left on her plate. But he shot away into the long grass when Mattson's El Camino and the other truck lumbered noisily into the yard. Lilly was sorry to have her idyll interrupted, but she knew she, too, had to get to work. A pile of assignments lay on the coffee table, ready to be corrected, and Lilly knew she couldn't expect to have any free time during this hectic weekend schedule in which to grade papers.

In the end, Lilly compromised. She picked up her green grade book, her pile of assignments, and a stack of quizzes from her linguistics class and took them back outside to grade. The time flew by, and before she knew it, it was once again quitting time for the lads. And they quit right on time, too. Lilly had no quibble with that as long as the job got done as quickly as it was going at the present time.

In fact, she was glad to see them go so that she could sneak into the kitchen and have a look at what they'd been doing all day. Several times during the afternoon she'd been tempted, but Mattson was so grumpy about Aunt Sylvia's interruption yesterday that Lilly decided to wait until they'd cleared off.

"Oh, it looks terrific!" Lilly couldn't help exclaiming aloud as she stepped into the transformed kitchen. The gleaming almond appliances and light-colored wood cabinets made such an excellent combination that Lilly couldn't wait to show Alec. More than Lilly's good taste was at stake here; Lilly was aware that she felt she had to prove something to herself by handling this project successfully.

Since moving to Fielding, Lilly had realized how good it made her feel to make decisions and carry them out. Until she got out from under the influence of her family, Lilly hadn't known just how heavy it was. Well, there wasn't time now to dwell on her glories, Lilly thought self-mockingly as she went upstairs to get ready. Alec had said he's stop by around six thirty, and so she had time for a leisurely bath.

As she splashed in the scented water, the bathroom door swung open and in came Mongo. Always more curious than was good for him, he'd lately become fascinated by bathwater. One leap had him balancing somewhat precariously on the tub's edge, and Lilly warned, "Be careful." Thus warned, Mongo sat back sedately and stared. Intent eyes followed each splash and slurp of the water as he patiently waited for Lilly to finish and get out of the tub, because what he was really waiting for was to watch the water go gurgling down the drain.

The phone was ringing when Lilly emerged, and she went into the bedroom to pick it up. "Hello?"

"Alec! How are you?" Lilly's voice warmed.

"Sweetheart, I'm afraid I'm going to be a bit late."

"How late?" Lilly nearly wailed, but managed to sound merely disappointed.

"Not much. An hour at the most. I just got back in, and an unexpected errand has cropped up." He sounded harassed, strained. In the background Lilly heard noises that sounded like a female voice.

"Are you still at the airport?"

"No. I'm at home. I tried to get a hold of you before I left yesterday. Mason or Mattson promised to pass on a message to you."

"He didn't, but it doesn't matter so long as you're

coming," Lilly said softly, uncaring of how vulnerable that admission made her sound. "I missed you terribly. Was your trip successful?"

"No. But I'll tell you all about it later, okay? Bye for now." The phone clicked down abruptly, and left Lilly feeling deflated.

Still, once Alec heard what she had to tell him, Lilly was sure that most of his bad humor would be dissipated. She told herself she would have to stop taking everything Alec said so much to heart. He always had too much on his mind, dividing his talents between too many things, as far as Lilly was concerned. But that didn't mean she wasn't important to him, wasn't loved by him.

It was just at about eight o'clock when Lilly heard the quiet hum of the Omega, and minutes later she was showing Alec into the remodeled kitchen.

"Don't you like the cabinets?" she asked, taking his arm and drawing him into the room in a blatant ruse to touch him.

"Yes, you've made some good choices. The place looks twice as big," Alec said, complimenting her, and suggested they leave for the restaurant since they'd already had to delay their reservation.

Halsted House was gorgeous, and Lilly was suitably impressed by the ambiance of luxury and privacy it gave off. The owner, related to the Thomas family, showed them to their table deep in a curving leather booth that overlooked the creek at a point where it grew enough in size to nearly warrant the name of river. Torches blazed from metal poles stuck at intervals along the bank and cast an attractive bronze pool of light over the bubbling surface of Fielding Creek.

They ordered a cocktail, and Lilly stared across the table at Alec with eyes that gleamed with suppressed excitement.

"You seem to be just overflowing with something,"

Alec commented, his blue eyes sparkling with curiosity.

"Oh, I am. But it can wait awhile. First, tell me all your news," Lilly urged. She and Alec sat close together on the curving leather seat, and Lilly felt the sudden hot press of his thigh against her own.

"Actually, nothing is new. I want you and need you. Do you suppose my cousin Paul would mind if I made love to you, right here on one of his pristine tables?"

"I think he might, a bit," Lilly said demurely, although her pulse jumped and she felt that familiar tightening in her lower stomach at the image that conjured up.

"Well, I've got a secret hankering to see you on one. I have from the beginning, so we may just have to check it out," Alec said as their drinks arrived. "To sturdy tables," he toasted wickedly, and the waiter was puzzled to see Lilly blushing so violently at such an innocuous, if odd-sounding, toast. He walked away shaking his head.

"You think I'm joking around, don't you?" Alec asked.

"No, I don't, and that's what worries me!"

"Say, did I neglect to tell you how you look in that outfit?" The sparkle was still in his eyes, although he tried to hide it by lowering his lids; Lilly could see it lurking between the starkly straight lashes.

"No, you didn't," she answered cautiously, not ready to accept this as a straightforward compliment just yet.

"I was just thinking that I liked the outfit you wore yesterday morning so much better."

"You liked...." Lilly started to question how he could prefer that simple blue shift over this expensive dress when his true meaning came through to her. "You are completely incorrigible, Alec!"

"Thank you. I can only try," he answered as though

she'd paid him a compliment of the highest order. Then he rubbed his index finger over an eyebrow in a gesture Lilly knew meant he was thinking about something that was bothering him.

"What is it?" Lilly closed her rather extensive menu and put it to one side. She always knew what she wanted at a place like this, and couldn't be bothered reading through exotic descriptions of other dishes. "Does it have something to do with this mysteriously called business trip?"

Lilly had tried not to sound too much as if she had a right to know his every move, for in reality she knew her claim on Alec, despite his declarations of love to her, went only so far as he let it.

"It's not all that mysterious. Say, did you pick up that copy of the script yesterday?"

Lilly nodded impatiently. "Yes. It's at my house somewhere; you can get it back when you drop me off, if you like."

"No, no. I wanted you to read it, and give me your opinion."

Lilly felt the breath go out of her. "You really mean that?"

This time it was Alec who nodded. "Of course. I think your opinion would be very valuable, especially since I heard from Jonathan what your opinion of *Twilight* was."

"Listen. I—the last thing I want is for you to get the wrong impression from my criticisms of *Twilight*," Lilly sputtered in an attempt to get the words out as fast as she thought them. She knew Alec was mostly teasing, but this as one subject that needed some serious attention, Lilly thought, and said so.

"It's because I think you're so extraordinarily talented, Alec, that it worries me that you forced the female character into what seemed to me to be a preconceived mold. She was your 'villain,' and wasn't allowed to have any excuses or extenuating circumstances, even though the details we learn of her in the course of the play make us want to sympathize with her." Lilly paused and shook her head ruefully. "If you were a talentless hack, it wouldn't matter what your opinion of life, or of women was, because you wouldn't be able to influence people. But you're so *good*, Alec!" Lilly grasped his forearm intensely.

"Have you ever considered public relations as a career move?" Alec teased, but his tone was deep and his eyes darkened with emotion as they moved over the features of Lilly's face one by one. "Have you read the new play?" he asked softly, and stroked her hand.

Lilly looked up in surprise to see the waiter standing patiently before them. For the last few minutes it had seemed to Lilly that she and Alec were so close that they could have easily been the only people in the room.

"Give us a few more minutes, will you?" Alec asked, and the round-faced young man disappeared.

"I think you'll find the new play an improvement," Alec said, and there was a ghost of dryness in his voice that Lilly picked up on, which made her think perhaps he felt she'd overstepped her bounds, even though he was looking at her in a way that made her ache to kiss and to be kissed.

Lilly found she had a passion for touching his skin. It felt like no other, and Lilly knew she could probably shut her eyes and tell which person Alec was merely by touching him.

"Now what are you smiling about?" he asked. "You are most elusive at times. I think you know it drives me crazy and you do it on purpose."

"Maybe I do."

"Anyhow, we got sidetracked, and I never told you about my so-called business trip. I just went to see a few people I know up in Minneapolis—"

"Backers?"

"Potentially, yes."

"But?"

"Didn't work out," Alec finished his drink and turned to motion to the waiter. "I'll simply have to wait until this whole suit business has blown over, and then reapply for the government stuff."

With great effort Lilly restrained herself until the waiter had their order and was moving again. "You won't have to do that."

"What? Now, Lilly, don't get any silly ideas about selling everything you own and investing in a play, please," Alec warned, only partially teasing, his eyes sharp.

"No, nothing like that." Lilly tossed that suggestion off impatiently. "Karen has been lying, and I found out about it! She never finished her degrees at Iowa, and no one from the department here bothered to check her out."

Lilly stopped, puzzled. Her bombshell seemed to be fizzling. Alec didn't even look surprised.

"Have you been telling other people this?" he demanded.

"You mean you knew she lied about her degrees?" Lilly asked, completely stunned by this whole thing. She'd thought Alec would be ecstatic. Instead he was looking at her with a great deal of irritation in his face.

"Well, have you?"

"No, I haven't." Lilly muttered in a small, lost voice. "I wanted to tell you first, and anyway, I thought it was your place to decide how to handle the news."

"God, that's the first break I've had lately," Alec said in a relieved tone. "Good girl."

"I don't understand. If you knew this all along, why didn't you stop her? She's hurting your career. She's keeping you from getting your play produced." Lilly spoke in short, jerky sentences. "If you don't tell the administration this, I will."

"If you care anything about me, you'll say nothing."

"Care about you! How can you say that?" Lilly cried, hurt and confused by what was happening. This was so far from the jubilant scene she'd imagined that Lilly was thrown totally off balance.

"Take a deep breath. Think about this from my angle for a moment," Alec urged.

"I am! Why do you think I went to all the trouble of sneaking around and getting the proof that she was lying, if I didn't care what happens to you?"

"Okay, okay, I'll grant that you interfered for all the right reasons, but—"

"*Interfered*? I just did the job you and the rest of that male bastion called the Fielding English Department ought to have done in the first place."

"Lilly, calm down," Alec pleaded, grabbing her hand as Lilly half rose. "Don't you think you could give me two minutes?"

Lilly subsided. "All right." She sank back into the plush leather, gazing pointedly at his hand, which gripped hers so hard there were white marks where his fingers bit into hers.

"Let's play this scene out, shall we?" Alec began, and relaxed his grip, obviously upset by her intent to leave. "It's very possible that even if I told the administration about Karen's lying, she might still take the case to civil court. You told me yourself just the other night, right?" Alec went on only after Lilly's reluctant nod. "A jury might be swayed, might feel that, lying or not, Karen has some claim. Especially if Godwin gave a great performance as the eyewitness to one of these incidents."

Lilly gave Alec a mulish look. His reasoning seemed absurdly weak to her, and she thought she knew the real reason Alec didn't want to act on this information—his love for Karen.

"Karen would be publicly humiliated. Once again, she'd be the laughingstock of Fielding."

"Why do you care about that? She deserves it, in my opinion. She's certainly trying to do the same to you," Lilly pointed out angrily. "I don't see why you feel obligated to protect her."

"Because I can take it, and she can't," Alec said in a hard voice.

"Anyway, it doesn't have to get to court. All you have to do is confront Karen with the facts, and common sense will force her to back down," Lilly went on with what she thought was perfect logic.

"I've already done that," Alec said, stunning Lilly completely. "And she hasn't backed down."

"When? How long have you known about this?"

"I've known since the beginning that Karen never finished her degree—"

"But I read the minutes of the committee. You confirmed—"

"Ahh, but wait a minute. I volunteered that Karen was at the Iowa Writers' Workshop at the same time I was, not that she'd finished her degree."

Lilly thought about that for a moment and realized Alec spoke the truth. "When did you know, then?"

"Oh, I did my own checking. I figured Schwartz would forget—Hey, what put you onto this, anyway?"

"A friend of mine, Mike. He called to tell me he's getting married, and he mentioned it." Lilly quailed a bit inwardly at the darkening expression on Alec's face.

"Is he likely to talk?"

Lilly shook her head mutely, and Alec went on. "I never expected Karen to last. She's no born teacher the way you are," Alec said with a rueful shake of his head. Somehow what ought to have sounded like a compliment left Lilly wishing desperately that she was dramatic and could bind men to her the way Karen Willis seemed to do.

Lilly couldn't understand it, really. Men always prided themselves on being so logical, so rational. Yet

Alec's desire to protect someone who was doing her best to do him in seemed to Lilly to defy all logic, and even self-preservation.

"But Karen didn't fail under the weight of her own incompetence, did she?"

"No. She hung in there pretty well."

"So when did you confront her with this?"

"Remember that night I stormed out of your house? Well, you'd finally managed to get through to me. I saw how serious things had really become, and I knew I had to stop her."

Lilly shivered. She'd been right, then, to worry on Sunday night when Alec slammed out of her house.

"The next morning I tracked her down at the construction site. I tried to offer a compromise. I was even willing to admit to some kind of guilt in the whole thing—anything to coax her into dropping the suit. But things had gone too far. I think she couldn't get past the fact that, once again, I would be 'winning' and she would be 'losing.'"

"But that's so childish!" Lilly interrupted angrily.

"But inevitable, given the history of the people involved," Alec reminded her firmly. "Anyway, as a sort of final effort, I told her I knew about her phony résumé."

"And that's when she took a swing at you?" Lilly felt the truth of that scene on the cliff dawn on her with sickening impact. Over and over Karen's body had tumbled, and Lilly saw it all once again, but in a terrible light. Because now she felt it had been at least partly her fault. And perhaps that was why she'd nearly allowed anger to drive her away from Alec tonight. Lilly admitted to herself now that she'd known things couldn't be that simple, but that she'd *wanted* them to be that simple. They were each of them twined and intertwined with each other now.

"Alec, I'm sorry I reacted so angrily before. I apologize. I knew deep down that this thing couldn't be as simple as just telling Karen, but I'm so afraid..." Lilly stopped, unable to continue with the clot of tears and emotions choking her throat. "Karen's at your house, isn't she?"

"Yes," Alec said simply. "She didn't have much other choice."

The waiter stopped just then and served their dinners, aromatic and artfully arranged. Yet Lilly just shook her head, and pushed her plate gently aside. "I'd like some coffee, please." She was pleased with the normal sound of her voice. The waiter came back almost immediately and set a steaming urn of coffee and a frosted pitcher of cream on the table. Lilly poured some, then added a whirl of cream that sank like a mocking question mark into the dark, fragrant brew.

The exercise gave her time to think, and the conclusions she came to were painful. Either she gave up right now, or she fought, for the first time in her life, for something she wanted. She'd always run away, either physically or emotionally, from things that could hurt.

"Jonathan has offered to buy out my shares of the house," Alec went on quietly.

"I don't understand? You mean Karen's there at his behest?"

"Oh, yes. Tonight was the first time I knew about it, although Karen was released from the hospital the day before yesterday."

"How is she?" Good manners compelled Lilly to ask.

"Prickly, fiercely independent and in general a pain to be around for more than five minutes." Alec laughed. "In short, almost back to her usual form."

"I would have thought she'd be thrilled at the way things have turned out. I mean, she's certainly gotten Jonathan completely on her side."

"And you don't think he was before?" Alec asked skeptically. "My brother has been in love with her for years."

"I know. He must be making progress if he wants to buy you out."

Alec shrugged. "It could be. You couldn't prove it by me."

"What do you mean Karen 'had no choice'? Do you mean Jonathan forced her to go to your house?"

"No. She needs help getting around, though. And no one at her house could be trusted with that. She'd be virtually helpless out there."

Lilly had a vivid mental picture of the desolate farm-yard, miles from anyone else, and felt a pang of true sympathy for the woman whose antics had caused her so much grief. One had to make some allowances for a background like that, she admitted to herself.

Somewhere beyond their sight, a combo began to play some lush, melancholy tune which was soon joined by the shuffle of feet on the dance floor. "Dance?" Alec offered, blue eyes focused intently on her, and Lilly nodded.

Once in his arms, Lilly felt a sigh of pure pleasure leave her, and she smiled against his neck. "What's so funny?"

"I was just laughing at the fact that I nearly left here in a huff, and I would have missed this luscious moment in your arms," Lilly whispered truthfully, and heard him breathe in sharply. One hand tightened on hers, and his other dropped dangerously below her waist to press her to him. Lilly thought she ought to protest, but being held against him felt so good, so right, that she said nothing.

"Why is there never an empty table when you need one?" His deep voice teased against her ear, and Lilly moved her lips softly against the beat of the pulse in his neck, wondering how someone could be both calmed and excited by someone else's physical presence at the same time.

"Don't drive up to Minneapolis, tonight, Lilly," Alec murmured. "Stay home, with me."

"Are you trying to impede my career, sir?" Lilly teased, pulling her head back to survey him in mock horror. To her surprise, though, Alec replied seriously.

"No. Just as you earlier needed to make it clear that you only criticized *Twilight* because you thought I could do better, I need to make it clear that I'm for your career as much as my own. I'm aware of the emptiness of mere words, so I'm taking this opportunity to take action. You need to be fresh and rested to do your best at this thing tomorrow.

"So off to Minneapolis with you it is. It's now around nine thirty. You ought to be at your parents' around eleven."

Lilly opened her mouth to protest, but Alec was already leading the way off the dance floor. He scrawled a signature over the face of the bill, and took her to the car.

"You could come up with me," Lilly offered in a small voice when he dropped her in front of her darkened house.

"And stay in your bedroom? Or rent a room in a hotel? Thanks, but I've had enough trouble with the law regarding fellow faculty members!" He was joking, but firm, and Lilly made her kisses lingering just in case she might change his mind.

"Excellent try, but no," Alec said shakily as he put her into the Corvette and went quickly back to his own car. All the way up to Minneapolis the warmth of their good-bye kept Lilly warm. She reveled in the way Alec had stood up for her career, and never once wondered if there was another reason he stayed behind in Fielding.

Chapter Thirteen

Lilly was half-way through her presentation when she saw Martin hanging around the entrance to the conference room. She paused, collected herself by taking a sip of lukewarm water from the paper cup in front of her, then continued. The question and answer period was long and animated. Indeed, her paper was one of the best-attended of the conference. My God, what is he doing here? Lilly wondered frantically as she outwardly answered questions about how she'd set up her questionnaire and possible further applications of her results.

"Like many theories about how students learn..." one white-haired, cherry-cheeked academic began pompously. Lilly tuned out momentarily, knowing it would take him a while to get to the point, if there was one, and continued to sit casually on the corner of the conference table, a look of bright interest on her face, and the bulk of her attention on the dark, thin man lurking at the back of the room.

Last night, when she arrived at her home, she'd been so full of Alec that she had mentally still been in Fielding, wondering what he was doing each minute, and anxious for him to arrive in Minneapolis.

"How would you answer those critics, then, Miss Burns?" The white-haired gentleman had finished his windy dissertation and looked expectantly at her, tapping his half-glasses slowly against a copy of her paper.

"Very simply, Professor Helmann." Lilly squinted up her eyes to read his name tag. Her experience in business had taught her the importance of using the opposition's name when they might least expect it. "I would ask them how much real, hands-on experience they've had in dealing with eighteen- and nineteen-year-old products of our secondary educational system. I'm not just creating theories out of thin air, sir. I work with these students every day, and I see how one-sided the writing experience becomes for them. As I stated earlier, most students see writing as an arduous, obstacle-strewn exercise in which they are trying to *please the teacher*—a task that makes most of them resentful and even fearful. All my theory suggests is that making them aware of their reader's response, not just the *teacher's* response, results in freer, better writing. It gives composition courses a purpose that they normally lack."

There was scattered applause after Lilly finished. She felt flushed with her success as she gathered up her possessions and stepped down from the podium. As always, her dread of public speaking outstripped the actual event. When it came down to it, Lilly enjoyed public speaking as long as she was well prepared.

"A great answer to old Helmann," a blond, fresh-looking young woman said as she came up to Lilly in the aisle, before she even got out of the room.

"Thank you," Lilly began, then exclaimed, "Jan! I didn't recognize you for a moment. You really look terrific!"

In fact, Jan had lost about thirty pounds since Lilly had last seen her, and was wearing her hair in a much more attractive style.

"Would you like to have a drink, or a cup of coffee?"

"Sounds good. I'm really parched after all this." Lilly spoke with determined lightness as she scanned the crowd for Alec's familiar form. But the crowd swallowed up all but those over six feet tall.

"Looking for someone special?" Jan asked good-naturedly as they flowed with the crowd toward the hotel center lobby.

"I'm sorry. Am I so obvious?"

"Only to someone else in love," Jan murmured wickedly.

"My goodness, of course. Best wishes to you and Mike, and don't you dare forget my wedding invitation." Both women laughed and, since they had headed up there, entered the lounge area of the hotel. Both ordered sodas, and sat back in the comfortable luxury of deep chairs. Several people came up to congratulate her. But still no Alec.

Then Lilly froze. A few others from Iowa had joined their informal group, and Lilly got up, excused herself, and tried to make it to the exit. Too late.

"Lilly. I've been searching this convention for you." Martin's voice sounded desperate.

"Whatever for? We certainly have nothing to say to each other." Lilly spoke coldly, anxious to be rid of him, and seeing no earthly reason why she ought to be even polite to someone who'd used her as callously as Martin Stone had.

"Look, I know I have gall even to try to approach you, but I have to talk to you. Please!"

Martin took her arm and Lilly moved with him into the bar proper, more as a way to avoid making a scene than through active agreement.

"What would you like? You used to love Tia Maria, I remember," Martin said when they'd edged up onto impossibly high leather stools. He'd kept one finger hooked possessively around the tender flesh of her elbow.

"I'll have a tonic water, and get to the point, Martin." Lilly tried to free her arm without success. Up close, Martin looked haggard, his usually impeccable suit had faint stains on the lapel, and his shirt looked not too fresh. That shocked Lilly, since Martin had always been meticulous to the point of fanaticism about cleanliness and his dress.

"You're more beautiful than ever, Lilly," he muttered jerkily as he downed a heavy Scotch and left the water standing untouched. His wet brown eyes never left her face.

"Are you on drugs or something? Look, I may be naive, but I'm not stupid. I was taken in by your act once, but never again."

Martin continued to cling to her arm, nails digging into her flesh. He muttered something to himself and then raised his free hand to cup her face. "It's not an act. I've always loved you. It's true!" he put in hastily at Lilly's exclamation of disgust. "I got a bit too caught up in my job, but you were always first in my heart."

Lilly closed her eyes as nausea rose in her. She couldn't believe she'd ever cared for this desperate, clinging phony. And the thought that she might well have married him made her shudder. Martin, ever the egoist, evidently took her shudder as a mark of pleasure.

"See, you still feel for me, too. We could make things good again. We could have it better than it used to be. You were so smart to get out of the company and the influence of your father. Now I'm no longer under it, either."

"I know you got fired," Lilly put in bluntly, deliberately nipping a possible lie he might have made up to cover that. A flash of irritation marred Martin's humility act for a second before he recovered himself. But that was enough for Lilly.

"If you could just see your way clear to having a word with your father—"

"Is that what this is really about?" Lilly laughed. She couldn't help it. "Well, you're stupider than I thought, or more desperate if you think I can get your job back—"

"Oh, no, I know you can't do that," Martin said hastily. He turned and spoke sharply to the bartender. He'd always been that way with those he considered beneath his good manners.

"But if you could see your way to asking him to give me a better recommendation. Lilly, I'm blackballed. I can't get a job in the industry if he says I'm poison."

Lilly sighed, an unwilling feeling of pity rippling through her now that Martin was being honest with her for the first time.

"I can try, but I can't promise anything," Lilly said slowly, and Martin grabbed both her hands in his and raised them to his lips, to Lilly's ever-escalating embarrassment.

"That's all I ask," he said humbly. He lay a few crumpled bills on the bar and stood up. "That's all I ask, Lilly."

"I was going to come up and congratulate you, but you seemed rather involved." Alec's gravelly tone interrupted Lilly's thoughts. She watched Martin weave his way through the crowded lobby, feelings of pity and dislike warring within her. Part of her knew that Martin Stone would always land on his feet, but she would keep her promise to him nevertheless.

"Oh, Alec, you startled me!"

"You two did seem in a world all your own," Alec acknowledged sarcastically. "Who's the lucky fellow?"

"That *un*lucky fellow is Martin Stone," Lilly quipped a bit tartly. She didn't like the way Alec was looking at her—as if she always went around picking up strange men.

"Ahh, the hapless fiancé." Alec nodded sagely, then rubbed his finger along the side of his nose, a sure sign that he wasn't as casual about this as he pretended. "Do I take it that you've decided to kiss and make up?''

"No, you don't," Lilly said shortly, annoyed with the whole situation. Martin made her feel unclean. She'd been afraid of something like this the minute she saw Martin lurking around the conference room door. "Martin got fired and is desperate to get a job. He wants me to talk to my father and try to get him to put in a good word for him in the industry.''

"I know just how he feels," Alec muttered, changing keys immediately. "Begging about describes my own activities lately." Something about him, a suppressed excitement Lilly hadn't noticed at first, made her think he had some new prospect in mind, though. But before Lilly could ask what, Alec went on.

"Caught your presentation." He stepped up near Lilly. "Not a bad job, Burns," he said softly, and the intensity in those blue eyes caught Lilly in Alec's web of attraction. His beaky bushy-browed face made her go weak and hot inside. Coherent thought seemed to bubble its way out of her reach, and all Lilly could think of was how much she loved Alec.

"Will you marry me, Alec?" Lilly whispered, leaning forward until her straight nose touched the end of his. With shaky fingers she traced the outline of his mouth, uncaring of the place or who might see her. Alec filled all her senses and her mind.

"Oh, you're a cruel wench," Alec muttered, and grabbed Lilly by the waist to swing her off the bar stool. He took her hand and hustled her out of the bar, and more than one set of curious eyes followed them out of sight.

They didn't go far. A discreetly marked door said it led to the garden area, and Alec lead the way out into a world of fountains and lush green bushes and grass where the noise of city traffic was muted.

"Why am I cruel?" Lilly prompted when Alec finally allowed them to sit on a secluded bench near the back of the garden.

"Because I had a whole evening planned around getting to those few sweet words, my love, and in one instant you beat me to the punch," Alec said ruefully, and pulled her into his arms. They kissed softly, their mouths fitting together lovingly.

"Oh, Alec, really?" Lilly asked, her hazel eyes shining gold with happiness.

"I love you. Will you marry me?" Alec countered.

"Yes, yes, yes. Oh, Alec, you make me so happy!" Lilly exclaimed, and held him tightly to her, almost as though she feared something would come between them.

"Are you sure? This is a big decision. You might decide that Martin is a better deal." Alec smiled as he spoke, but his eyes were deadly serious.

Lilly laughed lightly, happily, and shook her head. "You're what I've always been looking for, although I didn't know it. You're the one who has to be sure; you know I've been terribly jealous from day one of this Karen Willis person!" Lilly could joke about it now, but as with Alec, there was an underlying vein of seriousness to her words.

"You're crazy, you know that? Karen never made me feel the way you do. I need you, Lilly. Don't ever doubt that." Alec tenderly stroked the hair that fell in heavy waves around Lilly's face, and she literally purred under his touch. "Karen always needed to control me, and you're different."

"I don't see how you could have found a more perfect spot to ask for my hand," Lilly commented lazily as she turned up her mouth to ask for his kiss. She got it. Their bodies strained together, and it was only the very edge of Lilly's consciousness that caught a faint ringing of a bell.

"The conference! I'm supposed to—"

"Forget it. Let's just get out of here, and spend the rest of the day together," Alec growled against her neck, not loosening his grip as Lilly tried to sit up.

"Wish I could," Lilly said wistfully. "But I have another appointment in less than half an hour. I promised to have lunch with my aunt."

"Forget it. Tell her—"

"No one stands up my aunt Sylvia, Alec. Besides, I rarely see her, and I have a particular bone to pick with the lady," Lilly said firmly. She softened it by saying, "But dinner tonight?"

"Try and keep me away."

"Would you mind meeting my family?" Lilly asked shyly. "I know it would be nicer to be on our own, but—"

"No. I'd like to meet them. And I take this opportunity to apologize for those arrogant comments I made about them when we first met."

Lilly shrugged, and felt her cheeks grow hot as she remembered the way Alec and she had fought that night. "I guess it just shows there's been something between us from the start."

"Actually, this will work out well for me, too. I'm waiting for a phone call, and by the time we meet for dinner tonight, I may be able to relay some good news. For a change." Alec gave Lilly that wolfish grin that always made her heart pump faster. "I'll be in the lobby around seven, and I'll drive you to the house, okay?"

Lilly hurried out to the street, walking up Nicollet Mall to a small restaurant, Mitterhauser Cuisine. Her aunt rose from one of the gilded chairs with her usual effusiveness.

"Darling, you're here! You look positively radiant, Lilly. Is there something you need to tell your old auntie?" Sylvia asked when they were seated and their order had been taken.

Lilly dropped her eyes to the linen napkin in her lap, but was unable to resist the temptation. "I'm engaged to be married."

"To Alec Thomas, of course? Well, I think I may have an early wedding present for you, darling," Sylvia said mysteriously.

Claus himself chose this moment to come and check on their meal. He was an enormously tall Swiss, whose two-foot snowy-white chef's hat only added to the giant illusion. He was a bachelor, and the few times she'd eaten here with her aunt, Lilly had gotten the definite impression he fancied her small, plump aunt. Lilly smiled pleasantly, but was glad to see him retire to the kitchen.

"Delightful man, don't you think?" Sylvia said with twinkling eyes.

"Yes. Now what is this about some cryptic present? And before I forget, did you swipe my copy of Alec's script while you were down in Fielding the other day?" Lilly demanded, face stern.

"Yes, dear," Sylvia said smoothly. "Although I prefer the word *purloined*. It has such a deliciously naughty ring to it."

"Why?"

"That's a rather long story. But I can make it short for you. We're going to put Alec's new play into the Arlo schedule this season."

"You can't! Those schedules are set months in advance!"

"Yes, well, in a best of all possible worlds, I suppose they are," Sylvia said meditatively. "But in this imperfect world, no. I thought you'd be pleased. I think Alec will be."

"I'm flabbergasted," Lilly said with total honesty. "Does this mean you haven't told Alec yet?"

"Oh, we've put the feelers out. He seems interested. I've been given the go-ahead from the board of directors, and Stanislav is very positive about the whole thing. That was a tough and delicate nut to crack, which I did an excellent job of, I must say."

"You didn't do this just because I'm, er, fond of Alec, did you?"

"Well, I hope you're a good deal more than just fond of him, dear, if you're seriously going to marry him!" Sylvia said a bit tartly. "And no, as much as I love you, I couldn't rearrange an entire theatrical schedule."

"I bet you could if you wanted to," Lilly said with a slight shiver of awe.

"Thank you, dear," Sylvia said smoothly, "but back to the matter at hand. Our artistic director, as you know, is a brilliant man. But the poor dear has no business sense. None. And he scheduled the heaviest season imaginable. 'Educational' was the best you could say for it. Anyway, the box office has been disappointing and so many season ticket holders have called to complain. Then this followed by *Titus Andronicus*, a six-hour production to take place over two nights! Something had to be done, and fast."

"Well, I think this is a marvelous opportunity for Alec," said Lilly. She thought that was the understatement of her life. Of course, it wasn't Broadway, but he'd be reviewed by major publications, and the exposure would be invaluable. "But I have to say, having only read and seen his first play, that Alec's work is fascinating, and powerful, but scarcely—"

"Light relief? My dear, I'm not looking for Gilbert and Sullivan. What I want is something American. Something homegrown, so to speak. By the way, have you read *Sunrise*?" Lilly shook her head, and her aunt reached down below the table and pulled the red-plastic-covered copy from her capacious bag. "Read it, then. I think Alec is one of the most talented newcomers in years. This"—she tapped a nail on the cover—"is powerful stuff."

Lilly left the restaurant a dazed woman. For so many weeks she had been trying to find ways and means to get Karen's suit dropped, and now the biggest reason for it had vanished like a puff of smoke. Alec would no longer need to care about Karen's suit, because his funding wouldn't hinge on it. The switch was too much for Lilly to take in at once, and the source of Alec's surprise excitement earlier today was fully understood now.

Lilly walked slowly back to the hotel. She sat in on a presentation she assumed was good, but heard nothing of it. Her mind was totally preoccupied with Alec. This news was like manna from heaven, so bountiful and unexpected was it. And that, if Lilly was honest with herself, certainly overshadowed their engagement.

Lilly's aunt had told her the best opening date would be in January, and Lilly knew Alec would be extremely busy for the next weeks. She couldn't help feeling a twinge of jealousy because she knew he would have little physical or mental time to devote to her. Oh, he would try, Lilly knew. But this was his big break, and the kind of thing that possibly came only once in a lifetime. She could try to share in it with him, but Alec basically worked alone, and her role would be that of listener, sounding board. Well, that was important too, she pointed out to herself. Still, it was a somewhat subdued and thoughtful Lilly that waited for Alec in the lobby.

He came bursting out of the elevator, bristling with energy, blue eyes electric, and she knew her aunt had managed to get in touch with him.

"Hello, lover," he said exuberantly, and wrapped an arm around her shoulder, pulling her off balance so that she had, in the interest of balance, to put her arm around him, too, as they walked toward the parking lot elevators.

"Sounds like your phone call was good news," Lilly

murmured as they stepped out of the elevators that emptied into the musty coolness of the parking ramp. The sleek lines of the red Corvette beckoned to Lilly, raising her spirits as they always did. She started to ease out of her suit jacket, and Alec immediately began to help her. Or hinder her, Lilly couldn't tell which, but somehow her arms were trapped behind her back, and Alec's length pressed hers to the cool fiberglass. "Do you know I love you, and I missed you?"

"I was only gone a few hours, though." Lilly pretended to be puzzled, although her heart was beginning that steady thumping increase in beat that Alec always produced in her.

"I still need a refresher course, teacher," he murmured, and lowered his head to put his mouth on hers, and Lilly thought, how can something done so many times still remain so fresh? Her mouth opened eagerly, and Alec released her hands and they gripped his waist, pulling him closer against her in an openly sexual motion. A wolf whistle from a passing rattletrap going down the exit ramp jerked them apart, and they both gave the husky, shaky laugh of people who had just nearly stepped off firm ground onto nothing. The feeling teetered between fantastic and fearful.

Both were still breathing hard as Lilly unlocked the car and collapsed inside. Alec folded himself inside and tossed a small black box into Lilly's lap. Her heart, which had just begun to slow, sped up again.

"What's this?"

"Open it and see," Alec said with a grin.

"How lovely!" Inside was a ring with a large, oval stone of a dusky gold color. "Is it citrine?"

"Close. Topaz," Alec replied. "I thought it reminded me of your eyes, when you go all mysterious and far away. Do you like it?"

"Like it? I think it's gorgeous. Thank you, Alec!" Lilly slipped it on and it fit well. She turned fully to

Alec and said, "You must have had a busy day, or have you had this since the day we met?"

"Not hardly, but I wanted to claim you, that much I don't mind admitting, and I wanted to have something different, something—"

"Martin hadn't given me?" Lilly guessed, and leaned over the console, holding the ring to the faint light in which it glowed a rich golden brown. "Well, you succeeded." Martin had given Lilly a large diamond solitaire that she'd returned, even though he urged her to keep it when she broke their engagement. "This is the most wonderful ring, Alec." The more Lilly looked at it, the more she liked the gleaming topaz.

She watched it catch the light as she moved her hands on the steering wheel. The evening seemed to be in cahoots to provide a perfect setting. The sun flamed off the buildings of Minneapolis behind them, and occasional whirlwinds of brown and gold leaves ghosted over the road. Inside the car, soft music played over the stereo, and Lilly had the big car humming along just slightly over the speed limit.

"You're a good driver," Alec complimented her when the highway narrowed to two lanes each way and Lilly neatly fit the car in just where she wanted it.

"I like it. This car is a big love of my life, I have to admit," Lilly said, a grin seeming to hover constantly around her soft mouth. Each time she looked down at that ring, or over at Alec's profile, the corners of her mouth turned up. "I've always used it as a way to work out problems,"

"Ahh, that explains the way I've seen you tear out of the faculty parking lot in this red bomb. Just driving around?" Alec's head turned her way.

Lilly nodded, surprised that she'd admitted it. She felt closer to Alec than she'd ever felt to anyone, but trusting people with things still came with difficulty. It wasn't a deeply intimate secret in itself, perhaps, but Lilly was leery of volunteering any clues that might give someone a way to hurt her.

They stopped at a red light, and a teen-ager in a souped up Chevy Camaro pulled up next to her. He looked over once, then did a double take. Lilly was looking straight ahead, but was aware of him out of the corner of her bright hazel eyes. He gunned the engine, and although Lilly knew it was no contest, she felt her pulse quicken to his challenge. The traffic was thinner now that they were further from the city, and Lilly couldn't resist the impulse. She eased the clutch and timed it perfectly: as the light turned green she popped it out and the Corvette leaped out of the starting gate with a throaty growl that left the other car as if it were standing still.

Alec, who hadn't been tuned in to this, was flattened against the seat, and he slowly pulled himself erect and shook his head.

"I take it back. You're a crazy driver!"

Lilly laughed with a sound of pure joy. "Just making sure I have your attention, that's all."

"You got it, maybe more than you can handle." He flashed the teenager an irritated glance as the Camaro kept exactly even with them in the fast lane, then reached across to take Lilly's left hand, and held her very engaged hand. "Just try to remember your age and incipient married status, if you have any care for my health."

"Anyway, that kid wasn't interested in me, just in the car." "It's true!" Lilly insisted when Alec made a disbelieving sound.

"Say, did you get that phone call you were waiting for?" Lilly inquired casually as they neared the turnoff to her parents' home.

"Yup."

"And?"

"The Arlo Theatre will be producing *Sunrise.* The premier is January twenty-first."

"Alec! That's incredible news. Now you don't have to worry about Karen or her suit or any of that." Lilly had almost said I know, I heard about it before you did, but then decided to let this be his moment.

"It's a tremendous load off my mind," Alec agreed.

"And such a fantastic opportunity!"

"Yes, I was surprised, to say the least, when Sylvia Bellows called with the go-ahead. The most I expected was a maybe for two or three years down the line, or possibly another production at the Arlo II. *Twilight* drew the biggest box office they'd ever had there, did you know that?"

Lilly shook her head. A problem loomed on the horizon. She pulled up into her parents' long driveway, and her mind was furiously working at trying to find a way to keep her mother off the subject of her sister.

"That's great, Alec."

Unfortunately, her father loomed in the doorway.

"I hear congratulations are in order to you, sir," he said as he shook Alec's hand.

"Yes, isn't it wonderful, Daddy?" Lilly said in a desperate attempt to distract him. "Alec and I are engaged!"

She succeeded, as her father took in the gleaming topaz on her finger. In different circumstances, Lilly would have tried to break it to her parents a bit less dramatically, and indeed Alec shot her a quizzical glance as they followed her father down a long, dim hallway to the rather stiffly arranged Burns living room, where canapés, drinks, and another surprise awaited them.

"Aunt Sylvia, hello," Lilly said weakly, clinging to Alec's arm for more than just conventional support. "Mother, this is Alec Thomas, my fiancé. Alec, my mother, Millicent Burns."

Alec went through the usual polite measures, but Lilly had seen him stiffen at the sight of Sylvia Bellows.

"Is Uncle Phil coming too?" Lilly asked, and her aunt shook her head. "Too much business for him. He's in Chicago tonight and tomorrow, so your mother was kind enough to invite me to the celebration dinner.

"Congratulations again, Mr. Thomas. I wish you great success in our joint venture in the theater as well as in your marriage to my charming niece."

"Ahh, Lilly's your niece. I didn't know that," Alec murmured, and his glance said quite clearly that he felt Lilly ought to have told him. Too late, Lilly realized, she had seen the possibilities of his view of this.

But the dinner went smoothly, and Lilly saw another side of Alec, as he told amusing tales of the years he'd spent as an apprentice playwright. Several times Lilly felt her mother sending her approving glances that ought to have warmed Lilly's heart, since her mother's total approval was as scarce as hen's teeth. Instead, Lilly felt alternately hot and cold as she contemplated driving Alec back to the hotel. It turned out to be worse than her wildest imagination.

"You must have been laughing yourself sick over my little triumph today," Alec began bitterly as soon as they were alone. At least he waited this long, Lilly thought, in an effort to focus her attention on small things because she was terribly afraid that this might explode their relationship and the trust that had slowly built between them.

"No, no, I wasn't. Aunt Sylvia only told me of it at lunch. I admit I ought to have said I knew in the car, but I didn't want to spoil your triumph...."

"My triumph! What a joke! You and your family set this up. You people have to own others, control them. Well, you won't control me."

"Alec, you're not thinking of refusing the Arlo offer?" Lilly asked in alarm.

"Ahh, that's just what you'd like. Well, I'm not. But I am refusing *you*, and I hope you can learn something from this. Maybe the same lesson that you forgot since poor Martin. But I'm not getting in the same position to be tossed out like he was when you lose interest in me."

Lilly had never seen him in such a rage. He slammed out of the car, and with tears blurring her vision, Lilly watched Alec stalk up the stairs and out of her life.

Chapter Fourteen

The stage went black, and a crackling roar of applause came up out of the responsive audience as the house lights came on for the intermission. Lilly shifted and struggled to surface from the compelling drama in progress on the stage below. She hadn't meant to come. She still couldn't believe she was here, and told herself that she must be a glutton for punishment—at least the kind dealt out by Alec Thomas.

It was nearly three months since that terrible evening at her parents', yet Lilly could remember each detail of that day with painful clarity. After she dropped Alec off, she hadn't gone directly home, but had driven around for hours trying to decide what to do. She came to no conclusions.

Finally she'd gone home in the faint hopes that Alec might have calmed down, might have called Sylvia himself to find out Lilly had nothing to do with the Arlo agreeing to take on his play. There had been no phone call, and Alec had managed to avoid her after that weekend. That was no small feat on a campus the size of Fielding, and especially when the two people worked in the same department.

From her seat in the balcony Lilly had an unfortunately excellent view of her parents, aunt and uncle, and Alec as they stood and began to work their way out of the crowded main floor. Alec was shaking hands and several of the people around him looked like reporters. Lilly could hear her aunt's clear voice, thanks to the perfect acoustics, as she freely gave out Alec's credentials, past triumphs or future plans when he appeared too modest to do so. Lilly thought they made a superb team. She felt fairly safe up in her hideout in the balcony, and watched their slow progress out of the theater with mixed pleasure and pain.

She couldn't believe it was over.

When Alec didn't call, Lilly had swallowed her pride and had talked to her Aunt Sylvia, asking her to do whatever she could to straighten things out. "That is one stubborn man" was her only comment, and Lilly had nearly burst into tears when Sylvia said regretfully that she'd made no progress with Alec. "In fact, darling, I fear that I may have made things worse. He seemed to see my talking to him as one more proof of this family's attempts to control him."

Next Lilly had tried the philosophical approach. People fell in love, had problems, and couldn't work them out. Other promising relationships broke up every day. She shouldn't consider herself some sort of special case. But while Lilly could keep herself busy enough during the days, she found excruciating loneliness crept over her at night, or when she was tired. She hurt. She found herself with a growing list of things to tell Alec, things that would amuse, annoy, or interest him. Like the day she fought and won a battle against her aging heating system. Covered with soot and grime, but triumphant, she'd stood up in the cellar and wished with all her heart that Alec was there to hear the roar of it starting up and to feel the heat percolating its way through the house.

The philosophical approach had been a complete wash-out.

Lilly found she didn't care about other people's relationships, but she cared very much about hers and

Alec's. When she'd first gotten back to Fielding with Aunt Sylvia's 'purloined' copy of the script, Lilly had been too upset and depressed to read it. But when she did, the power of it left her weak and shaky. The Arlo was doing it justice, too, she thought, as she watched the black-clothed stagehands unobtrusively carry out piece after piece of the set necessary for the next acts. They took place in the kitchen of the heroine, Maggie, and each was placed precisely. Each chair and seemingly casually placed pan or stalk of celery had a set of pieces of tape invisible to the audience. Without such precision, actors could become completely fouled up by a casually placed or missing prop.

When Lilly heard those lines in the second act that Alec's students, Jill and Oscar, had rehearsed, she realized what a difference good acting and directing could make. Where Jill had shouted and sneered, the well-known actress playing the role of Maggie in the Arlo production used her body and subtle intonations far more effectively to convey her refusal to be intimidated.

Lilly sighed. She, too, had refused to be intimidated. When she'd finished Alec's script she had been determined to return it in person. That proved much more difficult than she'd thought. Not only was Alec skillful at avoiding her himself, but he had Hilda running interference for him.

"Mr. Thomas can't see anyone right now. He's in conference with his director," Hilda had told Lilly firmly when she arrived, red-covered script clutched tightly in hand. "You can leave that with me, and I'll see he receives it."

Lilly had raised her head and seen the shadowy outline of Alec through the frosted glass. He evidently was in conference over the phone, his booted feet up on his desk as he talked.

"I can wait." Her voice came out reed thin, but determined.

"I wouldn't," Hilda had warned, but Lilly refused to be warned off that day. When she heard the phone slam down, she opened his door and went in.

"Alec, we have to talk." She'd rehearsed those words so many times they came out only as meaningless noises that she prayed would at least give her a few minutes with him.

"I've got a play in production. I haven't got the time nor the interest in taking on another melodrama at the moment." Alec spoke crisply and moved to the long, narrow windows that overlooked the parking lot. When he turned back, his face was shadowed, and Lilly couldn't read it, although his intention to hurt was obvious.

"I heard Karen's suit has been settled. You must be very pleased that's no longer hanging over your head." Lilly swallowed, playing for time, although she'd been genuinely relieved to hear through the grapevine that Karen had agreed to an unannounced sum in exchange for refraining from further action, civil or criminal, against Fielding or its staff. Apparently word had gotten to the administration of Karen's forged credentials, and while they felt this invalidated Karen's claim to some extent, they also seemed to feel it prudent to get Karen's written agreement to take the case no further. After all, it had caused the college enough embarrassment already.

"Karen's happy with the settlement," Alec had agreed. "And the stringent hiring policy requirements should keep it from happening again."

"Did you tell them?"

"Yes. Because I knew they would react just the way they did. The whole thing had dragged on too long, and the whole administration was ready for any excuse to end it, with face-saving on both sides."

They had been in the same room for nearly five minutes without fighting. Lilly didn't care what they talked about; she just wanted to be with him. That question about whether Alec told the committee about Karen's credentials had been a sticky one, though. Somehow it seemed a test of whether he still cared for Karen or not. But his answer, logical as it was, left her frustrated. It didn't prove or disprove his addiction to Karen Willis.

"Any other chitchat or backstairs gossip you'd care to discuss?" Alec had asked.

"That isn't fair. I've been intimately involved in this from the start!" Lilly said heatedly. "It hardly qualifies as back-stair gossiping." That little dig had stung.

"I'll say you have! You've had your rich little nose poking and prying and manipulating from day one!" Alec roared back, and took a step toward her. That moved his face into the light, and the tired lines in it made Lilly gasp.

"Alec, please? Why do you need to hurt me? I love you." Lilly felt the words ripping out of her passionately. "I have never manipulated you, or even tried to. You must know that now that you've had time to think about it, too, that even with my 'rich' connections I couldn't have bought *Sunrise* a spot on the Arlo schedule. No amount of money or influence could have made space where there wasn't any!"

"Oh, grow up! Of course it can. And I want to succeed on my own. Why is that so hard for you women to understand?" Alec had asked, turning his head toward the ceiling as if at the end of his small store of patience.

"I do understand that, better than you know," Lilly had cried, thinking of her own battle to escape her dependence on her father's world. "It was an unfortunate coincidence that my aunt was on the board, but that's all. It—"

"Then why didn't you tell me you knew? Why did you let me babble on like some idiot when you knew all about my great news before I did?" Alec came close to Lilly. "Do you have any idea how much of a fool I felt when I walked into that living room and found out Sylvia Bellows was your aunt?''

He glared at Lilly for a tense moment, then said, "Oh, get out of here. You women can always come up with some lie to get yourselves out of things. Then when that fails, you just turn on the tears."

Indeed, tears were threatening in Lilly's hazel eyes, and she clenched her fists and took a deep breath in an effort to choke them back. Alec loomed over her, his anger a palpable thing that pressed down on her, but Lilly held her ground. "Just tell me you don't love me, Alec. Then I'll go," Lilly had whispered.

"Hilda!" Alec had bellowed the secretary's name and grabbed Lilly's arm while he swung wide the office door with his free hand. "Escort Miss Burns from this office immediately."

When he brought Hilda into it Lilly had known she had no choice but to go, and she went. But she'd learned something. What had been most deeply wounded was Alec's pride in his ability to do things for himself. Yet Lilly could think of no way to mend those cracks without making things worse, and her depression over their relationship refused to lessen.

One cold, bleak morning in early winter Lilly was out walking along the creek when, just as the first time they'd met, she was nearly bowled over by Jonathan's exuberant golden retrievers.

"Hello, Lilly!" Jonathan said, coming into view right behind them.

Lilly had answered with marked coolness. Jonathan looked healthy, bright eyed, and happy with life, and Lilly had resented the way that happiness seemed to be at the expense of his brother's.

But Jonathan's happiness had been so pure and, when Lilly forced herself to view the situation objectively, well deserved, that she couldn't really blame him or wish him ill. "How is Karen coming along?"

"Just great! Of course she's impatient with herself and thinks she ought to be out skiing by now. But the doctors are pleased, and she'll have the final casts off soon."

"That's great. I'm glad there's no permanent damage." She'd stroked the silky gold ears of one of the dogs, pulling it gently through her gloved fingers as he leaned against her. Patches of the first snow hung in the shadows, but the creek itself hadn't frozen over yet. The sky hung down heavily that day, and before it ended, a pristine blanket of snow covered the land. Just then a few large flakes floated past them.

"Look, I'm deeply sorry all this has spoiled our friendship, Lilly," Jonathan had said.

"It's your treatment of Alec that I think is so shabby," Lilly had said bluntly, and she was surprised when Jonathan agreed.

"I was jealous of him all my life, you know. The accident gave me the perfect excuse I needed to vent that jealousy."

"You've hurt him a lot." Lilly spoke quietly in the muffled quiet of falling snow. "He considers you an important part of his life."

A look of pain had entered Jonathan's navy eyes, and they began to walk on. He'd invited her up to see Karen, but Lilly had declined. She hoped that Jonathan might think about making it up with Alec, because the two of them needed each other.

The trumpets sounded for the start of the third act. Lilly came back to the present with a jolt. To her surprise, she saw Jonathan and Karen, who looked gorgeous in a dramatic off-the-shoulder dress of midnight blue, coming down the aisle to congratulate Alec. The two men shook hands; then Jonathan drew his brother to him in a swift embrace. Karen chose just that moment to look up and wave an arm at Lilly. She shrank down in her seat, and was thankful when the house lights began to dim in preparation for the next act.

When the first spotlight came up and flooded the stage with light, Lilly couldn't suppress her gasp of shock. When she read the play she'd noted that the final two acts took place in a kitchen, but she hadn't realized whose kitchen it was. There before her in exact detail lay Mrs. Jordan's extraordinary kitchen, with its enormous freezer and expansive, solid kitchen table. Maggie walked on stage. The drama continued and soon consumed most of Lilly's attention.

Not all, though. She told herself she was happy that Jonathan and Alec had reconciled, and tried to ignore the little voice that said, If he can forgive Jonathan, then why can't he at least talk to me? Because if she pursued that line of questioning, it led Lilly to conclusions she didn't like at all. Conclusions like perhaps Alec didn't really ever care for her as much as she cared for him. No, the kernel of hope still lay within her, and Lilly had one more trick up her sleeve to get a stubborn man to see the light.

At the end, Lilly was on her feet with the rest of them, program sliding to her feet and tears of pride in her eyes as Alec reluctantly took the stage when the lead actors beckoned to him with their open arms.

Lilly knew it was probably just her imagination, but it seemed to her that Alec stared straight up at her as he left the stage. The applause went on and on. Aunt Sylvia looked positively ecstatic, Lilly thought, as the principals came back for a third standing ovation before it was all over.

Strangely reluctant to leave the theater, Lilly sat watching as it emptied slowly. The young ushers moved swiftly up and down the aisles, picking up discarded programs, a lost chiffon scarf, and even a pair of glasses. Then they too were gone.

Lilly was alone in the theater with Alec's fantastic set

before her. She went sure-footedly down the narrow steps that led to the main floor. The lights were dim, but adequate. The soundproofing made it surprisingly quiet.

Lilly walked up onto the stage, which only minutes before had been pulsing with life and sound. Lines from the play ran through her head, and she was alone with her images of Alec and herself: That night he'd boosted her up into Mrs. Jordan's window as though they were a professional second-story team. The intense concentration he'd devoted to exploring the kitchen ought to have alerted her, Lilly realized, but so much had happened between that night and when she'd finally read the play that Lilly hadn't made the connection....

"Like it?" Alec stood in the middle of the center aisle. He wore black pants and a black turtleneck sweater that emphasized his well-muscled shoulders and flat stomach.

"It's absolutely fabulous!" Lilly said without restraint. "I felt a shock go through me when the lights went up and Maggie came on stage. Even the hum of the freezer and that horrendously rolling linoleum are exactly the same." Lilly made an expansive gesture with her arms, feeling strangely freer and less inhibited than she'd ever felt in her life.

"I had a hard time keeping myself from dragging you down here to see it weeks ago," Alec admitted in a quiet, deep tone. He took the distance between them in three long strides.

"That's not the impression you've given me over the last few weeks," Lilly said just as quietly, her fingers unconsciously turning her topaz around and around on her finger. Alec took both her hands in his.

"I know." His face twisted in a wry expression. "If it's any consolation, nothing was ever so hard or painful in my life."

"But why? What the hell was the point?" Lilly demanded angrily. "I know you love me, and I certainly love you. I've been so unhappy the last few months, Alec."

"Oh, darling, I know, and I've hated myself when I've caught a glance of your sad eyes watching me in the halls of the English building. And that day you came to my office!" Lilly felt his warm, solid hands begin to shake around hers. "Well, it was nearly over for me then."

"So you called in the reinforcements," Lilly concluded gently, still not understanding why he'd needed to torture them both, but growing more confident of their relationship by the second.

"You'd better believe it!" Alec said fervently. "You almost won before the war really got off the ground."

"But why did it have to be a war? I was so sure that once you had time to cool down, you'd see how impossible it would have been for me to *buy* this opportunity for you."

"Logic plays only a small role in love, though—"

"And you make that point so beautifully in *Sunrise*," Lilly couldn't help interjecting. "I guess I ought to have applied the lessons in *Sunrise* a bit more to our own situation," Lilly said.

"You think I'm that much of a moralist?" Alec's deep voice was thoughtful. "I guess you're right; although I tried, God knows, to cloak that this time in a good story, with the sort of believable female characters everyone thought were missing from *Twilight*."

"Maggie is wonderful, so strong yet tender," Lilly told him. "I identified with her thoroughly."

"You ought to, she's modeled on you," Alec said blandly, and shook Lilly to the core.

"My God! You're joking, right?"

Alec shook his head slowly back and forth, obviously well pleased with the reaction he was getting.

"But I'm not wonderful, not the way she is," Lilly protested. "I run from every possibly painful situation. She confronts them head-on—"

"I know that's how you think of yourself, always poised to disappear in the damned red Corvette, but it's not true." Alec took her chin in his fingers and made her meet his serious blue eyes. "Did you run when I hurt you?"

"I wanted to, several times," Lilly admitted truthfully.

"Ahh, but we're all tempted to do that. Did you actually run, though?"

"No, but—"

"No *buts*, Lilly. You stayed and you fought. Just the way Maggie fights for what she believes in, and against the odds."

Lilly's hazel eyes were shining golden brown as the truth of Alec's statement sunk in. He was right, only she'd beed too busy fighting to realize she was finally breaking old patterns.

"Is that one reason why you kept away from me, and kept me from you?" she asked tentatively. She saw the answer in his eyes. "I love you, Alec, so much it hurts."

Alec kissed her, his hands furrowing her hair. His mouth felt warm, rough, and right. Lilly breathed his scent in deeply and wrapped her arms around his neck to bring them into full contact from shoulders to thighs. She teased her tongue in and out of his mouth. He caught and held it with the strong ring of his lips, and Lilly slowly drew it out in a frankly suggestive movement. Alec groaned and buried his face in her neck, his lips moving toward her ear, outlining its curves with the tip of his tongue before pulling the lobe into his hot, moist mouth. Lilly felt sensation shoot arrow-straight to her stomach, and she pulled his mouth back to hers.

They swayed, and without knowing how they got there, Lilly found herself backed to the broad kitchen table at the back of the set. Alec's fingers shook over the buttons that ran down the front of her knit dress. "If you ever leave me, I'll die," he said as he opened Lilly's dress. Underneath Lilly wore only a thin, lacy garter belt that held up her stockings.

As if in slow motion, Alec drew his hand down the middle of Lilly's body until his fingers closed around the snaps of the garter belt. His hand was a hot, hard pressure against her soft flesh, and she moved beneath it; she couldn't help herself. Alec's fingers tightened and the snap sprang open. He lowered his head and swallowed hard.

"Is something wrong?" Lilly sat up in a satin smooth motion, taking that opportunity to take ahold of his belt, unfasten it, and reach for the zipper on his pants.

"Give me a minute," Alec said huskily, and stayed her hand. Lilly slid them both beneath his sweater, half caressing, half massaging the hard muscles of his belly and lower back. "Alec?"

He was staring off at some distant point in a very odd manner. "I wouldn't want to destroy this moment for anything, but isn't there a distinct possibility that someone might, er, come in?"

Alec looked down, laughed, and Lilly was relieved to see that strained look disappearing. "I already thought of that. The doors are all locked. We're as alone as you can be in a building with several thousand people in it."

"That's good," Lilly murmured a bit vaguely, and lay her head against his chest. "The thought did occur, you know."

"I know, oh, Lilly, I love you so much!" Alec held her closely and with such tenderness that tears formed in Lilly's eyes. "You're the most important thing in my life. If I hadn't had you in the back of my mind all these months, even tonight wouldn't have been worthwhile."

There was so much sincerity in his eyes, such seriousness in his words, that Lilly couldn't doubt him, and she felt her love for him grow and open even more than it had before. "You're the most important thing in my life, too, Alec. And I want our relationship to come first with both of us."

She touched her lips to his in a kind of pledge that quickly became passionate affirmation as this time he urged her fingers to stroke down the cool metal of his zipper. Lilly loved taking his clothes off, and when he lay full length against her, their skin telegraphing the messages of the flesh, she rubbed slowly, gently against him. All sensation, all focus, grew tighter and tighter into one pulsing need as her pelvis tilted and Alec responded on an exhalation of her name. They moved together in a rhythm that slowed, sped up, then roared toward heights that left them spent and gasping, their heated flesh nearly melting into the oneness they'd soared so near.

"You're exquisite," Alec murmured when he'd partially recovered his breath. His hand stroked the curve of her waist as he lay on one elbow. "And this thing," he snapped the garter belt, one finger following the path of a garter to her still nylon-clad thigh. Lilly just smiled. Utter contentment washed over her in succeeding waves. She couldn't summon the energy to do more than that. "That dress is pretty effective, too. I was noticing the flash of your, er, hips," Alec said with a teasing euphemism, "as you strutted around this stage."

Lilly felt her smile widen, but she kept her lids half lowered. "A less modest man than myself might think you were planning a bit of seduction, Miss Burns."

"And what's a modest woman supposed to think when a man locks her in a theater with him, and forces her to—" Lilly's lids flew wide open, and she gave Alec's shoulder a hard enough shove to send him to the floor with a thud. "You planned this! You and your toasts to sturdy tables!" All her weight on her locked arms, Lilly peered indignantly over the edge of an exceedingly sturdy table at her laughing fiancé, who was reaching for his scattered clothes.

"What's wrong with a bit of planning?" he wanted to know as he stood and zipped his pants, reaching for his sweater.

"Nothing. It's just that I was going to seduce you," Lilly said, dressing quickly. She wasn't going to loll around naked if he wasn't.

"Now, now. Does it really matter who comes out on top?" Alec said soothingly, and only the absolutely diabolical sparks in his intense blue eyes gave him away.

"God, why did I have to fall in love with a wordsmith?" Lilly demanded, and rolled her eyes. But she couldn't ignore the effects of his words on her body. "I think your basic plot was good, but it could definitely benefit from some directorial input," Lilly added as she slipped into her shoes.

"Now what?" She looked at him expectantly.

"You mean to tell me you don't have further moves planned?" Alec tutted in mock dismay. "Well, we'll just have to do things my way, then."

Mystified, but too happy to care, Lilly allowed Alec to lead her by the hand back up the narrow stairs to the furthest balcony exit. There Alec took a key from his hip pocket to open the door. As he did so, music poured over them, corks popped, and a loud mixture of cheers, cries of congratulations, and other slightly more ribald comments greeted them from the crowd. Two glasses of golden bubbling champagne were pressed into their hands, and Lilly stared in a dazed way at the sheer number of people that filled the semi-circular area.

"Just one or two informal shots of the happy couple-to-be," a toothy photographer pleaded, obviously having very fixed ideas of what constitutes informal as he arranged their arms and bodies like store mannequins. "Marvelous, darlings," he cooed when he'd contorted them to his satisfaction. "Now a big smile!" Lilly bared her teeth in what she hoped would pass as a smile to everyone else, and said into Alec's ear, "You'll pay for this, in full."

"Of course. Would I be such a cad as to order a party like this and then stick you with the bill?" he asked. In spite of herself, Lilly felt a genuine smile forming, and the photographer said "Marvelous, darlings!" and snapped away.

Now that Lilly'd had a moment to recover, she was touched by this absolutely unexpected gesture.

Alec took Lilly's arm, and she raised her free hand to take a generous sip of champagne as they approached the first group of well-wishers. It consisted of Karen, Jonathan, Susan Thomas, and Alec's mother, a slim, direct-eyed woman.

"I'm so happy to meet you at last," Mrs. Thomas said in a voice almost as deep as her son's. "Alec has kept you under wraps for too long."

"It's a pleasure to meet you, too," Lilly answered, and took her hand warmly. She liked Mrs. Thomas already. "Alec certainly kept this party under wraps!"

Around them Lilly watched the busy black-tie waiters whisking canapés and champagne to the clusters of people. Strains of Handel's Water Music bathed them and set the cascading banks of chrysanthemums, bittersweet, and spiky anthurium trembling in their background of glossy ivy and featherlike ferns. "This is so marvelous," Lilly whispered, hazel eyes shining, to Alec, and felt her insides melt at the look in his eyes.

"I just wanted the world to know we belong together, that's all," he responded.

"Congratulations, brother. You're getting a fine woman," Jonathan said, and once more the two brothers shook hands. Lilly caught the older Mrs. Thomas's eyes and saw the relief there. A waiter approached her with a loaded tray of cheeses, stuffed mushroom caps, and a glistening mound of caviar in the center, then moved around the circle of people surrounding Alec and Lilly. But when it reached Jonathan, there was trouble.

Jonathan's scrutiny of the tray was slow and methodical, but in the end he took nothing, only shaking his head sadly. "This is dreadful," he said, and waved the tray away. Lilly noticed he had no champagne, either, and her ripple of alarm seemed to be echoed by others in the group, who shifted uneasily.

Alec looked at his brother for a minute, then gave a shout. "Raspberry coffeecake! How could we have forgotten it?"

"That glutinous stuff?" Jonathan demanded, his expression affronted. "Oh no, I was looking for some chilis, and the funny thing is, I have a strong craving for a beer right now."

A prickle of tears stung the backs of Lilly's eyes as she watched the two brothers embrace once more. She shook herself to make sure this wasn't a dream, because over the past months she'd longed for the reunion of Alec and Jonathan almost as much as she longed to be with Alec herself.

The circle shifted, and for a moment Lilly was outside the laughing group around Alec and Jonathan. Karen stood beside her. "Best wishes to you," the redhead said tersely. She inhaled deeply on her ever-present cigarette, her neck a long white arch as she lifted her head to blow the smoke away from Lilly. By common consent the two women stepped to the railing where the room overlooked the expansive lobby below.

"I'm glad to see you've fully recovered from your fall," Lilly said. "You're looking really gorgeous."

That was said with honesty, since Lilly usually felt very ordinary next to Karen's exotic beauty. Tonight, however, Alec's love made her feel equal to anyone.

"Thanks." Karen paused, evidently wanting to say something more. "I—you, I just wanted to say I like and admire you—"

"Admire me! Why?"

Karen shrugged, and, putting her palms flat against the railing, she leaned forward to stare down into the lobby. A gyre of smoke rose from the cigarette in her right hand and dissipated into the lights. "You're the same kind of people as Jonathan and Alec."

"And just what are you? I think you are most definitely Jonathan's kind of person, Karen."

"I know, and that's the most wonderful thing that's ever happened to me," Karen said, and turned her head to look at him. Just then he raised his navy eyes above the heads of his sister and mother, obviously searching for Karen, and the look that passed between them did more than any words could to reveal the love between them. "And I so nearly tossed it all away."

"Why, Karen? Why did you set Alec up with that lawsuit?"

"Initially, it was because I wanted to humiliate him the way I thought he was humiliating me."

"You mean you felt he was responsible for you losing your position at Fielding?"

"Yes." Karen sighed, and lit a new cigarette from the stub of the old one. "Although underneath I knew it was really my fault, I just couldn't bear to fail, and the lawsuit was my way of saving face and hurting Alec's career at the same time. I was so obsessed with my own sense of inferiority that I really lost sight of the consequences of my actions." Karen gave a small, self-mocking smile. "Maybe that sounds unbelievable to you—"

"Oh, no, it doesn't," Lilly said emphatically. She

thought of her prodding of Alec that night that led to Karen's accident. "We were all guilty of tunnel vision, each seeing things only through our own angle."

"Well, the accident changed things, altered my angle of view, and made me take a closer look at my life." Karen smiled up as Jonathan came over and slid his arm around her. "Not without a struggle, though. But Jonathan is nothing if not persistent, and I was a captive audience."

"Did she tell you she's had another book accepted by the university press? And nibbles are out for Karen to start a midwest lecture tour—"

"Jon, you're embarrassing me," Karen interrupted.

"One thing you'll never cure me of is being proud of you, darling. So please don't try." Jonathan's tone was mild but firm, and from the flush along Karen's cheekbones, Lilly thought she must be enjoying the experience.

"Congratulations to you, then," Lilly said warmly. She realized she'd not spoken to Susan yet and excused herself to do so but was intercepted by Alec, who rushed her on to the next group, composed of mostly Lilly's own family. "Quite the party, huh?" Carlisle commented expansively, and Lilly was surprised and pleased to see that both her parents were enjoying themselves. "I admire a man that can carry off a coup like this."

"Like what?" Lilly asked, immediately suspicious of how much her father had actually seen. "Well, keeping this whole party a secret from you, and keeping you occupied looking at the set while the party was set up. Alec told us it was modeled on that kitchen in your rooming house. What else?" Her father gave Lilly a curious glance. "I couldn't keep something like this from your mother," he admitted with a grudging look of respect at Alec.

Lilly laughed and kissed Alec's cheek. "And you did

a magnificent job of keeping me occupied, didn't you?'' Alec looked from Lilly to her father and back again.

"I gave it my best shot, sir," he said to Carlisle, and Lilly fought to maintain a straight face.

"I'm afraid it's time for us to be going," Alec said only a short time later.

"Go? But we just arrived," Lilly protested, and looked around at all the people from the college she hadn't gotten a chance to speak with. "People will think we're rude."

"Can't be helped. We've got things to do." Alec said.

When they came to the front door of the theater and Lilly saw the gleaming black limousine waiting there, she halted.

"If we're getting married tonight, Alec, I insist on changing my dress," Lilly said in a firm voice before continuing to go down the steps to the waiting car. She was only partially joking. For at the speed Alec was moving, she just thought she'd better make her preferences clear.

"Married? Who said anything about getting married?" Alec asked, completely perplexed, as they settled back into the soft luxury of the huge car.

"It's the usual follow-up to luxurious engagement parties," Lilly commented a bit plaintively. "But don't let me manipulate you into anything you don't want to do." Lilly felt sure enough, safe enough now, to tease him, and was rewarded with a belly laugh.

"I'm sure I deserve that!" Alec admitted, and pushed a button that rolled back the smoky sunroof and revealed the velvet, glittering panorama of the night sky. It was chilly, so Lilly snuggled close, feeling the heat curl around her feet while the end of her nose grew chilled. "Too cold?" Alec asked solicitously, and Lilly shook her head.

"Where are we really going, Alec?" she persisted, feeling she'd had enough excitement for one day; and she had a fleeting wish for her own quiet space, her own home in Fielding.

"Home, darling," Alec murmured as he kissed her, and she felt warmed from the inside. "Just home."

Lilly thought nothing had ever sounded so simple and so good.

HARLEQUIN *Love Affair*

Now on sale

OPEN HANDS   *Rebecca Flanders*

Joe Ella was like a hummingbird that brought shimmering beauty into Cameron's world for a moment, then vanished. Over the years, their paths had crossed and recrossed, and though Cam understood Jo Ella's restless spirit, he couldn't stop hoping any more than he could stop loving her.

Cam's offer of temporary shelter was a balm to Jo Ella's soul, which had been battered and bruised by an ugly scandal. Jo Ella knew it wasn't fair to stay with him in Dallas, but for the first time in her life, she had nowhere else to go. . . .

THE HEART'S REWARD   *Vella Munn*

It was unlikely that Noah's Ark had contained a better menagerie than that which brayed, barked and roared on Scott Barnett's ranch in Oregon.

Rani found the ranch an exciting place to work and Scott an exciting man to work for, but she balked at Scott's suggestion that she and her three-year-old son, Dean, live there. For Dean did not mix well with assorted camels, llamas and cougers. And while Scott's teenaged son clearly enjoyed his duties as babysitter, Rani did not believe that he, or anyone else for that matter, could provide the constant attention and gentle care that Dean so badly needed.

FROM TWILIGHT TO SUNRISE   *Martha Starr*

To a man, the English Department of Minnesota's Fielding College objected to its newest staff member. Spearheading the opposition, Chairman Alec Thomas made it clear that he had no quarrel with Lilly's excellent credentials—it was her gender he minded.

Alec paraded his dislike of women at staff meetings, at social functions and in the plays he wrote. Lilly had no choice but to dig in and fight. First, she had to find the woman responsible for Alec's hostility. Then, Lilly had to find out whether Alec was still in love with that woman. . . .

Next month's titles

HEART'S JOURNEY   *Cathy Gillen Thacker*

Gwen Nolan looked at the face she had not seen in twelve years and heard echoes of all their breathless promises and whispered dreams. Memory stretched across the chasm of years and bridged the distance between them. Daniel Kingston spoke her name, as he had done so many times in her daydreams, and Gwen felt a fluttering in her heart.

But then the familiar pain came rushing back, the ache of all the secrets she had had to bear alone, and Gwen found she could say nothing at all to this man—the only man who had ever mattered!

PERFECT COMBINATION   *Sandra Kitt*

Dale Christensen was a visionary, pioneering medical advances that would some day restore happy, normal childhoods to sick and injured children. When Dale decided to take her first break from work, it was only because she hoped to exchange ideas with kindred souls at the convention in New Orleans. . . .

Damon Christensen was amused to discover that the hotel had mistaken his bags for those of another Dr. Christensen. The problem was speedily resolved, as were most problems in Damon's life, but this time a new problem replaced it: the distracting image of the other Dr. Christensen had lodged itself firmly in his mind!

THE WELLSPRING   *Pamela Thompson*

The town of White Rock was dying. Standing between life and death was Brent Archer, city manager of neighbouring Joplin. If Brent didn't find the cause of White Rock's malfunctioning water line, built by and running from Joplin, more livestock would perish, tottering businesses would collapse and the citizens would be bankrupt.

As White Rock's mayor, Jennifer Lyon knew it was not just a duty to see that the town had water—it was a moral obligation. Her course of action should have been simple but for the unforeseen complication that arose—one that risked her heart!

Rebecca had set herself on course for loneliness and despair. It took a plane crash and a struggle to survive in the wilds of the Canadian Northwest Territories to make her change – and to let her fall in love with the only other survivor, handsome Guy McLaren.

Arctic Rose is her story – and you can read it from the 14th February for just £2.25.

The story continues with Rebecca's sister, Tamara, available soon.